I OWE YOU ONE

BOOKS BY LAUREN NORTH

My Word Against His

She Says She's My Daughter

The Teacher's Secret

I'm Her Mother

For Better, For Worse

Perfect Wives

All the Wicked Games

Safe at Home

One Step Behind

The Perfect Betrayal

I OWE YOU ONE

LAUREN NORTH

bookouture

Published by Bookouture in 2026

An imprint of Storyfire Ltd.
Carmelite House
50 Victoria Embankment
London EC4Y 0DZ

www.bookouture.com

The authorised representative in the EEA is Hachette Ireland
8 Castlecourt Centre
Dublin 15 D15 XTP3
Ireland
(email: info@hbgi.ie)

ISBN: 978-1-80550-660-7
eBook ISBN: 978-1-80550-659-1

For Mel Ewings

PROLOGUE

Jess

My feet falter as I reach the cliff path, as though something buried deep inside me already senses what's coming. As though it knows the part I'll play in my sister's death and is trying to pull me back.

Stop.

Turn.

Run.

But I keep moving. Because it's already too late.

The path winds towards the cliff edge that overlooks Skelwick Bay. The wind picks up, a blustery shove against my back, like a playground bully trying to push me closer to the edge. The drop is steep. The rocks are jagged. One wrong step is all it would take.

Far below, the town is bathed in buttery-yellow spring sunshine, making the cafés and gift shops look pretty, hiding the peeling paint and weathered wood of the town and people who limp from one tourist season to another.

Sailboats line the harbour, golden sand stretches out around the coastline of Devon, and then there's the sea – dark blue and streaked with crests of white. It looks alive. A churning monster, waiting for its prey to drop into its depths and never be seen again.

I wrap my arms around myself. A lone gull wheels overhead. Its cry is sharp – the tip of a knife digging into my memories, prising out whispers from the sailing accident sixteen years ago. I want to remember. I don't want to remember. Always the same opposing thoughts war in my mind.

Another turn in the path and soon I see my sister hurrying towards me from her grand house on the top of the clifftop. Bryony is hunched over, lacking the polish and glamour I'm used to. Her skin is washed out, her eyes wide and wild. She throws a glance over her shoulder without slowing down.

I want to call out. To tell her to be careful. She's so close to the edge. But then we reach each other and her hand slips into mine. Her fingers are ice cold as they squeeze mine with a desperation that's tight enough to hurt.

'You came,' she says, her words breaking in a shaky sob.

'Of course I came,' I say, my own voice pulling tight. A thousand memories rush up of our shared bedroom, whispered secrets, all the ways she made me laugh when we were small. 'What's happening, Bry? What's wrong?'

She swallows hard. 'It's bad, Jess. Worse than I feared.'

My pulse stutters. 'He's—'

A frantic shake of her head, another furtive glance behind her. I follow her gaze. The sun is hitting the glass of her house, but for a moment I think I see a figure watching us.

'There's no time,' she says. Her grip tightens. Her eyes lock with mine. 'You have to help me, Jess.'

'Anything,' I blurt. 'Tell me what to do.'

For a moment, she can't speak. Her chest heaves. Her lips tremble. When she finally forces the words out, they make no sense.

'I need to die.'

My breath punches out of me. 'What... what are you talking about? No. Absolutely not.'

'Not really die,' she cries, the tears spilling onto her cheeks. 'But I have to make everyone believe I'm dead. It's the only way I can get out. I have to fake my death, and I need your help to do it.'

I stare at her, unable to process the words.

Fake her death.

Disappear.

Leave everything behind. Her beautiful house, her perfect life. And Mum. And me. Leave *me* behind.

Another gust of wind whips around us, lifting Bryony's hair – the same dark brown as mine, but highlighted blonde at the bottom. A sleeker, shinier version of me.

'There has to be another way,' I say. 'This is crazy.'

She shakes her head. 'If there was another way, don't you think I'd do it?'

'But I can't lose you,' I whisper.

She cries harder. 'I know. I'm so sorry. But this is the only way.' Bryony jerks her head back towards the house, pulling her hand away, stepping back. 'I have to go. I shouldn't be out here.'

I reach for her arm, not able to let her go. 'We'll think of something else,' I try again, desperate now to make her see sense.

She laughs – a horrible, broken sound. 'Jess, do you think I haven't thought of every possible way out? That I'd ever ask this of you if I had any other choice?'

We stand there, the silence dragging out between us. Our eyes are blurred with tears, but neither of us look away, like we're both caught at the edge of something enormous and terrifying. Below us, the sea is a distant roar.

Then Bryony steps closer, pulling me into a hug, whispering into my ear. 'You owe me, Jess.'

The words sap the last of my resolve. My knees feel weak.

'I saved your life,' she whispers. 'Sixteen years ago. I pulled you out of that water. I kept you alive. And now... now you have to help me fake my death.'

For a second, I can't breathe.

Then she squeezes my hand one final time before saying something I barely catch and tearing herself away.

She turns and runs back up the path, stumbling once, catching herself, not looking back.

And I'm left standing on the cliff edge, the wind still shoving, the sea still waiting.

She's right. That's the awful, terrible truth. She's right about everything. There is no other way. She saved my life. I owe her. And so now I must help her fake her death.

ONE

SIXTEEN YEARS EARLIER

Jess, age 13

I'm going to die.

Panic wrenches through my body, consuming every muscle, every cell, every single part of me. There's another thought clinging to the first, but I can't keep hold of it. Can't see beyond my own death.

I'm going to die.

No! I grab at the air rushing by, trying to stop myself as I hurtle towards the waves. Falling. Falling. The world blurs. Grey sky, screeching gulls, The bright white of our father's sailboat, the *Calypso*. Then a sound. A piercing scream.

Bryony. I try to shout, try to warn her about the shadow that crossed my vision just before the fall.

Where is she? I can't see her on the deck.

But I can't get the warning out. She'll be OK, I tell myself. Bryony is stronger than me. Smarter, too. At sixteen, she's three years older and the captain of our boat. Our kingdom, we call it.

What happened just now? One minute we were fine. Happy. Everything normal. The next...

The thought is knocked out of me with the force of a baseball bat as I stop falling and hit the water. It's like landing on the smack of the playground concrete at school. The pain is blinding. I think my skull has cracked open, my brain prising apart.

The world turns black. The gulls stop their shouts. The wind no longer roars in my ears along with my racing heart. The only sound is the muffled gurgle of water. Salt stings my eyes, fills my mouth. I'm under water. I'm sinking.

I want to swim. I want to save myself. Find the surface. Find air. But my arms won't work. My legs are lead. Icy cold steals everything.

This isn't like the long, hot summer. All the times Bryony and I jumped off the *Calypso*'s bow, when the anchor was down, the water as peaceful as a pond, and the tourists were colourful dots on the beach. It was the first summer we were allowed out on Dad's boat just the two of us. *'No friends, mind,'* Mum told us, tsking as she said it. Friends meant parties and wildness and out of control. *'Never take anyone else out with you.'*

We didn't care. Bryony and I just wanted to sail. The freedom, the boat cutting through the sea with ease and grace. Completely in our control. Except summer slipped into autumn and the sea is no longer a pond, but something churning and moody, like the late afternoon sky, slipping into that space between day and night when we should've been home with the curtains drawn and the TV on and the smell of dinner in the air, almost ready. Cosy. Warm. Safe.

Not here, where there's no air. Just water and cold and black. I force my eyes open, frantically searching for the light of the surface, but the sea is gripping tight. Not letting go. And I'm not wearing a life jacket.

Stupid!

Dad's voice echoes in my head. *'Don't forget your life jackets, girls.'*

Always followed by the chorus of, '*We won't,*' said somewhere between annoyance and amusement. We wore the orange bulky vests the first time we went out alone but never bothered after that. We didn't think we needed them.

So stupid.

The sea claws at me, tugging me down, wrapping me in its cold grasp. My clothes are like weights, my limbs useless.

No air. No breath. I'm drowning.

The side of my head starts to throb, the pain so bad, I open my mouth to yell out. Sea water rushes in, freezing my throat. A drill is being pressed into my skull and suddenly it's too much. I can't stay awake. But this place I'm being pulled to isn't sleep. It's dark and black and so cold it feels like my blood is turning to an icy slush.

We're always so safe. Always careful.

Except this time, everything has gone terribly wrong.

Just before I fell, I heard someone behind me. A shift of weight. A shadow that didn't belong to my sister. Someone else was there. I heard laughter. And now I'm in the water.

Now I'm dead.

TWO

NOW

Jess

As I slip my key into the lock of my childhood home, the pity and disappointment curdling in my gut is almost enough for me to double over. I left Skelwick Bay ten years ago when I'd just turned nineteen. I went to London with nothing but half a dream and a desperate need to escape. And now I'm back with nothing but pity and heartbreak to show for it.

The key sticks like always. The sea air does that, rusting the metal, eating it from the inside out until it gives up. I jiggle it until the latch clicks. A gull shrieks overhead – that long, hollow cry that sounds like a mocking laugh. My temple on the left side throbs. Always the left side. For an awful moment, I'm in the water, ice-cold sea stinging my lungs, my skin, inside and out.

The words of the hypnotherapist I saw a few years before moving out of London run through my head. '*Sound and scents are our biggest triggers for memory,*' she'd said gently, notebook balanced on her knee. Behind her, a row of houseplants wilted on the windowsill.

'*So what do I need to hear or smell to remember?*' I'd asked, almost in tears because her six hypnotherapy sessions had done nothing to help me remember the day of the accident. All I had were snatches of being in the water. Drowning. I thought she could help me remember and then the nightmares would stop.

'It's not that simple, Jess,' she'd replied. *'You have a block right now. And it's coming from inside you. However much you say you want the truth, part of you is shielding it. A part of you doesn't want to remember what happened when you were thirteen.'*

I'd gritted my teeth, wiped my tears and left. If I'd been Bryony, I would've demanded my money back, but all I said was, *'Thank you.'*

The therapist was wrong. I did want to remember. I still do. I want the nightmares to stop. I want the fragments of memory to fit together.

I drag my suitcase into the hall and slam the door, pushing aside the memory of the water. Thinking about that day always makes my head throb, and however much I want the nightmares gone, I need every scrap of strength I have just to survive the here and now.

The air in the house smells stale and musty, like damp clothes that have taken too long to dry. There's an emptiness that makes me wish I was a kid again, calling out, *'I'm home.'*

To hear my mum shout back, *'We're in the kitchen, Jess.'*

Bryony's laughter filling the house. *'Hurry up, I'm starving.'*

And Dad: *'Don't traipse half the beach in with you.'*

But the house is empty, and that part of my childhood ended the same day as the accident.

My eyes drag to the coat hooks by the door. Mum's favourite blue jacket is still hanging there. I'm surprised it didn't go with her to the care home on the other side of the bay where she's been living for the last year.

Her decline started slow. Calling me to tell me a story about our neighbour, Kelly, that I'd heard the week before. Then calling twice in the same day because she'd forgotten the first time. The diagnosis of dementia came when she was already skidding down a slippery slope of confusion.

When she started to forget her way home after a trip into town, Bryony hired Addie, a local carer, to come in twice a day. The two of them cared for Mum until even that wasn't enough, and Bryony found her a room in the care home.

Guilt swims through my veins. I was too far away to help. Too busy running the hotel to visit. Sadness and grief follow. Mum isn't dead, but I still miss her. I touch the smooth material of the jacket. I'll take it when I visit tomorrow. She loves this blue, the same colour as the shells I collected in a glass jar for her birthday one year.

My gaze sweeps across the hallway. Everything is exactly how I remember. The green floral wallpaper. The narrow telephone table sitting by the stairs with a chipped porcelain bowl for keys and change. The white banister stretching upward. All so achingly familiar.

A part of me still can't believe I'm here. Back in my childhood home, at rock bottom. Six months ago, I was someone. A name on hotel reviews and local business awards lists. Liam and I co-owned the Kilstern Hotel – a boutique eighteen-bedroom manor house tucked in the Oxfordshire countryside, a two-hour drive from London. *The Times* called it *'a hidden gem of understated luxury'*.

Six months ago, I was successful. I was happy. I was in love, Liam and I working side by side. Two years before that we'd built our dream from scratch. Now, it's all gone. I spin on my heels, as though if I can move fast enough, I can escape the self-loathing and pity. I catch my reflection in the hallway mirror.

For a second, I see the girl I was at nineteen years old, half in love with my best friend, Alex, and far too scared to tell him. Then I blink and it's me as I am now. My brown, shoulder-length hair is scraped back from my face, my skin pale in the dull light. My jeans hang loose on my hips from the weight I've lost. The jumper I threw on this morning looks old and shapeless. I look like a faded version of myself. I feel it too. I'm twenty-nine, single, heartbroken, jobless, hotel-less, homeless and broke. My chest tightens and my stomach knots. If this is rock bottom, then the ground I've hit is quicksand and I'm sinking fast.

My phone buzzes in my pocket and I pull it free. It's Liam. Again. Tears sting my eyes. I don't answer. I've ignored all his calls since our fight, when I yanked open the drawers in our tiny loft bedroom at the hotel, threw his clothes at him and screamed, *'Get out.'*

He's called almost every day in the months since. Left voice messages, begging and pleading at first, then just to talk. Listening to them is picking at a scab that won't heal, and I can't keep doing that. It's like Bryony said when I called her in tears last week.

'Come home,' she'd said. *'This can be a fresh start.'*

I'd been putting off the call. Putting off making a plan, but I was out of time, out of money, out of choices.

I press delete on Liam's voicemail without listening and tuck my phone back in my pocket.

I leave my suitcase by the stairs to carry up later and look at the house once more. It's an end-of-terrace house perched on the road that winds straight down to Skelwick Bay, where every road seems to slope towards the sea, as though drawn by the pull of the tide. The town fans out around the harbour with the little motorboats for hire, moored beside the larger sailboats owned by the townspeople. There are rows of Cornish pasty shops, fish and chips, overpriced coffee spots, gift shops and market stalls that come alive each summer when the tourists descend. They come for the vast stretches of soft yellow sand that bend around the west coast of England, the choppy waves perfect for surfing and sailing when the wind picks up.

The house is three bedrooms, though calling the third a bedroom is generous. It's barely big enough for a single bed and a chest of drawers. Bryony and I shared the second bedroom when we were little, giggling over her made-up games; whispering secrets across the gap between our twin beds until Mum called up the stairs: *'Go to sleep now, girls.'*

But when Bryony turned thirteen and I was ten, the gulf between our ages suddenly became a vast, uncrossable stretch, and she claimed the box room as her own. She was experimenting with lip gloss and hair straighteners, daydreaming about boys while I was still sprawled on the carpet with sketchpads and felt tips.

For a moment, I'm lost in the memories this house holds – our childish laughter and the echo of who we all were before that day on the *Calypso* when I almost died, and the aftermath that ripped my family apart in ways I still don't understand. Dad leaving. Mum crying and pretending not to. Bryony squeezing my hand as I lay in the hospital bed. *'It's all going to work out, Jess. You'll see.'*

Why can't I remember? What happened before I hit the water? Why does nobody talk about it?

I grit my teeth, reminding myself why I'm here – a fresh start, like Bryony said.

'You can live in our guesthouse,' she'd said last week when I'd called. *'Alex won't mind. He's at the studio all hours anyway.'*

Alex. My best friend. Or he was for a little while anyway. The boy I was secretly in love with a decade ago, who turned around and fell head over heels for my sister instead.

'Thank you,' I'd replied, sniffing down the phone. *'I thought I could stay at Mum's. Just to start with. I thought I could turn it into a holiday rental for the summer. The money can go to her care home costs.'*

'You don't have to—' Bryony had started to say, but I'd cut

her off. The thought of the care home costs twisted the knots in my belly tighter. The worry like a disease, eating me up inside. The cost hadn't seemed so bad when the Kilstern was fully booked for a year ahead.

'*I do,*' I'd replied. '*She's my mum too. I want to help. But if I could stay with you after the house is ready to rent, just for a few months while I get back on my feet, I'd appreciate that.*'

'*We've got so much space you can stay forever,*' she'd said, and I'd known she'd meant it.

I will make this the perfect holiday rental. If there's one thing I'm good at, it's a do-er upper. A project. And at least the roof isn't leaking and the electrics all work, which is more than I can say for the Kilstern the day Liam and I collected the keys and moved into a derelict manor house with nothing but flashlights, a camping stove and our dreams of opening our own hotel.

Still, Mum's house is in a worse state than I remembered. The wallpaper is peeling at the bottom; the cupboards hang slightly off their hinges. They need paint and care. The tap drips, and the linoleum floor is bumpy. Even the windows are clouded with salt, blurring the view of the overgrown garden and Dad's old tool shed.

There's a lot to do, but I can work fast. I can get the place ready for the summer months. I can do most of the work myself, like Liam and I did with the manor house when it held only empty, damp rooms. Then, when the house is ready, I'll manage everything from the bookings to the cleaning and changing sheets. I'll live in Bryony's guesthouse for a while, and I'll put the money I make into Mum's care, and slowly, with Bryony's help, I'll crawl out of this rock-bottom place.

There's a sound at the front door – the scrape of a key in the lock – and I spin round, already smiling as though thinking of my big sister has summoned her.

Except Bryony isn't her usual joy and laughter, starting a

conversation halfway through and expecting me to catch up, the way she always does. The woman who opens the front door is still Bryony. The expensive clothes in beiges and whites – cashmere and linen. Her brown hair, highlighted with a balayage and sitting sleek and straight an inch above her shoulders, her make-up perfect, her face devastatingly beautiful. But her eyes are wide and brimming with tears. She looks... terrified, I think.

I step towards her. 'Bryony?'

Her voice is a strangled whisper. 'Jess. Help me.'

THREE

Jess

'Bryony, what's wrong? Is it Mum?' I'm in the doorway in seconds, pulling my sister into a tight hug as the worry squirms inside my gut. She tenses just for a moment, almost a flinch, before leaning into my hug. The scent of her perfume envelops me – an expensive mix of white musk and something floral.

Her chest rises and falls too fast, and I tighten my hold. She releases a single sob, shoulders heaving against me. 'It's not Mum,' she manages to say.

The relief is fleeting. I've never seen Bryony like this. I'm the worrier; Bryony is the fixer. That's how it's always been with us. But now, my own problems disappear. All I want in this moment is to help her. We're so much more than sisters. I might not remember it, but that day on the *Calypso* bonded us together in a way I can't begin to explain.

It was the only thing that remained after the accident – our love for each other. How she'd risked her life to save me that day. Everything else changed. Before I'd even left hospital,

Mum and Dad separated. Dad took a job in Norfolk, and Bryony went with him. Three hundred miles and a six-hour journey away if the traffic was kind.

For five years, it was just me and Mum. I only saw Dad and Bryony in the holidays when I went to visit. But the distance didn't matter to me or Bryony. We stayed close, talking on the phone almost every night.

Outside, the weak spring sun is dipping low in the sky and the wind has picked up. Suddenly, the smell of salt and seaweed replaces Bryony's perfume in my nose. I pull her into the house and shut the door before another memory of the cold sea digs its claws into me.

'What is it?' I ask.

Bryony hesitates, her throat working as though she's trying to find the words. Then she visibly straightens and some of the polish of my sister returns. 'God, Jess, I'm sorry. I didn't mean to scare you. I'm fine. It's just... it's been a really bad day...' She trails off for a moment, blinking back tears. 'And then I thought about how you're here, you're back, and I can see you any time I like, and I think it all just got to me. I saw you standing there—' She gives a breathy, self-conscious laugh. 'It just came out wrong. I didn't meant to ask for help; I just mean it's so good to see you. To have you here.'

I search her face, sensing there's more she's not saying.

She gives a shaky smile. 'Jess, I'm fine. I was being dramatic. You know me.'

'If you're sure,' I say, not believing her.

She digs in the large tan leather handbag looped over her shoulder and retrieves a bottle of red wine. 'I thought we should celebrate you being home.'

'Commiserate my life falling apart, more like,' I reply.

She squeezes my arm, telling me without words that she's here. She understands. She loves me. 'You commiserate. I'll celebrate.'

Bryony shrugs off her coat in the hall, throwing it over the banister. It slips to the floor in a heap, but she's already disappeared into the kitchen.

'Where's the corkscrew?' she calls out.

'I've been back five minutes, Bry. How would I know?'

'I'd know if I was in your shoes,' she calls back.

I almost laugh picturing Bryony in my tatty trainers that used to be white and now are grey. She would never be in my shoes. Literally or otherwise. Bryony is one of those people that good things just happen to.

Like Alex.

I'd known him for months. We'd met on the beach and forged an easy and instant friendship, sharing our love of the coastline and searching for our treasures. For me, it was shells; for him, it was driftwood he'd make art pieces with. On my end, it was just a hobby, but Alex's art is known all over the world now. People flock to Skelwick all year round to visit the studio and buy an original Alex Raffety.

But he met Bryony and very soon he looked at her in a way he'd never looked at me. They married a year after I introduced them. And a few years after that, Alex was so successful, they bought Cliffview House – one of the huge homes that sits on the clifftop, overlooking the bay, tall and grand, like the houses know they're worth more than everything below.

'A magnet for luck,' Mum used to say about Bryony. *'And mess,'* she'd add, tsking at the clothes and the make-up and hair products, bed unmade, books scattered. The years I spent sharing a room with Bryony before she claimed the box room were like living with a miniature tornado.

I pick up her coat and hang it on the hook beside Mum's. I'm about to step away when something catches my eye. A spot of red on the sleeve, bright against the beige wool. My gaze fixes on that spot as Bryony's whispered *'Help me'* echoes in my head. It looks like blood.

I roll my eyes and tell myself to stop being ridiculous. It'll be paint from Alex's studio. One of his more colourful pieces, I think, picturing the driftwood art he still creates from the pieces he collects from the beach.

I step into the kitchen as Bryony holds out a glass of wine for me. I take a grateful sip before staring back at the glass. It's red wine, but it's not heavy or acidic.

'It's delicious, isn't it?' Bryony says, swirling the liquid in her glass. 'It's Pinot Noir.'

'It's so light,' I say.

'It's the only wine I drink now.' She clinks her glass to mine and we settle at the kitchen table. 'So you're really home?'

'As of five minutes ago.'

'Good. It's been forever since I've seen you.'

'It hasn't been that long,' I reply, although I cringe inside because I'm not sure that's true. When Liam and I bought the manor house, it swallowed us whole. First came the renovations – turning a derelict shell into a boutique hotel – then the launch, then the endless grind of keeping it running. We barely slept, let alone breathed, and even though Mum always said she was proud of me and understood, the truth is I've neglected her. I've neglected Bryony too.

Bryony would visit Oxfordshire every few months, sometimes bringing Mum if she was having a good week, but more often coming alone. She'd clasp her hands together and declare loudly to our guests how divine everything was. She'd wander the grounds or take herself off to the nearby market town to shop, and Liam and I would squeeze in a cup of tea or a glass of wine with her whenever we could. But we were always rushing, always halfway out of our seats to answer a call or deal with a booking or fix something that had gone wrong.

And suddenly I realise how much I've missed her. Her big smile. Her quick, dry humour. The way she can make even the most stressful days feel lighter just by walking into the room.

'You know we haven't seen each other since September?' she adds.

I try not to wince. Bryony's visit was just before it all started to go wrong, and I couldn't face her after that. Couldn't let my big sister see me failing.

I can pinpoint the moment everything changed. The memory hits hard. I see myself standing at the tall mahogany reception desk in the Kilstern's grand entrance hall, phone pressed to my ear, the scent of fresh coffee drifting from the lounge. I'd been talking to the events assistant who'd made the weekend corporate booking. We'd been speaking most days. Usually, she wanted to add a guest or check a detail for the awards dinner and evening entertainment.

'I'm so sorry,' she'd said, voice overly bright. *'But we're cancelling the booking. Unfortunately, we don't think the Kilstern is the right location for our event after all.'*

'But you're due to arrive tomorrow. You've paid a deposit. We've booked a live band,' I'd added, not to mention the extra fresh food and wine we'd ordered.

'Keep the deposit, of course.' Then she'd hung up, leaving me staring at the silent phone. It had been our largest booking to date. An entire weekend. Every room booked. Three meals a day. Cocktail receptions. Evening entertainment. All of which we'd already paid for.

Their deposit covered the band but not the food or wine or the salaries of the staff we'd put on rota. And it was too short notice to fill the rooms. I remember ending the call and sinking onto the edge of the reception desk, the wood digging into the backs of my legs, the phone still hot in my hand.

Liam had opened his broad arms, and I'd stepped in. *'It's a one-off,'* he'd murmured in my ear. *'We knew this could happen. Something else will come up. We'll get through it.'*

But then more people cancelled. All at once, with no explanation. It was another week before even Liam started to panic, dragging a hand through his dark-auburn hair over and over again. Then the suppliers broke their contracts and the chef was headhunted by another hotel. The bills started to pile up, and the rooms continued to sit empty week after week, and our dreams started to shatter. Our profits disappeared along with our guests, faster than water down a drain. That's what it felt like. Watching our dreams wash away.

And then one final guest booked a room. A woman travelling for work. Drinking alone in the bar with Liam. I bite the inside of my lip, not wanting to remember.

I blink back tears and look at my sister. 'I'm sorry it's been so long,' I say.

'I get it,' she says. 'You were having a difficult time. But I've missed you.'

I can see beneath her smile that it hurt her. The times she called and I didn't answer because it was just too hard to tell her how much trouble we were in.

'I think a part of me felt like telling you how bad things were was admitting the truth to myself. I was so focused on saving the hotel.' My pulse judders in my chest. Bryony knows about Liam and what happened between us, but she doesn't know everything. She doesn't know how much trouble I'm in.

I wish I'd called sooner. Especially in those final, lonely weeks after Liam left, when it was just me in the empty hotel, the bar lights off, the restaurant closed, chairs stacked upside down.

We'd sold the hotel to a chain. They wanted the hotel and the grounds, but not the bespoke décor we'd lovingly chosen, agonised over. They had their own décor in muted green and paisley. The sale cleared the mortgage and most of the debt. So I sold everything I could, clearing the final credit-card bill in our names.

All that work and love. All that grit and those big dreams, and what do I have to show for it? A broken heart and a humming anxiety that feels like it could take my legs out from under me any second.

'I forgive you obviously,' Bryony says lightly. 'And you're here now.' She glances around the kitchen, eyebrows raised. 'You really think you can turn this house into a holiday let?'

Typical Bryony. Always straight to the point.

I laugh. 'Never play poker, Bry. Your disdain is written all over your face.'

She laughs too. 'Sorry. It's just all so tired and—'

'I know,' I cut in. 'But wait until I'm done. Even if it's not perfect, the surfers will be happy to be close to the beach.

'I can help,' she says, taking a long sip of wine. 'Jimmy, our gardener, does odd jobs.'

I can't help a wry smile forming. Of course Bryony's offer to help means sending someone else. She doesn't mean to sound so dismissive. It's just her way. Her and Alex's world is polished and curated, full of art openings and magazine spreads where nothing is out of place. She's flawless in that setting, the perfect host and adoring wife, her smile effortless as she stands beside Alex, charming collectors and art critics. But rolling up her sleeves, paint under her nails, isn't Bryony. It never has been. The only time she works up a sweat is at the gym or when she's out sailing.

A tiny shiver races through my body, like a static shock. I'll never understand how she can sail after what happened. Both of us should be dead.

'I appreciate the offer,' I say. 'But the whole point of me doing this is to be able to help with Mum's care home costs. I feel like I have to do this on my own, Bry. And I'm more than capable.'

'I told you, don't worry about the care home costs,' she says.

'And I told you I'll worry anyway,' I reply.

We share a smile and it's like old times. The gentle back and forth that's woven into our relationship. She forgets sometimes that I'm all grown up. That she's no longer the captain and me the second in command.

A sudden noise, the thud of a door banging close makes me jump, and my first thought is that they've found me.

'Jess' – Bryony's tone is sharp, like all the times I was little and would cry in my bed because I was worried about the dark, and she'd tell me to go to sleep – 'it was just Kelly, next door. You've forgotten how thin the walls are.'

I give a shaky laugh. 'Sorry.'

Bryony rolls her eyes before lifting her glass to drink. That's when I notice the shift of her sleeve as it slips down her arm and a dark bruise on her wrist.

'What's that?' I ask.

Bryony's smile falters, and I swear her hand shakes a little as she readjusts her sleeve. 'I walked into the dressing table yesterday. You know me.'

I do know my sister, and I know how clumsy she is. Always knocking over drinks or dropping things. It used to drive Mum crazy. She refused to go anywhere without a change of clothes for both of us because of the number of times Bryony spilled something down herself or knocked something over me.

And yet, I can't forget the fear I saw in her eyes earlier.

'Bry?' My tone is soft. Probing.

A silence draws out before she exhales. 'It's...' She trails off, staring down at the table. 'I don't know where to start.'

I place my hand over hers. 'Start anywhere.'

She opens her mouth like she's going to speak, but then her eyes drag to the white clock on the wall and she jolts, draining her glass and fumbling to scoop up her bag. 'I have to go. Alex is expecting me at the studio.'

I shake my head, not understanding. 'You've only just got here.'

'I know, but we've got all the time in the world now.' Her reply is almost breathless.

I follow her to the front door, and she throws on her coat before she wraps me into another hug. 'I'm so glad you're back.'

She's out of the door before I can ask her again if she's really OK. Why she's rushing away when she's just arrived.

On the street, she turns back. 'Can you meet me tomorrow? Come to Cliffview House. In the morning. It has to be the morning. I think I really do need your help after all.'

Then she hurries to her car and is gone in a roar of engine and bright headlights. I shut the door, the silence of the house closing in around me. For a moment, I just stand there, in the hall of my childhood home, breathing in the lingering scent of Bryony's perfume.

In the kitchen, I pour my wine back into the bottle and push the cork in the top. My head is starting to throb. Wine is the last thing I need.

I've spent the last few months scrambling to save my dreams and my relationship, and failing at both. I've neglected visits to Mum and barely spoken to Bryony. The last time we spent proper time together was when she came to stay at the hotel for a few days last autumn. She'd seemed happy. Her life perfect, like always. What could've changed so drastically in six months? What could turn Bryony – the sister who never flinched, never faltered – into someone who looks this terrified?

My phone vibrates on the counter. I snatch it up and freeze. Withheld number. I know who it is. This is the reason I overreacted to the noise of a door banging. This is why I thought they'd found me.

My heart starts to race so fast I can't tell one beat from another. Nausea tumbles in my stomach, and my breath catches in my lungs. I stare at the phone screen, legs shaking, hands trembling, tears swimming in my eyes until the hallway disappears. I wish it was that easy.

'Go away,' I whisper. 'Please go away.'

Anxiety feels like a rope wrapping around me, pulling

tighter and tighter, so there's no space to think about Bryony or anything but my own problems. I know I have to answer this call. And I will. Soon. But not now. There will be a way out of this. There has to be. I just need to find it. Then I'll answer. I'll do whatever they tell me.

FOUR

Jess

A few hours after Bryony leaves, the house feels too quiet. I've unpacked my suitcase, slipping my clothes in the drawers and wardrobe of my childhood bedroom. I've wandered from room to room, using an old sketchbook I found on my desk to start a list of everything I need to do. It already feels overwhelming, and I'm fidgety and stir crazy. Hungry too I realise.

I need milk for tea, bread, something simple I can cook for dinner. After months at the Kilstern, where I never liked using the large hotel kitchen alone, surviving mostly on toast, microwave meals, and bowls of cereal eaten standing over the sink, it's no wonder my jeans are hanging off me. Maybe it's being home in Mum's kitchen, but I'm craving something wholesome and homecooked.

I grab my bag, pull my coat from the hook and step outside. The spring air blowing across the bay carries the tang of salt and sea, cold enough that I zip my coat right up to my chin. The sun is already sinking behind the cliffs on the far side of Skelwick, leaving the sky streaked with faded yellow and faint pink.

If I was still in Oxfordshire, if everything hadn't fallen apart, I'd be walking the grounds of the Kilstern now, checking the gardens were secure before the sun sets.

Mole patrol, Liam called it. *'Those bastards are taking over.'*

'They're cute though,' I'd say.

'Kittens are cute, Jess. Moles are malicious creatures hell-bent on ruining my lawn.'

'It's—' I'd start to say, Liam joining in, both of us laughing.

'Rustic,' we'd say in unison. The word we used for anything we couldn't repair or replace.

Here, the wind from the sea is cold, and I'm grateful for the deep pockets of my coat to bury my hands in. Gulls wheel overhead, calling to each other like they're trading gossip.

It's only a five-minute walk down the steep hill to the main parade of shops. The cafés are closed now, the outdoor tables and chairs packed inside. They'll open again first thing, serving coffee and bacon sandwiches to tradespeople heading to jobs, and hot pasties for the surfers and the swimmers mad enough to brave the cold sea.

If I kept going, I'd hit the car park and the long promenade that overlooks the beach, then the corner that curves towards the stone wall of the harbour. But the sun is sinking lower, and I'm tired and sad – full of the self-pity of being home. I don't have it in me to wander. So I slip into the small supermarket and pick up a basket.

The aisles are narrow, the shelves crammed with too many items for the space. In the mornings when the bakery items are still warm, I'm sure it smells of yeast and sugar, but this time of day, it smells of bananas and vegetables on the turn.

I move slowly, focusing on what will get me through the next day or two. Eggs. Pasta. Chicken. Milk. Basic things. Comfort things. Things that feel like normal life.

At the till, a bored-looking teen with chipped black nail polish starts swiping my items across the scanner, not bothering to meet my eye. The amounts blink up on the tiny screen, each beep making the knot in my stomach tighten. It'll be fine, I tell myself. It has to be fine. A queue is already forming behind me – impatient little sighs, the shuffle of feet, someone's keys clinking.

'Cash or card?' she asks, still not looking at me.

'Card,' I say, and a second later the machine lights up and I hold my breath as I tap my phone. Long seconds pass before there's a beep followed by a flash of red light.

'It's declined,' she says, looking up for the first time.

I don't need to stare back to know there will be a mix of pity and curiosity in her eyes. The same look from the buyers who came to collect the last furnishings I sold from the Kilstern. They were local enough to know the story of our little hotel that failed.

A hot flush climbs my neck. I grit my teeth and force out a light laugh. 'How strange. I know there's money in there,' I lie, the sound brittle in my own ears.

'I've got cash. Hang on.'

I drop my bag onto the counter and start rummaging, pretending my cheeks aren't burning. Somewhere in here is the money from the bookcases I sold last week. I know it's here, but my fingers close around nothing but crumpled receipts and an old lipstick. I'm seconds away from saying to forget it and run out, when someone leans over and taps a bank card to the machine.

'I've got this.'

The voice is deep and as familiar as the scent of woody cedar and paint hitting my senses. Alex.

I look up and there he is. My old friend and my brother-in-law. He's tall and weather-tanned. Sharp cheekbones and dark-brown eyes. He's filled out in the last decade, no longer scrawny but broad. Dark hair and muscular arms with scars on his hands from years of working wood – the kind of handsome that seems to get better with age. He's wearing a paint-splattered T-shirt under an expensive-looking charcoal jacket.

'Jessie,' he says, using the nickname he gave me in those early days. It pulls at something deep inside me, reminding me of how easy it was between us. Two people who shared the same passions and interests, who could talk for hours without drawing breath. 'It's so good to see you.'

He steps forward before I can react, wrapping me in a hug that is solid and familiar. I pull away, aware of the queue and the spectacle I'm making, expecting angry faces and impatience, but everyone is smiling.

'There's your receipt, Mr Raffety,' the teen says, no longer bored but starry-eyed.

'Marnie,' Alex sighs, good-natured, 'for the hundredth time – call me Alex.'

She giggles, smile widening. 'OK, Alex.'

Alex scoops my food into a bag, talking non-stop to the queue of people the entire time. Asking after jobs and children and parents and pets. No one seems in a rush to get home anymore.

Outside, he hands me the shopping and smiles, and I feel eighteen again, rain-soaked on the beach, watching him wade knee-deep into the tide to put back the stranded crabs he'd rescued. Eating cold beans straight from a tin. Washing his clothes in public sinks. Free, impulsive, wild. It was a friendship built on loneliness and a shared love of the beach and art. Seeing him up to his knees, jeans soaked, a crab in each hand, I think I fell a little bit in love with him in that very first moment.

The horn of a passing car beeps, making me jump, but when I look up, someone is waving at Alex.

'Is there anyone in Skelwick who doesn't adore you?' I joke.

He laughs. 'Someone at the council once made a graph showing the town does better in winter these days because people visit my studio. Ever since, I'm apparently the saviour of

Skelwick, like it wasn't doing just fine for a hundred years before I showed up.'

'They should give you an honorary title,' I tease. 'A key to the bay or something.'

'Oh, they've tried. I keep saying there's no need.' His eyes crinkle at the corners. 'It really is good to see you, Jessie. And I'm... I'm sorry about the Kilstern. And Liam.'

The warmth in his voice squeezes painfully at my chest. I nod because I don't trust my voice not to crack.

We stand there for a moment, both smiling, and it feels like no time has passed since I was eighteen and he was twenty-one and we'd walk the beach side by side, swinging from talking over each other to easy silences.

I wonder suddenly if he'd missed our friendship the way I had in that first year after I left for London. I hadn't known what I wanted to do with my life, so when Alex arrived, I was eighteen, working in one of the cafés after finishing my A levels. I'd planned to take a year out, half a mind to apply for an art degree.

I thought we'd be best friends forever; hoped one day we'd be so much more. But when Bryony came home and she and Alex fell in love, it was too hard to watch. I tried to be happy for them both, but it stung to see the man I thought I loved and my sister together. So two short months later, I found a job in London on a trainee management scheme for a hotel chain, and it was me who moved away. I'd always loved hotel stays. How small details could make someone feel special.

I've only seen Alex a handful of times since. At his wedding to Bryony of course. Then a few Christmases I spent with Mum. There have been other visits, but he was travelling for work or busy, and he never came with Bryony and Mum to the Kilstern.

'Thanks for that.' I nod to the shop as I slip my hand into my bag again. 'I've got the cash right here.'

He waves me away. 'Don't worry about it.'

I drop my hand, stomach still knotted with guilt and relief and a squirming discomfort that Alex has had to rescue me after I've been back in Skelwick less than half a day.

'I'm guessing you've seen Bryony already?' he asks, voice light, but it feels like he's studying my face as I answer.

'She came by earlier,' I reply. 'Is she OK? She seemed...' I trail off, unsure how to put it into words.

His expression shifts. His brow tightens, eyes narrowing a fraction. 'What?'

'I don't know,' I say quickly. 'Stressed, I guess.' I shift the bag of shopping from one hand to another, feeling like I've said the wrong thing, but I'm not sure what exactly.

'She's fine,' he says. 'I've got to dash. I've got some more work to do in the studio tonight.' He nods in the direction of the town car park. In the summer, cars queue for an hour to get a space, but right now it's almost completely empty. Beyond it is the scrap of land where Alex used to park his campervan and now it's where his studio sits. A huge wood barn-like building with a shop and a gallery at the front and a space at the back where he makes his art pieces.

He smiles a goodbye that feels too polished and lacks the warmth of his greeting, and I wonder again if I said the wrong thing when I mentioned Bryony.

I wave and call another 'thanks', but the unsettled feeling lingers until he turns back and makes a silly face, the one where he crosses his eyes and sticks out his tongue, how he would after drinking cider in his van and I'd won at cards again.

My stomach flips at the memory. I remember how I used to lean close when I reached for the cards, trying to catch the scent of his aftershave, hoping he'd feel the same electric pull I did, too scared to make the first move.

But that was ten years ago. My feelings for Alex were an infatuation. Nothing real, like what Alex found with Bryony.

Or what I had with Liam. The thought hurts as I make my way slowly up the hill, the shopping bag digging into my fingers.

I remember the day Liam and I opened the hotel. How the entrance hall still smelled faintly of paint, how we barely had time to shove the ladder into the utility cupboard before the first guests walked through the door. I was front of house – the general manager, the receptionist and the concierge all rolled into one. Liam ran the bar and oversaw the restaurant, working closely with the Michelin-starred chef we'd all but dragged from London to cook in our little country hotel. We were delirious with exhaustion, running on adrenaline and coffee, stumbling over each other in the narrow corridors as we rushed to get beds made and menus printed.

And then one night, early on, we stood in the bar after the last guests had gone to bed. The room was quiet, soft lighting from the chandeliers reflecting off the polished tables, the air scented with pine from the fire he insisted we lit every evening.

'You did it,' Liam had said, sliding an arm around my waist. *'Full house for the first week. You made this place what it is.'*

He always did that – always made it sound like I was the captain and he was following my lead. Even though he'd worked just as hard, bled just as much into those walls as I had.

'We did it,' I'd corrected him, stepping into his arms, feeling that warm, easy closeness settle between us.

We were a team. Right up until the moment we weren't.

The memory squeezes at something tender deep inside me. Tears spill down my cheeks as I walk, but I don't wipe them away. The hill feels steeper tonight, the wind colder, the sky darker.

My phone rings. I pull it from my coat pocket, expecting Bryony or Liam. But it's the withheld number again.

The warmth of the memory fades, replaced by something cold and tightening in my chest. My pulse races. I know exactly who they are and why they're calling. It's the mistake I made, that I'd give anything to undo, or at the very least hide from. But these people will not give up. And if I keep ignoring them, they'll track me down and things will be so much worse.

I take a breath, swallowing down my fear and crushing anxiety and humiliation.

'Hello?' I say, trying for breezy.

'Jessica Waters?' The voice is deep and carries a gravelly malice and authority that makes my stomach turn over.

'Yes,' I reply.

'I've been trying to contact you—'

'Yes, I'm so sorry,' I say too fast, regretting accepting the call. 'I've just moved and things have been chaotic. In fact, now isn't a good time. Can I call you back later this week?'

The silence feels weighted.

'I don't want to escalate this,' he says like he really does. 'But I will. You have until Friday. At which point—'

'Of course.' I end the call before I'm forced to hear more. For a moment, I stand in the middle of the street, breath coming fast and hard. It's my fault. My desperation to save the hotel led me to do stupid things. It became a wedge between Liam and me, but I couldn't give up as easily as him.

We both made mistakes in the end. But I was trying to save us. And he destroyed us. And now my mistake has followed me back to Skelwick and I'm sinking in quicksand with no way out. I don't know what I'm going to do.

FIVE

SIXTEEN YEARS EARLIER – THE WATER

Bryony

I can't feel my toes or my feet or my fingers. They are blocks of cement, weighing me down. My teeth chatter, and my arms ache with the weight of Jess's body. I think I'm crying, but the salty water keeps hitting my face so I can't be sure. All I know is that it's getting harder to snatch a breath from the air between each pelting wave, getting harder to keep Jess's head out of the water.

'Jess.' I hiss my sister's name. Her body is slippery in my grasp. Her face is pale, lips blue, hair slicked like weeds across her cheeks. She's too still. Too heavy.

How long have we been in the water? It feels like hours. Will anyone even be looking for us yet?

How did this happen? Dad's rules flash through my mind.

'Don't go out without permission.'

'Always wear life jackets.'

And Mum's: *'Never take anyone else with you.'*

I thought they were being boring. Treating us like babies. I didn't think it would end like this. I push my head a little higher, trying to keep my face out of the waves.

'Wake up, Jess. Please wake up!' I gasp, voice breaking as another wave hits me, filling my mouth with sea water. I gag and spit as the panic tightens in my lungs. 'I can't hold you for much longer. Please wake up.'

I kick my legs, desperately trying to keep us both above water. This is a bad dream. A nightmare I'm going to wake from.

We've sailed the thirty-foot bilge keel a hundred times before without a hitch. This time was different. I remember the shadow moving to my side. The hand reaching for the tiller. That awful laughter. How quickly it changed from something fun to something dangerous.

No one can ever know. We can't tell a soul. My throat squeezes shut. We might never get the chance.

The sea surges, slapping my face with a sheet of icy water. Thank God I grabbed the life jacket. A last-minute decision. Just the one jacket. I've shoved it between us like a float. It's not doing much, but it's something.

When I blink away the water, the sky seems darker. The last of the daylight has disappeared, eaten by clouds and the darkening sky. The *Calypso* bobs a little way off, a white shape rolling on the grey water.

'Help,' I shout. 'Help!'

The distance to the *Calypso* doesn't seem far. I think I could make it if it was just me. I could survive. But it would mean leaving Jess to drown, and I can't do that.

Frustration presses against the panic. I wish she wasn't here. But then would our parents even notice if it was just me missing? They've always babied Jess. If she's not home, they'll notice. They'll realise. They'll call the coastguard. It will be OK.

Except, Mum could still be out shopping, Dad not back from work. What if no one knows we're here?

Another wave hits, hard enough for Jess's body to slip in my arms. I haul her up, my own head sinking below the water for a moment. I force myself to kick harder as salt burns the back of my throat.

The world is shrinking to black water and black sky. Jess's dead weight drags me lower. My legs cramp.

This is all my fault. It was my idea to go sailing. I wanted to surprise her. I was the one who insisted. Jess has her young artist exhibit in London tomorrow, and I just wanted us to have fun. Let loose a little. She'd been working so hard. Now I don't know if there will be a trip to London. Maybe there'll be no Jess. No me.

Dad's voice echoes in my mind. *'Always stay calm when you're at sea.'* He used to take me out on the *Calypso* when Jess was too little, just the two of us playing pirates and pretending to have adventures. He taught me everything about the boat – how to trim the sail, how to keep the tiller steady when the wind shifts. I've spent hours studying the charts with him, tracing coastlines and learning to navigate by instinct.

I can do this. I just have to stay calm.

The words do nothing to quell the rising panic.

I close my eyes, wishing us back in time. Wishing I'd followed the rules. The sea is growing around us, pulling us down. It feels like a choice. We both die, or I live and Jess dies.

SIX

NOW

Jess

The next day, I'm back in town on my way to Bryony's house, and already I feel like I'm unravelling at the edges. It's my first full day back in Skelwick and it feels too much. I woke three times in the night, gasping, heart hammering, the same icy water dragging me under. Always falling. Always in the water. Never anything before, no matter how much I try to remember.

This morning, I continued my list of things I need to do to Mum's house to make it a holiday rental. Pages and pages of notes, starting with clearing out a lifetime of possessions.

The call last night is like a constant hand around my throat, squeezing. '*You have until Friday.*'

I'd thought coming home would give me space. A chance to hide. To breathe. But it all just feels the same. And worse too. Today is Tuesday. I have three days to find a solution when I already know there isn't one.

I reach the town and pass the supermarket and the cafés. My cheeks flame remembering standing by the counter, scrambling to pay for a few items of food. The day is overcast with a thick blanket of grey cloud and a mist from the sea that's left the pavements damp. Without the sunshine and the tourists, it's easy to see how worn out Skelwick looks.

I drop my head and hurry on towards the promenade. Bryony's house sits on the cliff on the opposite side of the bay with the other mansion-like houses, owned by the wealthy like Bryony. When I was little, my dad used to call them snobs. *'They never shop or eat in our town. They think they're too good for us in their fancy homes with their fancy cars.'*

Dad lives on the coast of Spain now. He retired there after Bryony came back to Skelwick and set up as a handyman for the British residents. We don't speak much. I stayed close to Bryony when she and Dad left Skelwick after the accident, but it was harder with Dad. We'd talk on the phone, but it seemed neither of us knew what to say.

The easiest way to get to the cliff by foot is to go down into the town first and then up again. I could've driven Mum's car, but I like to walk. I always have. Walking is the only way to settle my mind when it starts to spin in a hundred directions and I start to overthink everything.

I used to love walking the beach with Mum and Dad and Bryony, competing to see who could find the most interesting shell. After the accident, when I came home from the hospital, and we were no longer a family and no one would tell me why, when it was just me and Mum, I'd go out walking on my own. Feeling sad and lost. Five whole years of feeling that way. At first, I asked Mum what happened on the boat. How did we end up in the water? She said she didn't know. I asked why Dad left too, and why Bryony went with him. Her reply was always the same. *'Sometimes things don't work out.'*

Both answers felt like lies, and eventually I stopped asking. For five years, it was just me and Mum and school. And then I met Alex and it felt like I'd found my person. My best friend. Then Bryony came home too, and I was so happy to have her back, like a missing piece of myself had returned. We'd talked all the time, but it wasn't the same as sharing a cup of tea at breakfast, swapping gossip in our PJs on each other's beds.

I round the corner and I'm on the promenade overlooking the wide stretches of sand. The sea beyond is the same colour as the grey stone walls. There are a few swimmers in wetsuits and hats braving the cold and a group of surfers on their boards, waiting for the perfect wave.

Alex's studio is to my left, looking over the beach. He used to tell me we'd have a studio like that together one day. Him with his driftwood. Me with my shell art. Earrings and canvases and anything I could think of. I was happy to go along with it, but I never saw art as my life the same way Alex did. It was all he lived and breathed. All that consumed him until he met Bryony the summer she moved home.

Bryony became his muse and him her everything, and I pretended it didn't feel like I'd lost both of them in the same breath. I pretended my feelings for Alex weren't real, and I left Skelwick soon after. Then I met Liam when I was twenty-two and it felt like everything had slotted into place.

I keep walking. The wall bends round, past a toilet and shower block and the Skelwick Arms, where Dad would take us for a fizzy drink and a packet of salt and vinegar crisps after sailing on the *Calypso*. I'm half smiling at the memory when the door of the pub opens and a woman with a bucket of cleaning products steps out.

'Jess Waters? Goodness, you haven't changed a bit.'

It takes me a moment to recognise the woman. Her hair is no longer the bright red I remember but cropped short and completely white now. Still, the voice gives her away.

'Kelly,' I say, smiling even as knots twist tighter in my stomach. Does Kelly know I'm back because my business failed? Because *I* failed? 'Hi. How are you?'

'The same, love. Always the same.' She lifts the bucket of cleaning bottles like evidence, the plastic clattering. Her eyes are warm and twinkly, reminding me of the times she'd pop round from next door for a glass of sherry with Mum when Dad was at the pub, and they'd gossip and cackle and put the world to rights.

'Gosh, I'd forgotten how much you look like your sister,' she adds.

People have always commented on it, though you only have to look at our clothes or our hairstyles to tell us apart.

A memory nudges at me. Being eight years old and calling Kelly our aunty. She always let me come when she took Bryony and her own daughter, Helen, to the cinema, letting us fill paper cups with pick 'n' mix. Fizzy cola bottles, white chocolate mice, and the chocolate buttons with the sprinkles on them. Mum never let us have sweets like that; she'd tut about our teeth and say we'd spoil our dinner. But Kelly just winked at us and said it would be our secret.

I smile at Kelly, about to ask how Helen is doing, but she speaks first, tone soft and caring. 'I'm sorry about your mum. I tried to do what I could for her, you know?'

'I know – thank you,' I say, voice suddenly choked.

'It was me who found Addie to be her carer,' Kelly continues. 'Addie and I used to work together.'

'Thank you,' I whisper again. 'I didn't get to meet Addie, but she spoke to me on the phone regularly. I wish I'd been here more.'

Kelly steps forward, enveloping me in a hug that smells of lemon cleaning products and something Kelly-like that reminds me of my childhood. 'Oh, love, your mum was always so proud of you. She wanted you out there living your best life. Although I bet she's happy you're back for a while.'

Guilt pricks at me. I didn't make it to the care home yesterday. And this morning, instead of going straight to her, I'm heading to Bryony's. Mum doesn't even know I'm home. I'm not sure she'd remember anyway.

Kelly shifts the bucket from one hand to another. 'I heard you're turning her house into one of those holiday rentals.' Her tone sharpens, like it did when we were kids and we made a mess in Helen's bedroom.

'To pay for Mum's care home costs, yes,' I reply.

She gives a tight smile. 'It's a shame. There are no houses for Helen to rent here. She's in Merkshaw these days, runs her own mobile beauty salon. She wants to come back and find a steadier job, but there's nowhere to rent. And of course there's the falling-out with Bryony.'

I almost laugh. 'That was years ago.'

Kelly shrugs. 'Some people don't forget.'

I remember the argument. Helen and Bryony were in the same school year and best friends and neighbours. They were always together – in and out of each other's houses. It was a life of sleepovers and bike rides. Sometimes I felt like I had two big sisters.

Then when they were fifteen, Helen accused Bryony of copying her on a test, getting Bryony in trouble at school. Then Bryony accused Helen of lying. My sister, hurt and furious, swore she'd never speak to Helen again. As far as I know, she's stuck to her promise. It sounds like Helen has held a grudge too.

Kelly adjusts the collar of her coat and steps from the doorway. 'I'd better get on. Two more cleaning jobs to go. Say hello to Bryony from me. Addie mentioned she'd had some trouble at the house. I hope she's OK.'

I frown. 'What trouble?'

'Oh, it's not my business, love, and you know I'm not one to gossip,' she replies, although that's not how I remember her and Mum when they were together, heads bent and whispering. 'I'm sure Alex sorted it. We're all so proud of him. Did you hear he's going to America next month? They're putting on an exhibition in Long Island.'

Kelly gives a wave and disappears up the road.

Her words about trouble follow me as I continue along the seafront. My mind is on Bryony and her tearful plea for help yesterday, and yet, my feet still falter at the next turn as the harbour comes into view.

My breath catches in my lungs as I take in the boats, wishing I'd driven after all. They rest in neat rows at their moorings. The small motorboats are first. All of them painted the same red as the FOR HIRE sign that sits, weather-beaten, on the dock. Beyond them sits an assortment of sailing boats; most are small dinghies with tattered sails that don't look like they've moved in all the years I've been away.

The larger, newer vessels cluster at the far corner, where the water is deeper. It's impossible to miss Bryony's yacht. The long, gleaming white hull, the huge sail folded tight, the name *Odysseus* painted in bold black lettering along the side. It's bigger than the *Calypso* and twice as showy. Our father sold the *Calypso* after the accident. I've never set foot on a boat since. I never will, but Bryony still loves to sail, calling her own boat after the Greek legend, who was held captive by Calypso.

Just looking at the boats makes my mouth turn dry, my head throb. I back away, dizzy, lungs fighting to draw in air that's right there. In a distant part of my thoughts, I swear I hear Bryony screaming my name. Would these moments that haunt me still happen if I could remember what really happened that day?

I hurry on, striding as fast as my legs will carry me, around the corner, away from the cold sea and the boats and the danger and panic that still pounds in my chest. The road carries me up, past the church and the little graveyard, past the cinema that used to be a ballroom, past the care home that used to be a grand Victorian hotel.

Up and up. The houses grow larger and grander until I reach Bryony and Alex's, perched at the very top. I remember Bryony dragging me up here each summer, walking the cliff path that ran along the backs of the houses, pointing out which ones she loved. *'I'm going to live there one day,'* she'd say, and I'd laugh but I believed her too.

Cliffview House is like something from a magazine. Sleek glass and pale stone, all sharp angles and shine with a huge black front door. Floor-to-ceiling windows wrap around the house. Two cars are parked in the drive – Bryony's silver Mercedes and a black Land Rover that must belong to Alex.

My phone rings, making me jump. It's Liam. Again. Hurt slices through me. Instant tears threaten to fall. There are moments when it's hard to separate the failure of the hotel with the end of our relationship. But other times, like now, when I picture his face – the broad smile and that dark-rust-red hair flopping over his eyes – the pain for what we had and lost is sharp and fills me with a deep, unending sorrow.

I wish Liam was here now. I know I wouldn't feel at rock bottom if he was by my side. He was always steady, the voice of calm when things felt out of control. Like the time the booking system went down and deleted a booking. A newly married couple turned up at reception, expecting a room overlooking the gardens, expecting champagne and luxury, and we weren't prepared.

'Don't panic,' Liam had said as I'd excused myself from the couple and run to find him in the bar. *'First of all,'* he'd started, lifting his thumb like he was counting, *'we've got an empty room, right?'*

'Yes, but it's not ready.'

'Second of all, they'll be happy to wait. Bring them in here. I'll give them a glass of champagne and then a tour of the grounds while you sort their room out.'

'But—'

'Jess, it's going to be fine.'

I'd made to move away when he'd grabbed my hand. *'And third of all, I love you. You've got this.'*

And now there's no one to tell me all the reasons it will be OK, and I'm not sure it will. I'm not sure if there's a way out of this mess I'm in.

The hurt rises up again. I can't keep thinking about Liam. It's over. He made sure of that.

I cram thoughts of him into the corner of my mind, next to last night's phone call and the rising panic that I'm in more trouble than I can admit. Part of me aches to tell Bryony, to let her be the one I lean on. She always knows what to do. But something was rattling her yesterday. She wasn't herself. Before I ask for help, I want to know what's wrong. Because her visit yesterday has left me feeling off-kilter.

SEVEN

Jess

The woman who opens the door to Cliffview House is not my sister. She's younger. Early twenties, I guess, with glossy dark hair scraped into a tight ponytail and a heart-shaped face that would look gentle if not for her narrowed eyes. She's wearing black leggings and a loose white T-shirt, one wireless earbud still in her ear.

'Hi,' I say brightly. 'I'm Jess. Bryony's sister.'

She nods but doesn't move aside. Her hand stays fixed on the edge of the door like she's guarding something. Then, without taking out the earbud, she raises her voice into the hallway. 'Mr Raffety, you have a visitor.'

'Oh,' I say, shaking my head, 'I'm actually here to see Bryony,' I add quickly, surprised Alex is home. I assumed he'd be at his studio, but then I suppose he can choose his own hours.

The woman shrugs. 'I always call Mr Raffety.' She keeps her body angled in the door frame, just enough space for her but not for me, like she expects me to push past her.

There's the sound of footsteps tapping on the marble floors, then Alex appears. He's wearing jeans and a loose navy linen shirt, hair damp as though he's only just stepped out of the shower. There are shadows beneath his eyes, like he slept as badly as I did.

'Jessie.' His voice lifts with surprise, and he smiles. 'I barely see you from one year to the next and now it's twice in two days.' He seems pleased, and yet he's taken over the space the woman was guarding and hasn't welcomed me in.

'Hi,' I manage, feeling suddenly awkward, like I'm intruding. 'Bryony invited me for coffee,' I blurt out.

I think I must imagine the way the muscle in his jaw tightens because his voice is still friendly as he finally opens the door wide and waves me in. 'She didn't mention it, but come in.'

I step into their spacious entrance hall. The floors are marble, the walls white. Both gleam under the lights of the chandeliers, bright despite the fact the morning light is spilling into the house from the vast windows. My gaze is immediately drawn to one of Alex's driftwood sculptures positioned near the staircase – an intricate spiral of bleached wood pieces twisting upward like a frozen wave. The smooth curves catch the light in places, throwing soft shadows that seem to move as you walk around it. It's stunning, organic and deliberate all at once.

I've only been here once before, soon after Bryony and Alex bought it, when I was on a flying visit to Mum one Christmas. I'd forgotten how big it is. There's a centrepiece of white lilies on a round oak display table. Grand and understated all at once.

The air inside is warm and faintly perfumed, the kind of quiet luxury scent we'd use in the diffusers around the Kilstern, I think with a stab of loss. Liam and I chose eucalyptus and sandalwood, reminding the guests of spas and relaxation.

Alex motions at the woman in the white T-shirt. 'Have the two of you met? This is Paulina, our housekeeper. Paulina, this is Jess. Bryony's sister.'

'Hello,' she says, barely looking at me.

'Paulina works every morning for us, and honestly we'd be lost without her.'

Paulina beams at Alex. The look of adoration in her eyes reminds me of the teen in the shop yesterday. Kelly was almost bursting with pride, too, when she mentioned Alex's trip to America next month.

'Would you like me to make the coffee, Mr Raffety?' Paulina asks.

Alex shakes his head, still smiling. 'Thank you, but I'll make them and join the ladies before I'm needed at the studio.'

She flashes a wide smile in return and turns away.

Alex leads me down a long hallway with walls covered in life-sized black-and-white canvas photographs of Bryony. In one, she's laughing, head down, caught unaware. In another, she's staring moodily into the lens. In another, she's walking barefoot along the beach at sunset. There's another from their wedding. I remember Alex taking it, ignoring the eyeroll from the official photographer because he wanted to capture his wife's beauty himself. His devotion to her is evident in every room, for everyone to see.

The kitchen is as grand as the hall. An open-plan space with dark-blue cupboards, white marble countertops and a wall of bifold doors that lead out to a simple lawn that slopes down towards the cliff. Beyond it, the sea looks dark – almost black – under the pale-grey sky.

Alex busies himself making coffee, and I stand awkwardly beside the marble-topped breakfast bar, wondering where Bryony is, when she glides into the room wearing simple black trousers and a cream cable-knit jumper.

She hugs me gently, exclaiming loudly, 'Jess, what a surprise.' Before I can reply, she leans close to my ear and whispers, 'I'm sorry. Play along.'

The confusion on my face is real. 'Have I got my days muddled? I thought we were meeting today?' Then, seeing the plea in Bryony's eyes, I do as she's asked and play along in whatever game this is. I smack my forehead. 'You meant next Tuesday, didn't you? I'm so sorry. I can go.'

I make a step to the door, but Alex laughs and holds out a mug of coffee. The aromas are bitter and earthy, and – like everything else connected to Bryony – expensive. 'Don't be silly. It's fine, isn't it, Bry?'

She nods and takes the coffee Alex offers her as I study her face. Her smile is in place, make-up flawless, but I think I catch a tension lurking just behind it. Enough to cause the worry to return. I remember Kelly's words. *'Addie mentioned she'd had some trouble at the house.'*

On the surface, she seems normal. But I know my sister, and the silent plea in her expression just now, and that fear I saw in her eyes yesterday. And there's something in the air between her and Alex. The awkwardness morphs into tension as we settle on the sofas in the corner of the kitchen, looking out to the garden.

'I bumped into Kelly this morning,' I say, pretending I don't feel the strangeness between them or with me, I can't tell. For a moment, it feels almost like something menacing is standing in the shadows, just out of sight. 'She's not keen on Mum's house being a holiday rental.'

Bryony rolls her eyes. 'The entire community are against them. They have long and dull meetings about the lack of housing for locals. They seem to forget that those holiday rentals are for the tourists that keep Skelwick alive. Well, that and Alex's art studio anyway.'

'She mentioned Helen wanted to move back,' I add.

'I hope she doesn't.' Bryony sighs. 'People like that never change. She's a liar and a troublemaker.'

We fall silent. There's an electrical hum coming from somewhere in the house, but it disappears under the noise of Paulina's hoovering. I drink my coffee, wanting to ask Bryony if she's

OK, but whatever is going on, it's clear from her whispered, *'Play along,'* that Alex doesn't know.

Maybe they've had a fight. All couples do, I remind myself, thinking of Liam. We weren't the type for quiet brooding or sulks. We decided early on in our relationship that we were too busy for that. If one of us was mad, we'd say so. Blurt it out, then let it go. It usually came down to money.

'You can't keep spending on the credit card,' Liam had hissed at me once when we were weeks away from opening the doors of the Kilstern. *'What even is half this stuff?'*

'It's the luxury we're promising. Throw pillows, expensive blankets. Personalised cups and saucers in the rooms. We're not a budget hotel, Liam. We have to stand out.'

'First of all, I know we're not a budget hotel. Second of all, not all this stuff has to be in place on day one, and—'

I'd cut in. *'Third of all, you trust me, the same way I trust you with the menus. Are you scrimping on the meat quality?'*

'Of course not,' he'd said, and instantly his face had softened. *'Sorry. It's just a lot.'*

'I know. I'm sorry too. I'll hold off buying anything else until we take more bookings.'

Trust. The word is spiky and bitter. I thought nothing would break that – break us.

'What are your plans today, Jess?' Alex asks.

I look up and catch him glancing at the large station clock on the wall.

'I'm going to visit Mum after this. Then make a start on clearing the house.'

There's so much to do I can feel the weight of it pressing on my ribs. Clearing Mum's things. A lifetime's worth of memories she's struggling to cling on to. The wallpaper needs to be stripped. The walls painted. The kitchen floor needs replacing, and the cupboards sanded down and painted. Every item on my to-do list feels like a reminder of how far I've fallen.

But I'll push on. It might not be the fix I desperately need, but it's a step. It's something. 'The plan is to have the house ready by the summer and then—'

My sentence is cut short by the sudden shift of Bryony beside me. She knocks my leg as she moves. It's enough that my coffee spills over the rim and drips on the floor.

'Shoot,' she says. 'Sorry, Jess, did I get you?'

I shake my head.

'No harm done then,' she says, copying the words Mum used to say almost daily. 'Not as bad as that time I managed to knock over the entire fresh orange carton.'

I laugh, remembering the commotion and yelling as thick gloopy orange spilled over the kitchen table, the chairs and the floor. And all over my art project minutes before we were due to leave for school. I must have been eight or nine. I remember walking to school in heaving sobs. While I was at school, Mum dabbed the juice with kitchen roll and hung the paper on the line to dry. *'No harm done,'* she'd said later that night, when I looked at my slightly orange-tinged picture of a forest.

'I'll get a cloth for the floor,' I say, but Alex is already on his feet.

'No need,' he replies brightly, striding to the sink.

With his back to us, Bryony leans close, speaking in a low whisper. 'Ask me to come with you.'

'To see Mum?' I whisper back.

She nods before leaning back, expression blank, as though the exchange never happened. What the hell is going on here?

I wait for Alex to return and mop up the spill. 'Why don't you come with me?' I say to Bryony, a little too bright, too false. I've always been a terrible liar. 'I'm sure Mum would love to see both of us.'

I expect Bryony to agree. It was her idea after all, but she holds back, looking to Alex. He gives me a pained expression before taking Bryony's hand in his, fingers threaded tightly together. 'Sorry, Jess. I need Bry with me at the studio today.'

'You can't spare her?' I push.

Alex's smile is all charm, but his reply is clear. 'Not today.' He looks at the clock again. 'In fact, we'd better go. There's a lot to do. I'm hosting an exhibit at the studio at the end of the month.

He stands suddenly, and I follow. Neither Bryony nor I have managed more than a few sips of coffee, but Alex seems oblivious. He must be in the middle of working on a new piece, I think, remembering the days in our friendship when he'd close in on himself, barely talk, barely leave his camper, barely remember to eat.

'I'll walk you to the door,' Alex says, giving me the distinct impression I'm being dismissed.

Outside, I pull in a deep breath, grateful for the cool breeze brushing my face. The house felt close, airless, like standing too long in a crowded room. Bryony and Alex have always been intense – all passion and heat. Of course their arguments would be the same. *Don't overthink it.* I can't obsess and worry like I normally do. I'm barely holding it together with my own problems as it is.

EIGHT

Jess

By the time I'm halfway down the hill towards the town, I'm suddenly desperate to see Mum. I want her to wrap her arms around me, kiss the top of my head, tell me she loves me. '*There. See. No harm done.*'

I want her to make me a cup of tea and open the good Fox's chocolate biscuits she hides for guests and bad days and rainy days. I want to tell her the mess I'm in. I want to cry on her shoulder for the heartbreak of losing Liam and the hotel we worked so hard to build. I want to cry for what I saw him do and the betrayal that feels like a sharp scratch against my heart.

But I made a mistake too. One Liam begged me not to.

My stomach twists, a sick, sour knot as the memory hits. His voice firm as he'd said my name. '*Jess, please don't do this. We can find another way.*'

But there was no other way. We needed more money to save the hotel. And so I'd done it. I'd made the call. And now it's all come back on me.

'*You have until Friday.*'

Then what?

I'm in a stranglehold. No way out. My legs feel weak. Friday. Three days.

But I can't talk to Mum about any of this. Because the woman in the care home is not that version of my mum anymore. Even on her best days, she's still the one we now comfort, not the one to offer it. Tears sting my eyes as I draw in a shuddering breath and force myself to keep putting one foot in front of the other until the big white care home comes into view.

Once a grand hotel that promised opulence and ocean-air cures, it's now tired, the white walls cracked and streaked with dirt and salt from the relentless sea wind. But inside, it's clean and bright, even if the carpets are worn at the edges, the curtains faded from years of sunlight and the air over-perfumed, barely masking the smell of disinfectant and urine.

I introduce myself to a woman at the front desk. She smiles and nods to a visitors' book. 'If you can make sure to sign in and then out at the end please. It's a fire regulation.'

'Of course,' I reply. 'I've forgotten the room number,' I say, swallowing down the rock of guilt. I've only visited Mum once since she's been here. The Kilstern was so busy at first that it felt impossible to get away. And then when we weren't busy, when all the guests stopped coming, all my energy went into trying to save it.

'Room three-two-nine. Andrea is a lovely lady.' She glances at my name in the visitors' book. 'And she thinks the world of you, Jess. Would you like us to bring you some tea and biscuits?'

I smile. 'Yes please. Chocolate, if you've got them. They're Mum's favourite.'

I make my way up three flights of stairs and down a long corridor. Most doors are open, showing residents in armchairs or lying in bed. Mum's room is near the end of the corridor. I knock softly before stepping in. She's sitting in a high-backed burgundy armchair facing the window that looks out to the bay. She's wearing the blue cardigan I bought her for Christmas. The wool is now swamping her. Her hair is thinner too. My throat squeezes shut, sadness and guilt and love threatening to split me open as I take in her frailty.

Mum was so excited about our plans for the hotel. She was our biggest champion. Telling Liam and me to dream big. She was so proud when Bryony brought her to visit, cooing over every cushion and picture we'd chosen, back when the dementia was little more than forgetting to drink her cup of tea or where she'd put her glasses. I don't know how to tell her it's all over. Or if she'll even understand or remember if I do.

'Mum,' I say gently.

She turns, her face breaking into a smile. 'Hello, Jess.'

It takes me a moment to answer. To fight the waves of emotion and the relief that today is a good day, that she knows who I am. 'It's so good to see you. I've missed you, Mum.'

She starts to stand, talking about putting the kettle on and finding the biscuits. There's a moment when confusion settles over her features, and she stares around the room like she's never seen it before. I'm by her side in two steps and easing her back into the chair. I pull up a second smaller armchair and sit across from her, close enough to place my hand on hers.

'They're going to bring us tea and biscuits,' I say. 'I asked for the chocolate ones.'

'Your favourite,' she says with a playful tsk.

'And yours. You hid the Fox's from yourself as much as from me.'

'I could never find the bloomin' things half the time.' Her smile warms something in my chest. 'The best days were the ones I'd stumble upon a packet I'd forgotten about.'

We're still laughing when a staff member brings in a tray with a pot of tea and a plate of biscuits.

I pour the tea for us, and we talk about the care home activities. I try not to ask too many questions, remembering what the doctor told us about how easily questions can confuse Mum. How it's better to let her lead the conversation.

'How have you been?' Mum asks.

I hesitate, swallowing back the tears. I hate lying, but what good will it do to upset Mum with how terrible things are. 'I'm really well,' I say brightly. 'It's busy but good.'

Mum smiles but doesn't ask about the hotel. Maybe she doesn't remember. 'You've always been the clever one,' she says, patting my hand. 'Your dad and I were so proud when you won the national art competition. The awards day in London was very special.'

I nod, forcing a smile. 'It was.' I don't remind her that we never made it to the awards day. It was the day after the accident, when I was still in hospital. The only thing I remember from that week is icy-cold water and the sound of Bryony's screams echoing across the sea. But that was another thing the doctor told us about dementia. How it's best not to correct the memory slips. It only leads to more confusion and then upset.

So we talk for a while about small things. Like how the woman in the room next door has noisy grandchildren, how she loves watching the gulls sweep over the bay. I nod and listen, guilt gnawing at me. I should have been here more. I should have done more. I promise myself that now I'm back, I'll visit every day.

When Mum tires and her eyelids grow heavy, I squeeze her hand and tell her I'd better go.

Only then does her smile slip. 'I want to go home.'

Her words break my heart, and it takes everything I have to keep my voice bright. 'This is your home now, Mum, remember?'

Her eyes dart quickly around the room, then she nods. 'Yes, of course. Silly me.'

I stand and kiss her on the top of the head, like she's done to me countless times. 'I'm going to be staying in Skelwick for a little while, so I'll be seeing lots more of you. I'll come by tomorrow. I'll bring some photo albums we can look through together.'

'That would be nice.' Her tone is almost robotic, and I wonder if she's just pretending to understand and inside she's still desperate to go home.

It's as I'm pulling on my coat that she asks me, 'How's Liam?'

I turn to face her, surprised she's asked. She usually keeps her questions vague, like her answers. Masking, it's called. A way people with dementia trick those around them into believing all is well inside their minds. Her question hits me straight in the chest. 'He's fine,' I lie quickly. 'Love you, Mum. I'll be back tomorrow.'

The moment the door closes, the lie about Liam sits like a stone in my stomach. The truth is, I don't know if he's fine. I don't even know where he is. I assume he's with his parents in Bournemouth, but I haven't answered his calls to find out. I've even stopped listening to his voicemails. Deleted the last few without opening them.

Mum always had a soft spot for him. *'You're the kind of girl who's happy to stand in the shadows, Jess,'* she'd told me the first time she met him. *'And Liam's the kind of boy who wants to pull you into the sun. He's a keeper.'*

Outside, the sea air clears the cloying warmth of the care home as I walk into the town, cutting through the narrow street with the laundrette and the building that becomes a basement nightclub every summer.

I can't stop the memory coming of the day Liam and I first went to view the Kilstern.

'It's in our price range,' he'd said as we drove through the gates and up the long driveway.

'For a reason,' I'd joked, even though my heart was hammering.

The manor house was breathtaking, even with all the work it needed. Wisteria climbed the orange-red brickwork, creeping into gaps in the glass of the pretty sash windows that looked out over rolling lawns and a pond rimmed with reeds. We'd wandered from room to room like awestruck schoolchildren – imagining the chandeliers, the roaring fires, the polished floors, the laughter of our guests.

'I love it,' I'd whispered. *'But it's too much work.'*

'For anyone else, yes,' Liam had said, turning to me with that fierce, unshakable belief in his eyes. *'For you? Never. This is our dream. Right here.'*

'But what about travelling? You said you wanted to see the world too. We can't do both.'

'There'll be time for travelling when we're filthy rich with our own global hotel chain. This place is too special to pass up. We could do this, Jess.'

And I'd believed him.

Tears fall before I can stop them. I wipe them away, suddenly angry. I loved him with my whole being. I thought nothing could come between us. But he hadn't wanted to try everything to save the hotel. He told me it was pointless. That we should cut our losses and walk away, but I couldn't give up after all our hard work and we'd seen what success could be.

Maybe Liam's betrayal with the woman in the bar was the final nail in the coffin of our relationship. But if that's true, then I dug the grave first. Because I borrowed the money I couldn't pay back.

NINE

Jess

A week goes by. Friday passes. The calls about my loan start up again. Two, three, five times a day he tries. Always the same withheld number. Always the same sick twist in my stomach.

I don't answer.

Liam calls too. He's stopped leaving voicemails, but he still calls most days. Like he wants me to know he's giving me space, not giving up. I don't answer him either, but my thumb has started to hover over *Accept*, like one day I might finally press it.

At night, the drowning nightmare claws at me, dragging me under again and again. I wake gulping air, tears pricking my eyes, chest aching like I've been held under for real.

And every time, I try to remember.

The therapist with the wilting houseplants told me to work backward. '*Your clearest memories are the moments in the water, before you passed out. So start there. Imagine pressing rewind on a film. What happened just before that? And just before that?*'

It worked at first. Years of reliving the moments in the water and then I started to remember the fall too. I remember a laugh that didn't belong to Bryony. A force shoving me. Flying through the air. The snap of cold as I hit the sea. The best nights are when the impact jerks me awake. But no matter how hard I try, I can't remember standing on the boat. I can't remember how I went over the side.

In the daytime, I drink coffee until I'm jittery and nauseous. I visit Mum and I clear the house. I start in the dining room. We mostly ate at the kitchen table or squished on the sofas on a Saturday night. The dining room carries fewer memories. There's also less to clear, less to do. I box up old glassware and crockery and paint over the yellowing magnolia with a bright teal, and try to pretend I'm moving forward.

And in all this time, I don't see Bryony. I haven't heard from her at all except a breezy message the day after our coffee with Alex at Cliffview House. *Things are super busy. Let's catch up next week x*

It's not like I expected her to drop everything the moment I returned to Skelwick. I didn't think we'd see each other every day, but I thought I'd see her more than this, especially after how rattled she seemed. Especially when deep down I know she's my only way out. I need to ask her for help. Every time I think it, heat burns in my cheeks. Bryony is already covering the full cost of Mum's care. How can I ask her to help me on top of that? How can I not?

So when she messages this morning – a full week since I returned – asking me to meet her on the beach in an hour, I drop everything.

> *Don't go through the town past the studio. Use the top path that leads to the dunes. Don't be late. I won't have long x*

I stand in the hallway staring at her message, a pulse of worry flickering beneath my ribs. Why does she want to meet on the beach instead of coming here? Why does she want me to avoid Alex's studio? I try to read between the lines of her cryptic requests, but in the end, I grab my coat and do as she's asked.

The spring morning stretches across Skelwick Bay in soft yellow and pale blue. The air is crisp and clean, and fresh in a way only sea air can be. Like gulping down ice-cold water on a hot day. I zip my coat and set off, turning left before the town, following the narrow lane that skirts the back of the houses until it becomes an overgrown footpath.

Most tourists don't know this way to the beach. Locals barely use it except dog walkers and kids skipping school. Coarse, long grass brushes my legs. Sandy patches slide under my trainers. The path dips suddenly, the sea breeze strengthening as the dunes appear ahead – sloping mounds of sand and scrub that roll down to the beach.

With each step, my feet sink deeper into the soft grains, and I half step, half jump down the final steep dune as the beach opens in front of me. The tide is out. It's at least half a mile of sand to the water's edge, and three miles wide. Dog walkers and runners are scattered so far apart I feel completely alone with just the roar of the wind in my ears and the endless sky.

I breathe deeply and close my eyes, trying to let the worries go. This used to be my favourite place on earth. The place I felt most at home. Most myself. In the long months after the accident, after Bryony and Dad left, I would come here every day after school. Sometimes before school too.

This is the place where I met Alex when I was eighteen. Our friendship on this beach made me myself again when I hadn't even realised I'd been lost. It was on the dunes behind me when Bryony appeared and told me she was back. I'd been sketching the sunset, and she'd plonked herself down beside me like she'd been gone a week not five years.

'Some things never change,' she'd said by way of hello,

nodding to my sketchbook. I'd jumped half out of my skin, cried out, then hugged her fiercely. '*Surprise,*' she'd said.

'*What are you doing here?*' I'd asked.

'*I'm back.*'

'*For how long?*'

'*For good.*'

We'd chatted for hours, burying our bare feet in the sand and watching the sun disappear and the stars come out. She'd wanted to know everything, like I hadn't shared it all on our nightly calls. But I'd had questions too, ones I'd struggled to ask when she was gone.

'*Why did you leave?*' I'd asked.

She'd waved her hand, reply breezy, like it was no big deal. '*Mum and Dad had been fighting for years, Jess. You must remember?*'

I'd shaken my head. I didn't. I thought they'd been happy.

'*It all blew up when you were in hospital, and Mum asked Dad to leave.*'

'*And you went with him,*' I'd said, wanting to ask why again. Why my big sister, my whole world, who'd just saved my life and risked her own in the process, would leave me when I needed her so badly.

She'd stayed quiet for a long time. '*It didn't feel right for Mum to have both of us and Dad no one.*'

'*But it has to be about the accident,*' I'd pushed. '*You both left so suddenly. What happened on the* Calypso*, Bry? I don't remember.*'

Her face had paled. '*I'm glad you don't, Jess. It's better that way. I promise you.*'

'*But I have to know.*'

'*What's to say? We were stupid. We almost died, but we didn't. You think you're the only one who has nightmares? I relive it too. And I wish it was only the part in the water I remembered.'* She'd stood suddenly, brushing the sand from her jeans in angry swipes, tears spilling onto her cheeks. *'Please just drop it, OK? I don't want to talk about it. I'm back now. That's all that matters, right?'*

And so I never asked again about the accident or why she left or why she came back.

I see her then – a distant figure at first. A woman bundled up, hood hiding her hair. But I'd recognise that walk anywhere. She moves fast, long strides across the sand. I pick up my pace, closing the distance. By the time I reach her, my feet are wet from the damp sand and the tide's thin ribbons of water.

'Bry,' I say as soon as we're close enough. 'What's going on?'

She shakes her head quietly, eyes darting down the beach, avoiding mine. It feels like she's fighting something – words pressing at her throat but held back.

'Nothing,' she says too quickly. 'I just... wanted to see you. Things have been busy. Alex needs me at the studio all the time. I can barely get away.'

'But why all the secrecy? You told me not to walk through town. I could've come to the house, or—'

'I know,' she cuts me off, voice thin. 'It's just... complicated.' Bryony presses her hand to her mouth, shaking her head like she can physically stop whatever's trying to spill out.

'It's Alex,' she finally whispers. 'Things aren't good between us. We fight sometimes. It's... been hard.'

'All couples argue,' I say gently, repeating the thought I'd had last week. 'You and Alex are so good together. It'll pass.'

She nods, but I see doubt in her eyes and a strain that looks a lot like fear. The waves crash – a distant, animalistic roar.

'It feels like you're not telling me something,' I say quietly, even as guilt coils in my stomach about all the things I haven't told her either.

'There's nothing else,' she says, almost desperately. 'You're right. Alex and I are fighting a lot. It's intense sometimes, and I knew I'd feel better if I got some fresh air and saw you.' She glances over her shoulder. 'I should get back.' Her voice is strangled. 'I told Alex I was just stretching my legs.'

She turns away, like she's going to leave me standing here with nothing. But I can't let her walk away. Not when she asked me here. Not when her message screamed urgency.

'Bry, wait,' I say, stepping forward. 'Talk to me.'

I reach for her arm, and she flinches. Not a startled twitch but a full-body recoil, like my touch caused her pain. I don't think as I pull up the sleeve of her coat before she can stop me. And that's when I see a dark purple bruise blooming across her forearm. Not a wrist mark like last week when she told me she'd knocked into her dressing table. This one is higher. The width of my palm. Finger-shaped shadows marking her skin.

'I fell at the gym,' she says, pushing her sleeve down as she pulls her arm out of my grasp.

I shake my head. 'You didn't get that at the gym.'

Tears swim in her eyes. 'It's nothing. I said, it's nothing.'

'Bryony, what is this?' I ask, already suspecting but praying I'm wrong.

'I can't tell you.' Her voice cracks.

'I'm your sister.'

'You're... you're Alex's friend,' she whispers, voice splintering.

My stomach drops at the mention of Alex. He wouldn't—

'I was your sister long before that,' I say fiercely. 'Bry, please. Talk to me. Tell me what's happening.' I need her to say it.

I see the battle in her face. The reluctance and the fear. The way her eyes scan the beach like someone might be near, someone might hear. And suddenly I'm thinking about the tension I felt when I visited her and Alex last week. And the way she flinched when I hugged her. The way Alex's eyes narrowed outside the shop in town when I mentioned Bryony hadn't seemed herself.

'Alex...' I start, but the word barely comes.

A sob shudders through Bryony like it's been fighting to be set free for the longest time.

'He's been... struggling,' she whispers. 'His art. The pressure. He says something's broken in him. He gets so angry, Jess. He... he lashes out. He thinks it's my fault.' Another sob. 'I'm scared, Jess.'

I shake my head. I don't want to believe it. Alex was my friend. My best friend. The Alex I knew rescued crabs and collected wood and let me win at cards and talked endlessly of the art pieces he loved. But even back then there were dark stretches. Whole days he'd disappear, shut away in his van. Once, I saw him smash a sculpture until it was splinters because it wasn't perfect.

And his love for Bryony has always been fierce, teetering on obsession. All those photos he took of her. The way he used to follow her around like a lost puppy in those early weeks. How he wanted to be near her every minute of the day.

How much would it take to tip that obsession into something darker?

'I have to go,' she says. 'I was only supposed to be gone ten minutes. Alex likes to know where I am all the time. He even has Paulina and Jimmy spy on me when he's not home.'

I think of the way Paulina called for Alex. The way she looked adoringly at him, like she'd do anything he asked.

Bryony turns to leave, and I step alongside her, blocking her path. 'Bry, wait!'

'Swear you won't tell anyone.'

'You have to leave him,' I blurt out. 'Tell me you're leaving him or going to the police. We can go right now. I'll come with you.'

'I can't,' she cries, moving away once more.

She's a few paces away now, the wind whipping her hood, her boots sinking into soft sand as she turns to face me. Her voice is barely a whisper. 'He's going to kill me, Jess.'

And then she runs, hurrying across the sand, back to the town and to Alex. Her words echo through the salt air long after she's gone.

He's going to kill me.

TEN

Jess

I wake choking on water. It's in my lungs, cold and heavy, flooding my chest as I gasp for air that isn't there. I claw at the sheets, desperate to pull myself free, but they're tangled around my legs like seaweed. For a moment, I don't know where I am. I can hear the roar of the sea, taste the sea water. My head throbs.

I scramble for the light and find the switch. A second later, a soft orange glow fills my old bedroom. I'm alive. I'm safe. Bryony jumped in. She saved my life. My chest still burns as I heave in breath after breath. I force myself upright, palms pressed to the duvet.

'Imagine pressing rewind on a film. What happened just before that? And just before that?'

I close my eyes and fall backward into it. No air. Only blackness. Water pulling me down by the ankles. Hitting the surface hard, skull threatening to split. Falling through the air, trying to reach for something. The scream lodged in my throat. And then... nothing. A blank strip of film.

I try again. Rewind. Play. Expecting the same void. But

something shifts. A flicker, a feeling – a shape where there should be darkness. Shock snaps through me. For the first time in sixteen years, I see something more. I see the sail of the *Calypso*, white against the brooding sky. I feel my feet on the deck.

I remember being on the boat. It's just a fragment, but it's something. My temple throbs, and I rub at the side of my head. I can see the sail. I can see Bryony at the tiller, her smile bright. Hair whipping across her face. And then the laughter. A shadow of movement. Someone else on the boat.

I push harder, reaching for the memory, trying to see who it is. Who did we invite to come with us? What happened next? How did it all go so wrong? But there's nothing more.

Tears sting my eyes as my fingers find only the cool edge of the single bed, leaving me hollow. My treacherous hand reaches instinctively for Liam, remembering all the times he'd woken with me, tugged me into the crook of his arm. *'It's OK, Jess. I've got you. I've always got you.'*

I could've slept in Mum's room with the double bed, but it didn't feel right. The air in there still smells of her perfume and my childhood, making my chest ache with the knowledge that the memories I take for granted are the same ones slipping away from Mum. So I'm in my old room, which still feels like it belongs to a teenage version of me. There are posters of album covers on the walls. Bands I used to love with a deep obsession, knowing every lyric and what it meant.

The dressing table is littered with old trinkets and shells. And on top of the wardrobe sit my old teddies, the ones I grew out of but felt too much a part of me to ever throw away. This room should feel like comfort and home, but the truth is my teen years were rocky and confusing.

Always the same questions – what happened on the boat that day? How did I end up in the water?

My phone hums on the bedside table, breaking my

thoughts, making me jump, heart in my throat. I snatch at it, fearing it's Bryony telling me she's in trouble. The words she said on the beach today still haunt me. *'He's going to kill me.'*

But the name lighting the screen is Liam's. It's like he knows I'm awake. That I'm scared and need him.

My mind pulls me back to the day of Mum's diagnosis, soon after the Kilstern opened. Bryony and I had taken her to the appointment together. We were expecting to hear the word *dementia*, but it still winded me. Mum had sat between us, eyes bright but glassy, offering us comfort. *'I'm fine, loves – don't you worry about me.'*

It felt like we were going to lose her in slow motion.

I'd driven back to the Kilstern that evening feeling hollowed out, braced for the chaos waiting for me – emails piling up, bookings to chase, guests who always needed something. But when I'd walked in, the lobby had been calm.

'Where is everybody?' I'd asked as Liam stepped out of the bar to greet me.

'In bed,' he'd said. *'Everything's handled.'*

'Thank you. I'll check the bookings for tomorrow. I have to make sure we're—'

'First of all, you don't have to do anything,' Liam had said gently, taking my coat from my shoulders before I could argue. *'And second of all, I've got it covered anyway.'*

He'd taken my hand and led me up the stairs to our room. The ceiling sloped on one side and the shower barely trickled, but we didn't want to take one of the rooms we could give to a guest, and it was ours and it was cosy.

He'd opened the bathroom door – steam had billowed out, candles flickering along the tiles, a mug of herbal tea waiting for me on the edge of the counter.

'Third of all,' he'd murmured, brushing a strand of hair off my cheek, *'I love you. Take a moment for you now, Jess.'*

That was Liam, always looking out for me.

I scramble for my phone, suddenly desperate to speak to him, but I'm too late. He's gone. I stare at the notification of his missed call, thumb hovering over his name. I ache to hear his voice, even if another part of me can't bear it.

Then another sound. Not the phone. Something else. A soft rattle. I freeze, listening. It comes again, and this time I hear the clink of the letter box, the scrape of metal. Someone at the front door. Someone pushing at the catch, seeing if it's unlocked. Someone trying to get in.

Every muscle turns rigid. I don't breathe as I listen, heart pounding so loud I swear it's thudding through the house. A violent pulse of panic shoots through my veins as the thought forms – is this it? The escalation he threatened? Friday came and went and I didn't call. Didn't pay. My mouth goes dry. My skin prickles. Hot and cold all at once. I've never felt so alone or so stupid.

I should never have taken the money. It wasn't in the name of the hotel. It wasn't even in mine and Liam's name. It was personal. Just me. The debt is all mine. Money I couldn't pay back. Still can't. Liam ran the numbers over and over. With the improvements to the manor and the sale to the hotel group, who'd offered to buy the Kilstern the day we opened and had been badgering us to sell for years, we'd break even. Just.

'We'll be walking away with nothing,' I'd cried.

'We'll be walking away without debt,' he'd said, pushing a hand through his dark-red hair, just as stressed as I was. *'We can get jobs. Start again. We could even save to go travelling for a year.'*

'I can't give up,' I'd snapped, snatching my phone and striding from the room, already making the call that would ruin everything. I'd told myself it would be enough to cover the bills. Buy us another few months. Pay for some advertising. But all I managed was a scattering of bookings at discounted rates. A handful of guests. It wasn't enough to turn the tide.

A sick, trembling certainty grips me: everything I've been trying to outrun has followed me here.

I slip silently out of bed, the only sound my rushed breathing. I step over the floorboards that creak and make my way to the door and down the hallway. The only light is from the lamp in my bedroom and the streetlights outside. My feet are ice in the cold house. I shiver in my flimsy pyjamas, wishing I'd grabbed a jumper.

At the top of the stairs, I stop. The rattle comes once more, sharper this time. Louder. Someone is at the door. The sound stops as suddenly as it started. The silence presses in, as thick as fog that rolls off the sea and lingers over the bay in winter.

I creep to the landing window and peer through the curtain to the road outside.

At first, there's nothing but the still of night. And then headlights. An engine. I hold my breath and watch as a Land Rover pulls away from the kerb and disappears.

I can't be certain in the dark, but I think I know that dark Land Rover. Just like the one I saw on the drive of Cliffview House, parked beside Bryony's Mercedes. It's Alex's car.

My stomach twists – a cold, nauseating roll. What was he doing outside? Does he know I met Bryony on the beach? I'd made her tell me what was happening and then she ran back to him. I think of the wild fear in her eyes. The awful bruise on her arm. The way she flinched when we hugged, like there were more injuries.

I still can't wrap my head around what she's told me. I thought Alex was still the intense but gentle boy I met on the beach collecting wood a decade ago. It's not like I believed they never argued. Bryony is so different from Alex. She loves the lifestyle his art allows them, the socialising and the events – the spotlight. For Alex, it's always been about creating the art. All that comes with it, he endures because it allows him to keep doing what he loves.

Of course they clashed sometimes. His distraction to her abrasive. The way she doesn't let things go versus how he'll stop mid-sentence and walk out of a room because an idea struck him and he wanted to work on it then and there. But I never thought—

Could never have imagined—

And now he's parked below my bedroom window in the middle of the night, trying the door. Did Bryony tell him I know? Has he come to explain himself, to convince me it's not what it looks like. Promise me it won't happen again. Or maybe he's come to make sure I stay quiet.

I bite my lip to stop it trembling. Bryony begged me not to say anything. Not to do anything. But standing here in the dark, staring at the patch of road where he'd been moments earlier, my own problems fall away. Bryony is the one in danger. And I need to find a way to save her.

ELEVEN

SIXTEEN YEARS EARLIER – THE JUMP

Bryony

Jess is in the water.

The thought doesn't feel real. But it is.

Move, a voice screams in my head. *Do something.*

The sea is a roiling mass of dark waves slamming against the hull. Jess is just a flash of red sailing jacket. Then nothing.

'Jess?' The single word is a scream.

Indecision tears through me. Seconds pass like hours. If I do nothing, Jess will die.

I have to do something.

I should clip in, grab a line – that's what Dad would do – but there's no time. The sea roars back at me, and so I grab the life jacket sitting on the bench, the same one we promised Dad we'd wear. My body trembles as I step onto the edge.

I pause again, allowing the fear to freeze me in place and the doubts to take over. Then I jump into the sea after my sister.

The water feels like ice freezing my blood. The waves a slap that steal my breath and make my lungs seize. Saltwater fills my mouth. My limbs feel instantly numb, my body heavy. And for one awful moment, I'm completely submerged in the water. I kick and kick. Then my head breaks the surface and I start to swim, scanning the waves.

Where is she?

Nothing but grey sea and white foam fills my vision. Then something. A flash of red. And hair drifting like seaweed. I cry out. Relief and fear. 'Jess.'

My chest tightens until I can't breathe. 'Don't be dead,' I murmur as Jess disappears beneath the waves again. 'Please don't be dead.' Panic and instinct take over. I dive down, the sting of salt burning my eyes, lungs screaming. Then I see her again, just barely able to catch her arm and haul her up, a dead weight that makes me feel like I'm sinking.

Jess's face breaks the surface. Then mine. Her eyes are closed, lips blue. My arms move under her shoulders, and I keep kicking, fighting, trying to use the single life jacket to keep us both afloat. My arms ache instantly. Waves crash into us, trying to push us apart. I tighten my hold on Jess's body.

I gasp, choking on the icy water. 'Don't you dare die!'

Even through the panic, the truth hits me with the same force as the slap of a wave. If Jess dies, it will be my fault. I'll be the girl who took my little sister sailing and didn't bring her back. I can't let her die. My world doesn't look right without Jess.

TWELVE

NOW

Jess

The wind blusters against my jacket as I climb the cliff road to Bryony's house. The day is bright again. It's even warm out of the wind. Across the bay, the dark-blue sea is broken by the crests of white waves and the splash of colour from a group of surfers. I squint against the sun, wishing I'd brought my sunglasses, but too determined on my mission to turn back. It's been two days since I saw Bryony on the beach. Two days of silence. She's not answered my calls or my messages, not been to visit Mum as far as I can tell from the names written in the visitors' book.

And now it's Thursday and I'm worried for her. I can't shake the image of the Land Rover pulling away the night I woke from the nightmare. Someone trying to open Mum's front door. If Alex guessed she'd told me about his abuse, what would he do? I need to talk to her. She seemed adamant she couldn't go to the police or try to leave him. But why?

I've thrown myself into clearing the house, moving from the dining room to the living room. The more I do, the more it feels there is to do. Liam hasn't called since that night. I hate that I miss him. He's the first person I think of each morning, the one I want to tell things to. But our last fight still feels like a fresh wound. Liam's voice, desperate and pleading.

'I was a mess, Jess. I don't know how I got so drunk. One minute I was having a drink, the next she was kissing me. I swear, she threw herself at me. It was nothing. It meant nothing.'

'It means something to me,' I'd replied, forcing myself not to cry.

He'd reached for me, but I'd drawn back, so angry I could barely share the same air as him.

'I know,' he'd said. *'And I'm sorry. I'm so sorry. Please, Jess. We've lost everything. Please, I can't lose you too.'* His voice had cracked like it was my fault we were standing there. The enormity of what was happening was overwhelming. He was right. We had lost everything. Our careers, our dreams and now our relationship.

'You should've thought of that before messing around with a guest. Just get out, Liam. Get out.' I'd covered my face with my hands and turned away.

He must have known there was no reasoning with me when I was so angry. So hurt. He'd packed his things in silence. The last thing he said before he left was: *'I'm going to keep trying, Jess. I'm never going to give up on us.'*

I'd taken charge of closing up the hotel and arranging the sale alone. It's been two months and he's stayed true to his word. He hasn't given up.

The man has called about my loan. Every day. I'd turn my phone off, throw it in the sea, if it wasn't for Bryony. Besides, I know deep down they'll find another way to reach me.

At least Mum has been bright the times I've seen her. She's enjoyed looking at the photo albums I've brought from the house, happy to live in the past where her memories are clearer than the present.

But nothing I've done has been enough to distract me from Bryony. The worry sits in me like a stone, grinding against my ribs as I walk up the path to Cliffview House. I step onto the drive, relieved to see only Bryony's silver Mercedes parked beside the garage. No Land Rover. I hope this means Alex is at the studio and that Bryony hasn't gone with him.

I'm halfway to the front door when I see a man I don't recognise standing beside one of the front flowerbeds. He's in his early fifties with a shaved head and a strong nose. There's a rake in his hand, but he freezes when I approach. I falter then remind myself I'm doing nothing wrong. I offer a polite smile, remembering Bryony's mention of a gardener – Jimmy. He doesn't return it. Instead, he reaches into his pocket and pulls out a phone, tapping a message. Is he telling Alex I'm here? Unease coils tight inside me. Bryony's voice echoes through my mind. *'Alex likes to know where I am all the time. He even has Paulina and Jimmy spy on me when he's not home.'*

A cold shiver runs down my spine. I look away and hurry to the door, feeling his eyes on me. Feeling exposed. I knock on the front door and wait for a long time before Paulina is standing before me in the same T-shirt and leggings. The same blank expression on her face.

'Hi, Paulina. I'm Jess, Bryony's sister. We met the other day.'

I expect Paulina to step back and motion me into the hall, but instead she stands her ground. 'Mr Raffety isn't here at the moment.'

'I'm here to see Bryony.' I force a bright smile while the hairs on the back of my neck prickle. I don't need to turn around to know the gardener is still watching me.

'Mrs Raffety is unwell and can't be disturbed,' she says and starts to close the door.

'Could you tell her I'm here?' I ask.

Paulina shakes her head. 'She's not to be disturbed.'

The door closes with a resounding thud before I have a chance to reply.

I take a step back, frustration and worry prickling my insides. Bryony is in the house, but I can't get to her. Is she hurt? Upset? Trapped?

It's just as I'm turning to leave that I see a flicker of movement from one of the upstairs windows. A creamy silk blouse, a face. Bryony. She lifts a hand, finger pointing to the side of the house, mouthing something I think is, 'Cliff path.'

I nod before backing away and walking down the road, to where a narrow stony footpath takes me to the cliff where the hikers trek the clifftops of the west coast. The unease follows me, deepening with every step. The urge to run whips through me with the same force as the wind, but I have to see Bryony.

I make my way along the hard ground, overgrown ferns and shrubs brushing against my legs, until I can see the glass of Cliffview House stretching up above me. The path is empty. There's no sign of Bryony. The battering wind seeps through my clothes. Then she appears, hurrying towards me, hunched over, coat pulled tight, gaze darting back to the house.

'You came,' she says, her words breaking in a shaky sob, reaching out to take my hand. Her fingers are ice-cold.

'Of course I came,' I say, my own voice pulling tight. 'What's happening, Bry? What's wrong?'

She swallows hard. 'It's bad, Jess. Worse than I feared.'

'He's—' I can't finish the sentence. Can't bring myself to imagine what Alex has done to my sister.

A frantic shake of her head, another furtive glance behind her. I follow her gaze. The sun is hitting the glass of her house, but for a moment I think I see a figure watching us. Is it Paulina?

'There's no time,' she says. Her eyes lock with mine. 'You have to help me, Jess.'

'Anything,' I blurt. 'Tell me what to do.'

For a moment, she can't speak. Her chest heaves. Her lips tremble. When she finally forces the words out, they make no sense at all.

'I need to die.'

My breath punches out of me. Fear grips every cell in my body. 'What...' I cry out, 'what are you talking about? No. Absolutely not.'

'Not really die,' she explains as tears spill onto her cheeks. 'But I have to make everyone believe I'm dead. It's the only way I can get out. I have to fake my death, and I need your help to do it.'

I stare at her, unable to process the words.

Fake her death.

Disappear.

Leave everything behind.

'There has to be another way,' I say. 'This is crazy.'

She shakes her head. 'If there was another way, don't you think I'd do it?'

'But I can't lose you,' I whisper.

Another sob escapes. 'I know. I'm so sorry. But this is the only way.' Bryony jerks her head back towards her house, pulling her hand away, stepping back. 'I have to go. I shouldn't be out here.'

I can't let her go. I reach for her arm. She's trembling. 'We'll think of something else,' I try again, desperate now to make her see sense.

She laughs but it sounds nothing like humour. 'Jess, do you think I haven't thought of every possible way out? That I'd ever ask this of you if I had any other choice?'

We stand there, the silence dragging out between us, our eyes blurred with tears.

Then Bryony steps closer, pulling me into a hug, whispering into my ear. 'You owe me, Jess,' she hisses then. 'I saved your life. Sixteen years ago. I pulled you out of that water. I kept you alive. And now... now you have to help me fake my death.'

For a second, I can't breathe.

She squeezes my hand.

Then her head snaps towards the house. A gasp slips from her mouth. I follow her gaze and my stomach drops. Alex is striding towards us from the direction of the garden – fast, purposeful, his shoulders squared against the wind like he's been watching us from the moment we stepped outside.

'Don't say a word,' Bryony whispers, her voice suddenly bright and brittle. In a heartbeat, she smooths her expression into something sunny and flawless.

Then she's hurrying towards him, her laugh high and cheerful on the wind. Her tone is perfect. '... just out for a walk and I saw her... popped down to say hi...'

Alex leans down to say something into her ear, and Bryony nods quickly before heading straight back towards the house. I stand rooted to the cliff path, trying to remember how to be normal around this man. This man who used to be my best friend. Who once made my heart ache with wanting. Who I begged the universe to let see me. He saw Bryony instead. Friend, brother-in-law, artist, monster. Who am I talking to?

'Hey, Jessie,' Alex says lightly, as though nothing is wrong. 'Enjoying your walk?'

I conjure a smile that feels more like a grimace. 'Perfect day for it.'

He studies me for a moment, head tilted. 'I thought you preferred walking on the beach to the cliffs.'

For a second, I think he's talking about when I met Bryony, but then I realise he means our shared past. I try to laugh. 'Both.'

The wind roars up the cliff face, tugging my hair across my eyes. Alex steps closer. His tone hardens. 'Be careful, Jessie.'

My pulse picks up. The voice in my head screams, *Run.* 'What?'

He nods towards the cliff edge just metres from where we stand. 'A hiker fell last winter just there. Slipped and went over the edge. Died on impact.' His gaze lingers on me a moment too long before he adds, with a tiny smile. 'What did you think I meant?'

I swallow, trying to calm my racing hard, as I force another laugh. 'Nothing. Just... nothing.'

I step away before he can say anything else, the path blurring slightly as I walk. The urge to look back claws at me. I feel his eyes burning into my back as I round the corner and move out of sight.

Bryony's voice echoes through my skull as I half stumble, half run towards the road.

I have to fake my death.

I wrap my arms around myself. She can't mean it. There has to be another way.

THIRTEEN

Jess

It's the following day when Bryony appears without warning, her key scraping in the lock of Mum's front door. I race down the hall, pulling it open before she's had a chance to turn the key.

I'm a mess. Hair unwashed and tied in a loose ponytail at the nape of my neck, clothes dusty from moving the sofas in the living room. But my insides are worse. The worry is a tight band squeezing and squeezing. The phone calls won't stop. The talk of escalation no longer feels like a threat so much as a matter of time. The one person who could help me is in her own personal hell.

I barely slept last night, staring at the ceiling, mind swinging from my problems to Bryony's and the words she whispered on the clifftop. *'I need to die.'*

'Are you OK?' I blurt the second we're in the hall with the door closed. I search her face. *How many times does he hit you?* I suddenly want to ask; don't want to know.

'Yes,' she breathes, and we hug tightly. 'I'm OK.' I don't

know which one of us she's trying to convince, but I doubt either of us are.

'I didn't think he'd let me leave the house,' she says, words rushing out. 'I asked him if I could visit Mum with you today. He only said yes because he knows I haven't seen her for a week and he's worried what people will think. But he said he wants to come too. He's had to go to a meeting at the studio then he's coming here. We don't have long.'

'Oh, Bry.' Tears sting my eyes. There are no words for the hurt I feel on behalf of my bright, joyful, carefree sister, who is no longer any of the things that make her who she is.

I bite back my own fear at the thought of seeing Alex. Anyone who'd been watching yesterday would've seen his words as friendly on the clifftop, but I still feel cold every time I think of his warning to be careful and the mention of a hiker falling so easily to their death.

Bryony's hands shake as she unbuttons her coat. I take it from her, hanging it on the hook. I don't search for the spot of red I saw on the cuff. The one I told myself was paint but now I'm certain is blood. Bryony's blood from where Alex hurt her.

I feel sick as I follow her into the kitchen. None of this feels real. She picks up the bottle of wine she left here over a week ago and pours herself a glass. She takes two long gulps before steadying herself against the counter, and a part of me wonders if I should do the same. It's not yet eleven in the morning and it feels like we're both fraying at the seams. If a glass of wine is what's keeping Bryony from crumbling to the floor, so be it, but I've never been a big drinker and the last thing I need is my head clouded by alcohol.

'He's under a lot of stress,' she says on a deep exhale. 'He's got his exhibit coming up and then the Long Island trip. He just—'

I shake my head. I've barely wrapped my head around a reality where Alex is hurting Bryony, but that doesn't mean I can let her explain away his monstrous behaviour as stress. 'Don't make excuses for him.'

'He's so paranoid, Jess. He thinks I'm planning something.' She pulls her phone from her pocket. 'I got this notification on my phone as I was driving here.'

She taps her screen, showing me an alert. *AirTag found moving with you.*

'What is this?' I whisper.

'Alex is tracking my car,' she says, voice trembling. 'He always wants to know where I am. Once I left my phone at home by mistake, and he totally lost it.' She stops, swallowing hard. 'I thought he was going to kill me last night.'

Goosebumps rage across my skin. 'Bryony, this is insane. You have to leave him. You have to go to the police. And don't tell me you can't because you can. I'll help you.'

Bryony is fierce. Smart. Beautiful. She's always stood up for herself. But she's also loyal. And this is Alex. The man she loves, who gave her the house and the life she always wanted.

Her voice is raw when she answers. 'I *can't*.'

'I know you love him, but if he's hurting you—'

'You don't understand,' she cries. 'I can't leave. I want to, but I can't.'

'Why not?'

'There are a hundred reasons. But for starters, I physically can't leave him. I meant what I said at the beach. Jimmy and Paulina watch me whenever I'm in the house and report anything unusual to Alex.' She swallows, struggling with the words as though the memory is painful. 'About a month ago, I tried to pack my bags. Alex came back early and caught me. He locked me in the basement until I promised to stay.'

My heart lurches. 'He locked you in the basement? That's insane.'

Tears spill over her cheeks. 'He said it was for my own good, that I wasn't thinking straight.' Her voice breaks. 'He wouldn't let me out until I promised not to leave him.'

A sickening guilt twists in my belly. I'd been so distracted trying to save my dreams and everything with Liam, I cancelled her visits to Oxfordshire. I ignored her calls. I thought only of myself and my own trouble. I didn't think that Bryony might need me.

She takes another sip of wine, pressing her trembling fingers to her mouth. 'He wants to know where I am every minute of the day. I'm allowed to drive to the gym, shop twice a week, and if I don't make trouble, I can take the *Odysseus* out and sail around the bay when the weather is good. When I'm good. That's my freedom now. People think I've got it all, but I'm barely more than a prisoner.'

I place my hand over hers on the kitchen counter where we used to stand side by side baking fairy cakes and cookies, Bryony helping me with the stirring when my arm got tired. 'You have to call the police,' I say again.

'He's built everything around me,' she whispers, like I haven't spoken. 'And now he's falling apart, and I'm the one paying for it. I'm his muse.'

Her words hit hard. I remember when Alex first called her that. It had only been a few weeks into their relationship. His career was just taking off. An art dealer holidaying with his family had seen Alex's art pieces on a market stall and had given him his first exhibition. Every piece sold and was quickly followed by a grant from the arts council. I thought it was perseverance, talent and a bit of luck, but Alex was convinced it was Bryony. That his love for her elevated his art to a new level.

'If Alex is going through a difficult time, then he needs to deal with it,' I say. 'You can't live like this. You're a prisoner while he's walking around being loved by everyone. You think he'll be so adored by the town if they knew he was doing this to you?'

Bryony laughs, the sound hollow. 'Of course he will be. Wake up, Jess. He'll deny it, and they'll believe him over me. Everyone in this town loves him. He's Skelwick's saviour. His studio brings coachloads of tourists every week. He alone is keeping the town alive outside of the summer months. They won't want to believe me. They'll say I'm hysterical or jealous or ungrateful.'

'So then you leave,' I say, desperate now. 'I'll come to the house with you while you pack a bag. He won't be able to lock you in the basement if I'm with you. And then you come here or leave Skelwick. You could visit Dad in Spain for a while.'

She shakes her head. 'It's not that simple.'

'Why not?' I cry out.

'Because we have to think about Mum,' she replies.

I frown. 'What do you mean?'

'You weren't here, Jess. You didn't see how awful some of the care homes I visited were. She's at the best facility in the area. She's in Skelwick, where she's spent most of her life. But they didn't have a room available when we needed one, so Alex spoke to the owners, and suddenly they found her a room with a balcony and sea views. Do you think that just happened? If I leave him, that room goes. He'll make sure of it. Mum will be out within a week, and then what? She's settled there, Jess. I can't see her move to somewhere else that won't take care of her. It will kill her.'

I open my mouth, wanting to argue, but Bryony continues.

'The entire community will turn on us. On you as well. You think they'll let you run your Airbnb? You said it yourself when you spoke to Kelly,' Bryony continues. 'They hate holiday rentals. Every year there's tension. They make sure any new rentals are slammed with council visits and paperwork and regulations. The only reason you'll have the place up and running for the summer is because of your connection to Alex.'

I shake my head, not wanting to hear any more. 'It can't be that bad.'

She shoots me a look I remember from our childhood. The one where she's questioning if I'm really that stupid. I think of the adoring look from the teen in the shop on my first day back. The way the queue of people behind me smiled and joked with Alex.

'You remember Damon Bartlett?' Bryony asks.

I think for a moment. 'The man with the fishing and gift shop? Tackle and Tat?'

She nods. 'His sister ran a bakery too. He went to one of the town meetings last year. He said Alex was using too much driftwood. He claimed it was destroying the fish's natural habitats and affecting fishing. He was going to petition the council to protect the driftwood in the bay.' She snorts softly. 'Word spread. The town found out he was going against Alex, and that was it. No one spoke to him. No one shopped with him or at the bakery. Within a few months, they were both gone. Three generations of Bartletts, and they ran them out like criminals.'

I stare at her, horrified. 'That's awful.'

'It's exactly what will happen to us,' she finishes. 'To you and to me and to Mum.'

'But you being safe is more important,' I reply. 'It's all that matters.'

'You don't understand,' she hisses. 'There is no safe. He'll find me. We'll implode our lives, lose Mum's room in the care home, lose everything, and it will all be for nothing because he'll use all his wealth to find me and he'll drag me back. He won't ever stop searching for me. I'm scared, Jess. And—' Her voice breaks off.

'What?' What could be even worse than what she's already said.

Bryony busies herself with adding another inch of wine to

her glass. Her hand shakes causing drops to splash on the counter. 'It doesn't matter,' she says.

'No.' My voice is sharp enough that Bryony spins towards me. 'I haven't been here for you or Mum and that's on me, but I'm here now, Bry. I want to help you, but you can't keep things back. If we're going to get you out of this, I need to know everything.'

She stares at the floor for a long moment. Then she nods. 'When he unlocked the basement,' she says quietly, 'he told me what would happen if I ever tried to leave again.'

My stomach tightens.

'He said he'd find me.' Her voice trembles. 'That he'd bring me back. But he wouldn't kill me.'

I let out a shaky breath. 'Because he needs you.'

'Because I belong to him.' Her lip quivers. 'He said he'd keep me locked up. Forever. But... I'd need to be punished for leaving. So he... he said he'd bring you to me. To the basement.'

The room suddenly feels too small.

'You're the most important person in the world to me, Jess,' Bryony continues. 'He knows that. Just like he knows you're the one I'd turn to for help. If I told you what was happening, you'd help me leave. But if you're not around anymore, I'd have no one to help me and I'd... stay. I'd have no choice.'

'What are you saying?' I ask.

Her voice breaks completely. 'He said he'd make me watch while he killed you. So I'd understand what it costs to choose someone over him.'

The words knock the breath clean out of my lungs.

Alex would happily kill me. My old best friend. My sister's husband. The man everyone in this town trusts without question. I thought I'd already hit rock bottom – with the hotel, the end of my relationship with Liam, the debt I can't pay. I thought I understood what danger was, but I had no idea.

'And he's right,' Bryony cries. 'I've told you now, and I'm

asking for your help. I've put you in so much danger. I'm so sorry, Jess.'

'But if you stay,' I whisper, barely able to voice my fear, 'he'll keep hurting you. He'll kill you eventually.' My skin prickles violently with cold as my words land in the silent kitchen.

Bryony hugs her arms to her body as though she's trying to hold herself together, her sobs quick and shallow. She's a barely there version of the outspoken, fun woman she was seven months ago when she last came to the Kilstern to see me and Liam.

I grab her hand, gripping hard. I want to tell someone, to scream out loud what Alex is doing to my sister.

'What are we going to do?' I whisper, my voice breaking too.

Her gaze lifts to mine. 'I've thought about it over and over. The only way out of this is if he thinks I'm dead. Then he won't come after me and he won't cause trouble for you or Mum. He won't have any reason to threaten or hurt you if he thinks I'm dead.'

I feel the same jolt of shock I felt on the clifftop yesterday. But this time, I see she's right. Alex believes Bryony is his muse. He's always been obsessive, never giving up on anything. If Bryony runs, he'll find her. And then he'll come for me. He sees me as Bryony's escape route. The person she'd turn to when she finally breaks. It's true. There's nothing I wouldn't do for my sister. If I'm gone, she has nowhere to go – and he knows it.

Fear coils tight in my chest. He'll kill me as punishment. And he'll keep Bryony locked away forever, knowing she'll never dare try again.

I can't let that happen.

Even with the fear pounding in my ears and shaking through my body, I won't let him win. But Bryony's right too. If we go to the police and speak out, he'll turn everyone against us, and Mum will lose her home. And then he'll lock Bryony away and kill me anyway. There's no escape from him for either of us.

'You have a plan?' I ask, barely able to believe we're talking about this. How is this my life? I came back to Skelwick to escape. To hide from my heartbreak over Liam and try to somehow – and I still haven't figured out how – claw my way out of the trouble I'm in. And now I'm supposed to help my sister fake her death because the man she loves is going to kill us both if she doesn't.

She draws in a deep breath, and I can tell by the way she straightens her shoulders that she can see a way out.

But before she can say another word, a knock rattles the front door. We both freeze. Bryony's eyes go wide.

'It's Alex.'

FOURTEEN

Jess

'Don't let on you know anything,' Bryony hisses under her breath, pushing me towards the front door.

My mouth is dry. I bite the inside of my cheek, hard enough to hurt. I'm certain the truth is written across my face as I force my feet down the hall. I'm certain he'll see it instantly, the fear, the knowledge, the fact that I know what he's capable of. For one selfish moment, I want to step back, not answer, never see Alex again. But if I don't open it, he'll know.

Panic is a vice-like hold. I stop breathing.

'Jessie.' Alex's smile is wide as he steps through the door, bringing with him the scent of his woody aftershave, mixed with faint hints of paint and salt from the sea. The smell hits me first, a memory flooding my senses before my brain can protect me.

Every muscle in my body is rigid with fear, and my heart races, but there's something traitorous beneath the terror. Because a small, stupid part of me still feels that pull towards him I once felt. And I hate myself for it.

How can I stand here trembling, terrified of what he's

capable of, knowing he threatened to kill me, and still feel that old stupid ache in my chest? Still remember the way I once wished he'd choose me? And the charm – God, the charm – rolls off him in waves, effortless and easy as he smiles at me.

Monster, a voice whispers in my head. *He's a monster.*

I close the door behind him and the walls shrink inward. And I realise with a cold, sinking certainty that this is more than fear. It's the knowledge that if I make one wrong move, say one wrong thing, this man won't hesitate to destroy my sister and me along with her.

'I hope you don't mind me joining you,' he says as he glances around the hallway. 'I've been so busy getting ready for my exhibit next Thursday night, but I've been meaning to swing by and see Andrea. I thought it might be nice for her if the three of us went together.'

I manage to nod, but my voice still trembles when I reply. 'She'll like that.'

He stares at me for a long moment. A cold, assessing look.

He knows I know, a voice screams in my head. My legs threaten to give way, but I hold myself steady, force myself to smile. Then his gaze moves to the dining room and the teal walls and the tidy space – the one room ready for guests. 'Looks like you've made a good start,' he says. 'I know Bryony said she'd help, but perhaps I should be here too. Bry and DIY don't exactly go hand in hand.'

His eyes dance as he looks at me, and I force a laugh. The offer seems kind, but it's impossible to miss the undercurrent of tension now I know better. Like a veil has been thrown back. His offer to help is just another way for him to keep an eye on Bryony.

'And where is my lovely wife?'

'I'm here, darling,' Bryony calls, appearing in the doorway to the living room with her wine glass in one hand and an old holiday snap in the other – a faded print of the four of us in

Spain when we were little. There's no sign on Bryony's face of the tears and terror I saw only a few minutes ago. She's a better actor than I am, but then I think sadly that maybe she's had to be to survive.

I glance at the photo. I look about four, which means Bryony must be seven. Dad's arm is around Mum, Bryony on his other side, me clutching Mum's hand. The sky behind us is impossibly blue.

'We looked happy, didn't we?' Bryony says, catching me staring. 'You wouldn't know Mum and Dad were fighting five minutes before this was taken.'

'Were they?' I frown.

'Maybe you were too young. We were playing a game near the pool. Mum thought it was too noisy. Dad said it was fine.' She shrugs. 'Typical.'

Her comment stirs a faint memory. Running along the pool's edge, Bryony's laughter echoing, my foot slipping. Mum's gasp as I'd come close to falling in. I wasn't a good swimmer as a young child.

But then, I'd been a strong swimmer when I was thirteen and it hadn't made a difference when the sea tried to swallow me. For an awful moment, I'm plunged back into the darkness of those scattered memories. My temple throbs, and I sway on my feet, remembering again the moment of standing on the deck and the unfamiliar echo of laughter.

Alex's smile is still fixed in place as he moves to kiss Bryony's cheek. She shrinks a fraction against the door frame. The tightness in Alex's posture says he notices. Without a word, he plucks the glass from her hand, moves into the kitchen and tips the wine down the sink. There's a loud clink as he places the glass on the counter with too much force.

I don't dare look at Bryony as Alex turns and walks back into the hall. It's taking everything I have just to hold myself together in front of him. If I see my sister trying to do the same, something in me will break. The truth – the terror – will spill out, and he'll see it. He'll know.

I bite down on the inside of my lip, hard enough to stop the scream clawing up my throat. I want to shout. To grab Bryony and run. To tear her out of this house and shove her into the car and drive until the sea is nothing but a line in the mirror.

A metallic tang hits my tongue. I've bitten too hard.

She has a plan, I remind myself, forcing a breath as the fear threatens to take over. *We'll find a way out.*

'Shall we go?' Alex asks, wrapping an arm tightly around Bryony.

Something cold slides down my spine. I no longer see love but cold control.

'Yes, let's,' Bryony replies, that wide smile still pinned in place.

'Oh, Jess,' Alex says at the front door. 'This exhibition at the studio next week. It's a preview of the collection I'm taking to Long Island. You will come, won't you? I want you to see my new pieces. I've been experimenting with the wood – burning the grain before sealing it, giving it that blackened, scorched effect so when the light hits it, the texture almost glows. I'd love to hear what you think.'

'Of course,' I hear myself say, gaze darting to Bryony. Her expression is still pleading. She's telling me to agree. To be normal. 'Wouldn't miss it.'

'I've got a few ice sculptures to display as well,' he replies, twisting the gold band of his wedding ring around his finger.

'Ice? That's new,' I say. My voice still feels strange. Not my own.

'Bryony's idea. It's just something I'm trying. There's something poetic about the fact that its time on earth is finite. Don't you think?' He laughs. 'God, I sound pretentious. That's what happens when you spend too much time with art critics. I need to hang out with you more, Jess, now you're home. You can make me feel normal again.'

It feels like there's a hidden message in his tone. *Because Bryony doesn't.*

Outside, we walk to Alex's Land Rover together, parked in the same place on the road I swear I saw it in the middle of the night when he'd tried the front door. My mouth turns dry. What did he want?

Alex opens the passenger door for Bry with a chivalry so smooth it feels like theatre. She slides in, spine straight, eyes forward.

On the short drive to the care home, Alex fills the silence with easy talk on how the tides were high last night, how Mrs Penrith's dog bit through his shoe, how the new drift came in heavy with blue rope. He's so attentive, so charming, I feel myself relaxing and slipping back towards our friendship. But then he touches Bryony's knee, and I see the way he squeezes and how she flinches.

At the care home, the act continues. Alex is all warmth for the reception staff. First names, compliments, a laugh that rings down the corridor. He asks after one staff member's mother who's just had an operation, and they all come out to greet him, flocking around us like he's a celebrity. It feels like the entire care home brightens under his attention. It's another reminder of how adored he is in Skelwick, and how much we've all been fooled by this man.

In Mum's room, he is the perfect son-in-law. He pulls the chair closer to her window, so she can see the boats. He lowers his voice when she seems tired. He squeezes my shoulder when he says, 'Our Jessie's back for a while. Isn't that good news, Andrea?' and my chest tightens because it sounds like he really cares.

How can they believe these lies? How can they not see the monster he really is?

'He said he'd make me watch while he killed you.'

I don't know how I hold myself together. I'm quiet, barely speaking, but I don't cry or scream or run. I'm frozen with the enormity of what this man is capable of and the threat I now know is looming over me and Bryony.

Later, when he's driven us back to Mum's house and he's pulled to the side of the road with the engine running, he says, 'I've got time when I'm back from America to help with the house. No sense you doing it alone, Jess.'

'It's fine,' I say. 'I can manage.' I don't know how to tell him that I *have* to do this alone. It isn't just that I no longer recognise the man I used to think was my friend. It's that working with someone who isn't Liam will be too painful.

Liam and I used to do every job together, side by side. If we were painting a wall, I'd do the edges and he'd do the middle. We'd have a radio on, belting out the pop songs I used to pretend I was too cool to like as a teen but still feel nostalgic listening to now.

I thought renovating the manor house was the hardest thing I'd ever done, but when I look back now, I ache to be there again with Liam, when things were still good between us. I suddenly wish he was here with me. He and Bryony always got on well during her visits. He'd want to help her too. He'd know what to do.

'Nonsense,' Alex replies. 'We're family. We help each other.'

He turns to Bryony. 'You'll follow me to the studio now,' he asks, nodding to where her car is parked.

'Of course, darling. I'll just grab my scarf from the house and I'll be right behind you.'

'See you at the exhibit next Thursday night, Jessie. Seven p.m.' Then he grimaces. 'It's formal dress code, by the way. I hate it, but my agent insists.' His gaze drifts down to my old jeans and the corner of his mouth quirks. 'I hope that won't be a problem.'

I manage to laugh. 'I'll find something, don't worry.'

Bryony and I climb out, and Alex pulls away with a wave. Only when his car disappears around the corner does Bryony lean against me, shuddering with a sob.

'Come on – let's go inside,' I reply, guiding her into the house.

'I only have ten minutes. As soon as he gets to the studio, he'll check I'm on my way.'

We settle in the kitchen, Bryony collapsing into a chair at the table while I make us cups of tea, my hands shaking so much, I spill hot water all over the counter.

'Can you believe he poured my wine away like that?' she says bitterly. 'He hates when I drink.'

Tears prick my eyes. 'I'm so sorry, Bry,' I reply because what else can I say? 'For everything you're going through.'

She shakes her head. The same stubborn look in her eye I remember from childhood when Mum would ask us to tidy our room and Bry would fold her arms across her chest and stamp her foot and shake her head, just as fierce as she looks now.

'No. I'm sorry you had to pretend like that. Believe me, I know how hard it is. And now you've got to come to the exhibit with us too.'

'At least there'll be lots of people there. He won't be able to hurt you.'

Bryony's lip trembles. 'No. He'll wait until afterwards. God, it better go well.'

Or what? I want to ask but don't dare. 'What's your plan?' I ask her instead.

'I won't risk him hurting you. Or me.' Her voice cracks. 'I have to get away from him.'

The isolation and the fear in her voice presses in on me. 'How will you do it?' I ask.

'Alex has his exhibit next Thursday, and then on the Sunday, he's flying to America. He'll be gone for five days. It's my only chance. I was supposed to go with him, but my passport expired, thank God. I need time to set up a new life, and I can't do that if he's tracking me or if Jimmy and Paulina are reporting back to him that I'm leaving the house at odd times, not coming home for hours.' She looks straight at me. 'That's why I need you, Jess. I can't set up a new life and be here acting like everything is normal at the same time. This can only work if Alex doesn't get suspicious while he's away.'

My pulse is a loud drumbeat in my ears. Bryony is talking like the answer is obvious and yet none of this is making sense. 'I don't understand.'

'I need you to pretend to be me for a few days,' she says.

'What?' I choke out. 'How could I possibly—'

'We look alike,' she says, urgent now. 'If you get your hair cut and a few highlights, wear my clothes, drive my car, stick to my routine with my phone, people will think you're me. You can reply to Alex's messages. He'll never know.'

She grabs my arm, talking fast, laying out her plan.

'While Alex is away and you're me, I'll set up my new life, and then I'll come back and take the *Odysseus* out around the bay and not come back. I can use a small inflatable dinghy and land up the coast. When the coastguard find the yacht drifting empty, everyone will assume I fell overboard and drowned.'

Like I almost did, I think, feeling sick. I can't believe we're even talking about this. 'This is insane, Bryony – you can't leave your entire life behind.'

Her voice breaks. 'If I stay, he'll kill us both eventually. It's getting worse, Jess.'

'What about Mum?'

Sadness streaks across Bryony's features, but she carries on. 'She barely knows I'm there most days. She won't notice I'm not visiting.' She takes a hurried breath, and her next words change everything. 'You won't have to worry about money. I took out a life insurance policy last year and put it in your name. It's enough to cover Mum's care and to set up on your own.'

'Last year?' I stare at my sister, forcing myself to ask the question even as my mind snags on the mention of money. 'How long has this been going on, Bry?'

Her lower lip trembles. 'A while, but it's never been this bad before. I've been saving my own money too. Bit by bit, so Alex wouldn't notice.' She pushes a hand through her hair, smoothing out the tangles. 'When it's safe, I'll contact you. We'll find a way to see each other again.'

I stare at her, mind racing with everything Bryony is suggesting. There are too many questions. Too many holes. Too many ways it could go wrong. This isn't a plan – it's madness.

But a little voice whispers in my mind. *This could save you too.*

FIFTEEN

SIXTEEN YEARS EARLIER – THE FALL

Bryony

I tip my head back, facing straight into the wind, feeling happy and free. Laughter rises inside me. These are the moments I love – the ones that leave me feeling alive. Like we're flying. The *Calypso* glides across the waves, cutting through the water like a blade, the sail taut and gleaming the brightest white. The sea spray catches in my hair, cool and sharp against the flush of my cheeks.

The day is slipping away from us, the horizon bruised with the promise of night and maybe even a distant storm. It's almost time to turn back. Almost. What's one more minute? One more minute of the wind in my hair and the exhilaration in my chest. Then we'll head home and I'll do the homework I ignored yesterday, and I'll sit through dinner while Mum and Dad talk of nothing but the trip to London we're all taking tomorrow for the art competition Jess won; pretending to play happy families even though I overheard their hissed argument last night. Sadness tugs in my belly alongside a bitterness I can't name. I wish I hadn't heard them. I wish they tried as hard to shield the truth from me as they do from Jess.

Mum is so excited for the trip. It's all she can talk about. What to wear, what route to take, where we'll have lunch. It's like she thinks we're going to New York instead of just spending a few hours on a train.

I shake the feelings away. They're waiting for me on the shore, but here, I'm free. One more minute of just me and Jess, then I have a surprise for her. I glance to the cubby that leads into the cabin and then to where Jess is standing, cheeks just as flushed from the wind, but she's not laughing, not happy like I am. Like she should be.

She looks nervous – a frown tightening her brow. She always worries. I keep telling her there's never anything to worry about, but she does it anyway.

'It's fine!' I shout, biting back that niggling frustration that she should just be happy for once. This was supposed to be fun for both of us. 'We're fine!'

A clatter sounds from below deck, a hollow thud that draws both our eyes to the open hatch. I smile, mouthing to Jess, 'It's nothing.'

The boat lurches slightly, and when I look up, Jess is shouting something, a finger pointing towards the sky where the clouds seem to have darkened in the minute since I last looked. I can't hear her over the roar of the wind and the sea, but I know what she's saying. She wants to turn back.

There's another sound from below, and for a heartbeat I tense, shoulders tight, holding my breath as I feel a presence beside me.

The movement happens fast. One swift motion. Hard. Violent. Like the wind has caught the sail from the opposite direction. The boom moves – a fast, sudden swing across the deck exactly where Jess has twisted around to talk to me.

I scream her name, but she hears it too late, and the boom

strikes her across the side of her temple. It all happens so fast, but even over the sound of my warning cry, I hear the crack as it hits. Jess's body crumples like an empty sack. The sound of laughter echoes across the boat, but this isn't funny.

Just as fast, Jess's legs give way and she is tumbling, not just down but over the edge. One second, she's there. The next, she's gone. Lost to the sea. I don't even hear the splash.

Sickening panic hits me just as hard as the boom hit Jess, and for the longest, most awful moment of my life, I'm frozen. Dad's warnings from all the times he taught me to sail echo in my ears. *'Every second counts when someone falls overboard. You have to act fast.'*

But for that awful moment, I'm stuck, wresting to get the tiller back in my control, eyes fixed on the place where Jess should be and isn't.

'She's overboard,' I shout.

Every second counts.

The tiller jerks again, dragging the *Calypso* sideways. Instinct takes over. I wrench the tiller hard, bringing her head into the wind. The sail flaps violently, the sound a crack like gunfire. I yank the mainsheet free and lash the tiller so she drifts slow and useless. Spray lashes my face, stinging my eyes.

I grab the orange buoy from the stern and hurl it towards the place she went under. For a heartbeat, I can still see her – a flash of red against the grey water – and I fix the image in my mind. Don't lose her.

'Jess!' The word rips out of me, snatched by the wind.

But there's no answer. Only the endless roll of the dark churning sea.

SIXTEEN

NOW

Jess

Alex's workshop smells of resin and salt and something smoky, reminding me of late-night bonfires on the beach. It's warm inside and stuffy. Too many people and not enough space. I'm wearing a simple black cocktail dress I bought for Liam's parents' thirtieth wedding anniversary. It hugs my figure before sweeping out in a skirt that stops at my knee with a black lace petticoat. I've blow-dried my hair and left it down over my shoulders and put on make-up. I barely recognised the face of the woman in the hall mirror as I slipped on my coat earlier.

It's been another week where I haven't seen Bryony. I thought she'd message or call to tell me she's had another idea, something less extreme, but I've heard nothing, and as I move through the crowd, I'm nervous. Alex leaves for America in three days. Is Bryony still planning to set up a new life, for me to help her, to fake her own death?

The studio is lit by strings of fairy lights woven around the wooden beams and carefully placed spotlights highlighting the driftwood art pieces, positioned around the room. Some are big ostentatious pieces. Others are small and intricate. Some hang from ceilings, others rise from the ground. Some are on walls, others in display cases. Even through my worry and fear, I can see the detail and work that's gone into each piece. They're breathtaking.

In the centre of the room is an intricate ice sculpture depicting the crest of a wave. I swear I see a hand hidden inside the ice wanting to grab and snatch and pull me under. I shiver and look away.

Last night, I'd woken from the same nightmare. I'd rewound the memory in my head once more, remembered the fall, then standing on the deck. And then a little more. A moment where Bryony shouted my name. A warning. I remember spinning round, gasping as the shadow loomed, then something hit me and I was thrown into the air. I spent hours trying to remember more, wondering if it's my return to Skelwick after so long that's unlocked these snatches of new memory. But I'm still frustrated. Still desperate to remember the time before it all went wrong.

The windows of the studio are black mirrors, reflecting the mingling crowd of art dealers, private collectors, journalists and some of the local community who made the invite list, like Kelly and a few other faces that seem vaguely familiar.

She sees me and waves me over as I take a glass of champagne from a passing tray. 'Jess, you look lovely,' she says with a smile. Her cheeks are rosy from the warmth or the champagne. 'How's your mum?'

'She has her good days and bad days,' I reply, thinking of this morning when she thought I was a care assistant and told me her daughters don't come to see her anymore, and I cried all the way home. 'I've been taking in old photo albums. I think she finds it easier to talk about the past.'

'And the house? You'll be ready for this summer, I expect?'

Her question feels loaded. I hesitate, taking a sip of cold, fizzing champagne just to buy myself a moment to think. I've cleared the living room, parts of the kitchen and the box room this week. Grateful for the distraction. But the truth is, I don't know when the house will be ready or what my plan is anymore.

Bryony had offered me their guesthouse as a place to stay for a while. Did she think my presence would protect her from Alex's abuse? I can't blame her for that, but there's no way I can stay there now. If she goes through with faking her death, it will only be Alex at the house. I could never stay so close to him. But without a rent-free place to live, how can I turn Mum's house into a holiday let? I'll be homeless.

Bryony's life insurance, a desperate voice whispers in my ear. That's the answer to all my problems. I can pay back the money I borrowed, cover Mum's care and then... I don't know what comes next. I still dream of working in a hotel again, maybe even owning my own place again one day, but doing it without Liam feels wrong.

'I'm not sure,' I reply honestly. 'I hope the house will be ready for the summer, but I'll make sure you're first to know, and of course, I'll make sure it's in the rental agreement that noise must be kept to a minimum. No large groups.'

I expect Kelly to smile at that, to thank me even, but her lips are pursed. When she speaks again, there's a wobble to her voice. 'I understand. It just feels wrong, that's all. Your mum and I were neighbours for so long. I'd hoped...' She trails off, waving her hand like she can shoo away the thought. 'It doesn't matter.' She starts to turn back to the group she's with before she gasps. 'Oh, Jess. I almost forgot. A letter came for you. They needed a signature so I took it for you. I've got it here.'

She pulls the envelope from her handbag before I have the chance to tell her it can wait. I see the white letters inside the red stamp. The two words that cause nausea to burn the back of my throat and the corners of the room to blur. *Final Notice.*

'Thank you,' I manage to say, taking the envelope and stuffing it in the pocket of my dress. 'It's probably a bill we forgot to pay for the hotel,' I mumble, turning away before I can see the doubt and pity in Kelly's eyes.

My cheeks are still burning as I down my champagne. I take another glass from a table and weave through the crowd until I find a quiet corner to stand in. Inside my pocket, the paper crinkles like a taunt. I can't pay and I'm out of options. I want to call Liam. I want to ask him what I should do. It was his hotel too. He made everything sound easy. Like we could do anything. I miss him so much. It hits me then that he hasn't called for over a week now. I wonder if I'd have answered if he had. But I can't ask him what he thinks I should do anymore. Or I won't. Not after how it all ended.

I'm so lost in thought that I don't see Bryony until she's leaning against the wall beside me, sipping a glass of champagne. She's radiant – hair impossibly glossy, lips a careful rose. Her dress is a simple pearl-white off-the-shoulder gown that flows to her ankles. Nothing that could upstage the artwork but stunning nonetheless. I feel instantly dowdy in comparison.

'We need to talk about next week,' she says without looking at me or breaking the bright, welcoming smile on her lips. To anyone passing by, we look like we're admiring the art and exchanging small talk.

'Now?'

She nods. 'Alex is busy with his agent. They're talking to all the dealers from London.'

I follow her gaze to where a stocky man with a receding hairline is moving Alex through the crowd.

'I've made an appointment at the hair salon I use for Monday,' she says. 'Alex knows about it. He thinks it's for me, but really it's for you. We can drive together in my car. You'll have your hair styled like mine. Then you'll change into my clothes at one of the changing rooms at the department store, and you'll drive my car back here. I'll disappear for a few days. It's safer if you don't know where, I think.'

The worry continues to gnaw at me. I swallow hard, trying to think clearly. I know we talked about this. I know I agreed to help Bryony, but this feels unreal. Monday is only four days away. It's not enough time to plan and be sure.

'What do I do while you're away?' I ask.

'You'll be me. Drive around town, go to the gym, visit Mum. I'm sure if you keep my sunglasses on and wear my clothes, people won't look too closely. They'll see the car and the hair and they'll assume you're me.'

'What about Paulina and your gardener? I can't exactly wear sunglasses in the house, and we might look alike from a distance but not up close, and they're at the house all the time.'

Bryony nods. 'I know. I was worrying about that too, but I think it will still be OK. Jimmy only works outside, and both only work mornings. Paulina always cleans the kitchen first. Wait in my bedroom until you hear her start the dishes, then hurry downstairs and straight out the front door. Call out that you're going to the gym and leave.'

'And Mum? She'll know I'm not you.'

From the corner of my eye, I see Bryony's expression falter. 'She might not realise,' she says softly. 'I know it's awful to confuse her, but if she thinks you're me, don't correct her. It'll be easier that way. You'll have my phone,' she adds. 'Alex will be tracking it, so stick to my routine, answer immediately if he messages. He'll get suspicious if you don't. He hates calling, so he won't try to talk to you.'

I nod slowly, a numbness creeping through me. I take a long gulp of champagne, forgetting I'm supposed to be keeping a clear head. This doesn't feel real.

Bryony continues. 'I'll come home Thursday and be me again. Then on Friday afternoon before Alex gets back from the airport, I'll take the *Odysseus* out and disappear. Everyone will assume there was an accident.'

Her words hang between us in the silence. Can we really do this? It feels like madness.

'How will I know you're OK?' I ask.

'I'll get an unregistered phone,' Bryony replies, like she's thought of everything. 'I'll message you when I make it to shore.'

'What if we're caught?'

She grabs my hand, her grip ice-cold. 'We won't be. It's the only way I'll ever be free. Please, Jess.'

I stare at her, unblinking. My head fills with the sight of the bruises and the desperation in her voice and the wild fear in her eyes.

'OK. Monday. I'll be ready.'

I want to ask her one more time if she's sure, but then a glass is clinked and the room falls silent to hear Alex talk. He beckons Bryony over, and she glides through the crowd towards him like a woman in love.

'Thank you for being here tonight,' Alex says, voice carrying with practised ease as he raises his glass of champagne. 'Next week, these pieces will be on display at the Vellion Gallery in Long Island.' He pauses as applause breaks out. 'But you all know that Skelwick is my heart. These pieces are born from this coast – its wrecks, its tides, its stories.' He gestures to the nearest sculpture, wood burned and sealed so it gleams like ink. 'And so all that's left now is to thank you all for coming and ask you to keep drinking the champagne, as it's already been paid for.' He smiles broadly, taking a sip from his glass as laughter carries around the room. 'And finally, I must thank my beautiful wife.' He turns to Bryony. 'My muse. My anchor. I can't live without you, darling.'

The room seems to sigh, obviously charmed. But to me those words carry the menace of a threat. A promise that he'll never let her leave. I watch Bryony's throat move as she swallows and lifts her glass, and still, even in her state of fear she stays on his arm throughout the evening, and I wonder if I'm the only one that sees that Bryony is strung too tight – a wire, vibrating, ready to snap.

She catches my eye as they sweep past a cluster of collectors and, for a second, she reaches out, leans close, fingers gripping my hand, breath hot in my ear. 'I'll pick you up at twelve on Monday.'

Before I have a chance to reply, she's turning back to Alex, staring up at him with an adoration that could fool kingdoms. The perfect hostess. The perfect wife. The perfect muse.

Bryony has always been good at putting on a show. At our cousin's wedding, when I was eleven and she was fourteen, she took over the dance floor like she owned it, spinning my aunt under the fairy lights, making the whole marquee laugh, even when she knocked over an entire tray of drinks and it spilled over my new dress. She was more upset than I was. Crying in the toilets, offering to swap dresses with me. I was happy to change into the skirt and top I'd bought to wear the following day. I hadn't liked the attention my dress got me anyway. All those, *'Jessica, look how you've grown,'* comments.

It's as the evening is winding down, and the important people have left for the last train back to London, that Alex finds me. 'Jessie, you came.' His voice is warm, maybe a little champagne slurred too. My back is to the wall, and he's leaning close enough for the masculine scent of his aftershave to fill my senses. He's lost his suit jacket, shirt sleeves rolled up to his forearms.

'Wouldn't miss it,' I manage, hoping it isn't obvious my heart is racing with fear of him – the monster he is beneath the surface – and for what we're planning. 'You must be so pleased with how it's gone,' I force myself to say, trying to sound normal. 'The pieces are outstanding.'

'They're all' – he rakes a hand through his hair and sighs – 'what's expected of me.'

I study his face. My insides feel like liquid. This is the man who said he'd kill me. I want to ask why he thinks he's lost his touch. Why he hurts Bryony when he used to adore her. But those questions lodge in my throat, stuffed down with the need for politeness and the fear that anything I say could push him over the edge and make things worse for Bryony.

A waiter brushes past me with a tray, and there's a flash of annoyance on Alex's face. 'Excuse me for a minute.'

I watch him follow the waiter into the back room of the studio. I don't hear what words are exchanged, but it's clear Alex is angry about something. The waiter seems appeasing and apologetic. Almost cowering.

A hand touches my arm, and I jump, turning too fast. 'Relax,' Bryony whispers. 'You look like you've got a gun to your head.'

'I feel like I have,' I reply.

'Next week, as soon as it's clear—' she starts.

But Alex is suddenly looming, voice loud and curious. 'What are you two plotting?' His smile is still in place, but there's a hard look in his eyes.

This is exactly what he meant – what he feared. That Bryony would come to me for help and I'd give it. That we'd find a way for her to escape. If he suspects it's happening, then what? Will he come to the house in the middle of the night? Will he invite me over, lock me in the basement? Will he go through with his threat to kill me so Bryony is completely alone in the world?

My mouth drops open. I have to laugh. To lie. To convince him this is nothing. But all I have is the truth. *Next week, as soon as it's clear, I'm going to pretend to be your wife so she can set up a new life far away from you.*

Luckily, Bryony doesn't miss a beat. She laughs and lays a

hand on Alex's chest. 'Plotting, darling, really? I was talking about the *Odysseus*. The weather is supposed to clear next week. I thought I'd take her out for her first sail of the year. I'm trying to coax Jess into coming with me.'

Alex looks at me, one eyebrow raised. 'Jess on a boat?'

'Exactly,' I say, finding enough strength to smile. 'Never going to happen.'

It's the truth. I will never set foot on a boat again. Never. Not a small yacht or a car ferry or a cruise liner. Nothing where there's only a railing and then the vast dark sea threatening to snatch me away again. It's not just boats I struggle with either. The idea of being submerged in any kind of water causes panic to shoot through my veins. I don't paddle in the sea. I don't swim in hotel pools. The only thing I can manage is the occasional bath, and only if the water is near scalding.

There's a silence I want to fill, but I don't know how.

Alex studies us for a heartbeat too long. My pulse thunders. Then he leans in and kisses Bryony's cheek. 'Come help me charm this local collector,' he says. 'He's drank his body weight in champagne and still hasn't bought anything. And you know I'm always better when you're by my side.'

They move away together, and I realise my nails are digging into the palms of my hand, hard enough to sting.

Ten minutes later, I find my coat and say a quick goodbye. 'Good luck in America,' I add.

Alex sighs, smile slipping. 'I don't know why I agreed to it. They never buy my work. I'll probably cut it short. I hate being away from Bry.'

I try to keep my face blank, but my eyes dart to Bryony. Her smile is casual, seemingly unaffected by Alex's comment. If he comes back early… if he finds me in his house…

'You always say that,' she coos, sliding her arm through his. 'And then you have a good time, and people do buy your work.'

'I'm just not sure what I'm doing this all for anymore,' he says. 'This isn't how I imagined my life would be.'

'You're just tired from tonight, darling. Look, the Joneses are waiting to say goodbye.'

She turns him away, her gaze still on me. Something sharpens in her look. A warning or a plea, I'm not sure.

I button my coat and push through the doors into the cold black night. The air is heavy with the sulphurous smell of seaweed. The tide must be out; the sound of the waves hitting the shore is distant. A halyard clinks somewhere in the harbour – like a warning bell, I think.

Next week, Alex goes to America.

Next week, I become Bryony.

Next week, my sister will be gone.

SEVENTEEN

Jess

On the drive to Merkshaw on Monday, Bryony talks me through the plan two more times. Her voice is low and fast. How she'll disappear until Thursday afternoon. How I'll live in her house. Drive her car. Wear her clothes. Sign her name in the guest book at the care home when I visit Mum. Reply to Alex's messages. Be her.

Each repetition tightens something in my chest. I sit in the passenger seat with my legs refusing to stay still; my knee keeps bouncing. Even the seat belt feels too tight.

'What will you be doing in the next few days?' I ask. My voice comes out thin.

'I'm going to set up a little place for myself, hidden away. Somewhere he won't be able to find me. I want everything ready so that when I disappear, I can stay hidden for a while. It'll be safer for both of us that way.'

I open my mouth to ask again, but the words die there. It feels like the time for questioning is over. And Bryony is glowing. Bright. Excited. Back to the confident, joyful sister she was before Alex's shadow started swallowing her whole.

So I say nothing.

We fall into silence, and I turn towards the window. The sea has become a constant companion in the three weeks I've been back in Skelwick – the salty wind, the roar, the shifting blue-grey. The rolling Devonshire countryside seems foreign somehow. It's a stitchwork of every shade of green, broken by hedgerows that grow over the narrow lanes, brushing the side of Bryony's car.

Eventually, the lane widens into a busier road with houses and shopfronts and endless traffic lights and roundabouts before we turn into the market square car park where Mum used to park when she'd bring us to get new school shoes. Afterwards, we'd get ice cream if we were good – vanilla for me, mint choc-chip for Bryony. The memory is so ordinary next to our reason for being here now that it hurts to think about.

The salon is down a cobbled side street just off the square. Even from outside it looks expensive – polished brass handle, frosted glass, a sign in elegant script reading *Giana's*. Inside, soft lighting glows against the mirrors framed in wrought iron. Leather chairs gleam. Shelves are lined with bottles in pastel shades. The faint, perfumed scent of hair products lingers in the air. It screams money. Privacy. Exclusivity.

'Bryony!' a woman calls, breezing towards us from the back of the salon.

We're the only customers here. I can't tell if that's planned or if the place is simply so high-end that they only take one client at a time.

'Julia,' Bry says warmly, leaning in to air-kiss the blonde woman. Julia looks somewhere in her forties, rake-thin and immaculate wearing a black jumpsuit.

'Same as usual?' Julia asks, gesturing Bryony towards the nearest chair. She gives me only the faintest side-eye, polite but dismissive, like I'm clutter she hadn't expected to deal with today.

'Yes.' Bryony smiles. 'But not for me. For my sister, Jess.'

'Oh.' Julia's gaze shifts from Bryony to me, and she plasters on a sweet smile. She steps closer, taking a lock of my hair between her fingers the way someone might lift a dirty sock they're not sure they want to touch.

'We want it to look exactly like mine,' Bryony says, dropping into one of the salon chairs and snatching up a magazine like this is any other Monday.

I know it's an act. Bryony is as scared and nervous as I am. I see it in the look she gives me. That half pleading, half warning, *'Play along.'*

I want to reach out and take her hand, offer comfort – be comforted. I will do anything for my sister, including this. But I never thought I'd lose her.

'Your sister's hair is a little thicker than yours,' Julia says to Bryony, not to me. 'So I'd actually recommend—'

'Exactly the same,' Bryony repeats, and beneath the command, I sense the urgency.

Julia nods, ushering me into the identical chair beside Bryony. A cape is thrown around my shoulders, a comb dragged through my hair. The smell of chemicals fills the air as Julia starts mixing bowls of colour.

There's nowhere to look but straight at myself. At the dark circles beneath my eyes. At how small and worn down I seem under the harsh lights.

I watch as Julia separates sections of my hair and folds them into foils. Each movement feels like another step into something I'm not ready for. A transformation I agreed to but don't truly understand – or want.

I try to remember the last time I had my hair cut, but instead my mind pulls back to the time during the renovations of the Kilstern when my hair got so long the ponytail kept dipping in the paint tin every time I bent down. We didn't have the time or money for me to book in anywhere, so I gave Liam the kitchen scissors and told him to do his best. We laughed so hard at his impression of a hairdresser that he could barely cut straight, but I didn't care and nor did he.

Two hours later, my plain brown hair has vanished beneath honeyed highlights and a honey-blonde balayage. Julia pulls each strand taut between her fingers and cuts the final strands. The urge to tell her to stop rises and falls with every snip of the scissors. I liked my hair the way it was, but it's far too late now. So I bite my tongue, reminding myself it will grow back. If I'm still here to let it.

If Alex finds out—

I cut the thought dead. I have to be strong for Bryony. Alex might have threatened to kill me, but he's already hurt Bryony countless times. The danger she's in feels more immediate, and I have to protect her.

When Julia finally removes the gown, I almost don't recognise the woman staring back at me. My hair is sleek and glossy, the cut sharp, sitting just above my shoulders, framing my face in a way that makes me look sophisticated and glamorous. Makes me look like Bryony.

'You could be twins,' Julia says as Bryony steps beside me, beaming.

'We could, couldn't we?' Bryony says a little too brightly, tapping her bank card to the machine without even glancing at the total.

The moment we step outside, she's rushing, no longer pretending to be anything but scared. 'Come on,' she says, striding towards the entrance to John Lewis. Her shoulders are rigid; her jaw tight.

We push through the tall glass entrance doors. Warm air heavy with the scent of perfumes hits me at once. Bryony doesn't slow; she grabs clothes off rails without looking – a top and a jumper, a pair of jeans before she beelines for the changing rooms. I trail behind her, nearly breathless from the speed, from the fear, from the strangeness of all of this.

We slip into two adjacent cubicles. I strip out of my baggy jeans and my best jumper. It looked passable at home but under the sharp white lights looks worn, bobbled, cheap. Like a costume from a life that's about to end.

'Are you ready?' Bryony whispers through the thin partition.

'Yeah,' I manage.

And then her hand pushes a bundle of neatly folded clothes through the curtain, just as she reaches under mine to take away what I was wearing.

When we step out to the large mirror, I stop dead.

I'm... transformed. I look just like Bryony.

The tailored trousers fit my legs perfectly, soft fabric skimming my hips like they were made for me. The cashmere jumper is warm against my skin, not just elegant but complementing my figure.

I turn to Bryony, expecting to see her in my clothes, but instead she's stuffed them in a bag and is wearing black activewear and an oversized grey jumper. Casual but still chic. Still Bryony.

She smiles warmly and pulls her hair into a ponytail, adding a baseball cap before throwing her arms around me. 'My bank card is in my purse,' she says. 'The pin is my birthday. And there's cash in there too. If you need money for petrol or anything like that, use it. It's not like I can,' she adds with a small, light laugh.

I wish I could say that in the madness of this moment, money didn't cross my mind, but it would be a lie. For over a week now, since Bryony told me about the life insurance policy she's put in my name, a voice has been whispering in the back of my mind that this is my way out. But it could be months before I see that money, and the debt I owe can't wait that long.

My heart starts to race as the questions I don't want to ask myself start to form anyway. I'm trembling with fear as much as relief. Bryony will be away until Thursday, and then on Friday she'll fake her death. Would she even notice if I used some of her money? Just a little bit. A down payment on what I owe. Enough to stop the phone for a little while?

'You'll be fine,' Bryony says, and I wonder if she's felt the tremor in my body and assumes I'm worrying about her.

I draw in a quick breath and can't stop myself asking: 'What if Alex comes back early? You heard what he said the other night.'

'He won't,' she murmurs, drawing away from me. 'He always says that. But he never does it.'

Before I can push or question or change my mind, she steps back. And it's as though she knows if we stand here a moment longer, I'll find a reason to stop this whole insane plan. She mutters a hurried, 'Thank you,' pulls the hood up on my coat, and with her head down, she disappears out of the changing rooms.

I wait a few minutes, heart thudding, making sure she's not coming back before I pull Bryony's purse from her bag and open the expensive leather. I gasp at the size of the wad of cash inside. Tears spill onto my cheeks despite the knotty, disgusted feeling in my belly that I'm stealing from my sister. She said I could use the money if I needed it, but she said for petrol or food. Not the debt that's been looming over me for months. Why didn't I just ask her for this money? She would've given it. But there never seemed to be a right time. I was already embarrassed to be at rock bottom without asking Bryony for help. And besides, I feel like we've been on a one-way path to this moment since I arrived back in Skelwick.

I'm making excuses. But however much I loathe who I am in this moment, I know exactly what I'm going to do.

Outside, on the busy street, people drift past with bags and coffees. I scan the crowd for Bryony, but she's nowhere. Already vanished. So I slide her Gucci sunglasses over my eyes and walk to the bank. Every step feels alien; I feel exactly like the imposter I am.

Later, the drive back to Cliffview House is slow and careful, my hands clammy on the wheel. Every unfamiliar control, every polished button, every faint whiff of Bryony's perfume lingering in the car makes my stomach twist. I'm scared of being recognised. Scared Alex will arrive home early. Scared Bryony will call me and ask why I withdrew money from her account.

By the time I pull into her driveway, there's a notification on my phone with the same alert Bryony's phone gave her. *AirTag found moving with you.*

A bolt of fear races through me. A reminder of what matters and why we're doing this. Alex might be on the other side of the world, but he's still tracking Bryony. Tracking *me.* Claws of worry sharpen as I slip into Cliffview House and pretend to be my sister.

EIGHTEEN

Jess

There's someone in the house.

Panic freezes me in place. I'm stuck, lying in Bryony's bed and trying to remember how to breathe, when all I can think is that there's someone else in this house. The realisation pins me to the silk duvet that feels too soft, too slippery against my skin. The pillows feel cold and the whole room unfamiliar. Her life. Her bed. Her house.

And there's someone else here.

My gaze shoots to the window. I must have drifted off because it's almost dawn. Too early for Paulina to be arriving. And Bryony said she always comes at nine sharp. Jimmy, their gardener, never comes in the house. He doesn't even have a key. And it can't be Alex because he's in America.

I want to tell myself I'm being paranoid. Ridiculous. The insides of my eyes feel scratchy with lack of sleep. It feels like I've slept less than an hour, and now the first stretches of daylight are creeping in. Not even the gulls are awake yet, but I'm wide-eyed, heart racing, just as I was for most of the night.

Scared.

Embarrassed too.

I want to go downstairs, make a coffee. Make a mess in the kitchen. Something for Paulina to clean when she comes in at nine, giving me time to slip out the front door like Bryony planned. Last night, I made myself a noodle stir-fry and then washed up the pan before realising that Bryony would've left it for Paulina. I love my sister, but it never would've crossed her mind that leaving the pan on the side and the sauce to harden will make cleaning it ten times harder for someone else.

I can't even describe why I think there's someone else in the house. There are no doors banging. No footsteps on the stairs. No strange smell or lights being turned on or off.

It's more a feeling. That same dark tension I felt when I visited Bryony for coffee. But now, with just me in the house, it's more like a crawling awareness that I'm not alone. I felt it the moment I slid Bryony's key into the lock and stepped into the house after the drive from Merkshaw, telling myself I was just spooked by the size of the place. Another ridiculous lie. Because all the nights I spent alone in the final weeks in the Kilstern, when there were no guests, and Liam had packed his bags and left, and it was just me, I never felt like this.

Still, I checked every room last night. Found nothing. Forced myself to cook dinner and watch TV, only allowing the fear to sweep over me as I'd climbed into Bryony's bed. Maybe I'm the strange presence. The one who doesn't belong. I ache to be back in my childhood bedroom with the posters on the wall and peeling stickers on the dressing table. But then I picture the way Bryony flinched at Alex's touch in the car, and how she begged me for help, and how yesterday, she was so much lighter, and I know I won't leave.

I owe her this.

I sigh and reach for the lamp on the nightstand, but my fingers find something else. A glass jar, the silk of a ribbon. I turn on the light, surprised to see the jar of blue shells, tied with a matching blue ribbon, the colour time-faded but still tied perfectly. I can't believe I didn't notice this yesterday.

Suddenly, I'm twelve again, walking the beach for hours until my toes and fingers are numb with cold, my hair knotted with the salt in the sea air and my cheeks flushed red. A small bucket in my hand, sifting through the debris left from the retreating tide for the blue shells. Mum's favourite colour. It took me weeks to find enough for the jar. Rinsing off the sand, leaving them to dry, placing each one carefully inside. Tying a ribbon I'd bought from the gift shop in town. Bryony tied the bow so perfectly, and we gave it to Mum for her birthday. From both of us, we said.

The jar disappeared the next week during one of Mum's cleaning frenzies. She cried when she realised. She thought she'd thrown it out by accident. *'I'm so sorry, Jess,'* she kept saying.

I told her it didn't matter. *'No harm done.'*

But it can't have been thrown out after all. I smile, thinking about how Mum probably tucked it away somewhere safe, like the chocolate biscuits she'd hide years later when it was just the two of us in the house, both of us pretending we didn't notice the quiet stillness left behind by Dad and Bryony.

Mum must have found the jar after I'd left for London and given it to Bryony. Seeing it feels like a connection to the past and the time when I thought we'd all been so happy. All families argue of course. Bryony would refuse to tidy her room and Mum would get cross. I'd stay up reading past bedtime and Dad would tell me to go to sleep. Silly things. Normal things. Then the accident. And nothing was normal again.

I can't lie here for a second longer. So I force back the fear and slip downstairs to make coffee.

The carpet runner on the staircase is soft under my bare

feet, and the house is silent except for a low hum I noticed last night too. It must be the heating or the boiler, and yet something about it still makes me pause.

In the kitchen, streaks of dawn push in through the windows. I pick out one of the dainty china mugs hung from hooks below the worktop, and within minutes the smell of rich coffee fills the room. I lean against the counter, my hands wrapped around the heat of the mug as I stare out to the garden. Beyond the dewy grass and the trees and cliff, there is a slice of steel-grey sea on the horizon, two shades darker than the sky that looks like it's emerging from it.

A movement flickers in the corner of my vision. My heart jerks. I blink. And suddenly there's a figure standing in the middle of the garden. Jimmy. Motionless. Back ramrod straight. Arms hanging at his sides. Staring directly at me through the window. Why is he here so early? A chill slides down my spine. His stare doesn't shift. Doesn't narrow. Doesn't blink. I force a smile and raise my hand in a quick wave.

Nothing.

Seconds pass. Then, slowly, he lifts his hand in return. No smile. Just that stare. I give a sharp, awkward nod and make for the stairs, my heart thundering painfully against my ribs. Did he know I wasn't Bryony?

He was all the way down the garden. Far enough that I should have been nothing more than a blurry outline in a window. And the sun was hitting the glass; he couldn't possibly have seen me clearly. And yet the way he stared unnerves me.

I hurry to Bryony's bedroom like I'm being chased, and dress fast. Ten minutes later, I'm ready, sitting on the edge of the bed, fear and worry circling like vultures as I wait.

Paulina arrives right on time, the front door opening quietly then shutting with a click.

'Good morning, Mrs Raffety,' Paulina calls up the stairs.

I bite my tongue, trying to remember all the rushed instructions Bryony gave me. *'Don't tidy up. Don't say hello to Paulina. I never do.'*

I move to the door, my hand on the handle, waiting until I hear Paulina in the kitchen so I can make my escape. I catch my reflection in the mirror on the wall and almost do a double take. With my hair neat and straight, my make-up and Bryony's black workout set, I really do look just like her. I tug at the waistband. It fits fine, but I prefer my clothes looser.

The buzz of a phone startles me. But it's not mine. It's not Liam. It's been over two weeks since he last called. And three since he left a voicemail. He's given up on me. On us. I expect to feel relieved but instead feel hollow and hurt.

I yank Bryony's phone from the side pocket of the leggings and tap in the passcode she gave me. It's a WhatsApp message from Alex: *How are you, darling? Missing you!*

Bryony's warning shoots through my thoughts. *'He'll expect a reply straight away. Don't keep him waiting.'*

It must be the early hours of the morning in Long Island, but still I tap a short reply, thinking of Bryony's breezy tone in the messages she sends me. I hope it's the same for Alex. I wish I'd asked. I wish she'd told me more. I wonder what else we've forgotten.

Just off to the gym and to visit Mum with Jess. Missing you too!

I add a kiss and stare at the tiny blue bubble until my lungs hurt. I half expect Alex to call and say, *'Nice try, Jess.'*

The dots appear. Disappear. Appear. Another message pops up, and this time my stomach drops and horror races through my blood. *Send me a photo at the gym. I miss your face.*

A cold dread seeps into my chest, like sea water in my lungs. He wants to see a photo of Bryony – his wife. To check she's doing exactly what she said she'd be doing.

And that's a problem. If I send nothing, he'll grow suspicious. If I send something, he'll see the truth instantly. Every option feels like a trap tightening around my throat. I realise with absolute clarity that this is how it starts: one wrong word, one mistake and the whole fragile lie shatters. How did we ever think we could get away with this?

NINETEEN

Jess

I grab the gym bag Bryony left for me, shove my feet into her trainers, slide the designer sunglasses over my eyes and move. Down the stairs, past the canvases of my sister's face, staring down at me, reminding me I'm an imposter. My hand finds the front door handle and then I'm outside, footsteps crunching on the gravel, inside Bryony's car. Engine started. Gone without seeing Paulina or Jimmy.

Still, it feels like I barely breathe as I make my way through Skelwick. The town is waking up. Locals out for dog walks and meeting friends for coffee. People on their way to work. I crawl slowly through the school drop-off traffic, feeling exposed.

I catch a few people waving at this car. Others nod. I almost cry out when Kelly appears as I'm stuck behind a delivery van.

Shit!

Her cleaning bucket is in her hand, and she's heading in the direction of the Skelwick Arms. I expect her to wave, to duck down at the window to say hello. Instead, she glances at the car, stares right at me, a frown deepening her features before walking on. No wave. No friendly greeting. But after a few metres, she glances back, eyes narrowing. My hands tighten on the wheel.

By the time I'm parked in the gym car park, I'm a mess. Hands shaking, jittery and nauseous. It's a large gym halfway to Merkshaw with tennis courts, a pool and a spa. More a health club than a gym, but even so, the last thing I want is to work out. The lights in the gym will be too bright, people too close. Bryony insisted yesterday that no one will talk to me. *'I'm not one for small talk when I'm sweaty.'*

But they don't need to talk to me to realise I'm not my sister. There are a hundred small ways we're different – the shape of our smiles, the scar at my hairline that throbs when I'm stressed. Not to mention, I haven't set foot inside a gym more than twice in my entire life. I have no idea how to use any of the equipment.

In the end, I hurry through the glass entrance doors and through a dimly lit lounge area, up the stairs to the gym floor. I take a photo of my trainers – Bryony's trainers – next to her water bottle and a dumbbell, sending it to Alex with a 'too sweaty for a face photo' comment I hope is something Bryony would say.

Alex's replies are fast but not suspicious. He tells me to say hi to Mum and to message again when I'm home, then asks me to wish him luck for his exhibit later. Each reply I send feels like stepping on a rotten plank of pontoon wood that could give way any second and send me falling to the dark choppy waters below.

I've been living Bryony's life for less than twenty-four hours and already I'm exhausted. It's only when I reach the care home that I start to relax a little. It's busy with visitors this morning, so no one pays me attention as I sign Bryony's name in her looping handwriting and make my way to Mum's room.

Mum is awake in her chair, a blanket over her knees, the sea slanting silver through the window beside her. She looks up and smiles, the expression so familiar my eyes sting.

'Hello, darling. I wasn't expecting you.' Her greeting is vague enough for me to feel uncertain. Does she think I'm Bryony, myself, or does she not recognise me at all and is masking it with a warm smile and a friendly comment? In the last week, I think she's known I'm her daughter only twice.

I keep my own reply just as vague. Like the messages to Alex, it feels like playing with fire, except I feel awful. The worst kind of human to lie to my mum when she's already confused and struggling. 'I had some spare time and thought I'd swing by.'

'Where's Jess?' she asks as I sink into the chair opposite her.

I bite the inside of my cheek and swallow down how much I hate myself and play along. 'She's busy today, Mum. I'm here.' The lie sits heavy in my stomach.

'I'd like to see Jess,' she says stubbornly.

The guilt rushes through me. I made a promise I'd come see Mum every day. I'm here, but I'm not here, and I don't know how to make it right. 'She'll be in tomorrow.'

Mum turns her gaze to the window. I try to make small talk, but she's quiet, barely responding. After a while, her eyes drift closed and I think she's asleep. I rest my head against the back of the chair and fight back tears.

Suddenly, it all feels too much. My own problems and Bryony's on top. Mum's failing memories. I can't carry it all on my own. I'm not strong enough. I try to swallow, but it's like a rock is lodged in my throat. Sharp and painful. I miss Liam with a fierceness that steals my breath.

'I'm never going to give up on us.'

But he's stopped calling. The hurt is a physical pain that streaks across my chest. We had something so amazing. We built something spectacular, and now it's all gone, like a sand-castle washed away by the tide.

I met Liam in London when we were both on the trainee management scheme of a leading chain hotel. I was the day shift. He was the night. And for an hour in the morning and an hour at night, our paths crossed and we'd hand over the duties and the problems of the day.

'I want to ask you on a date, but we're in different time zones,' he'd said after a month where those two hours were the best in my day.

I'd laughed. *'I think I've got a day off next month.'*

'I don't want to wait that long. Come in an hour early tomorrow. I'll skip my lunch break.'

'Why?' I'd asked.

'For our first date,' he'd replied, making it clear he knew even then there would be more than just one.

The following evening, I'd arrived an hour early to find a picnic blanket and candles set up in the poky manager's office. We'd had a dinner of sandwiches and lemonade and talked non-stop. Liam told me about his plans to travel the world before coming back to England to set up his own hotel. I'd been working in the hotel for a few years by then and had come to love it. Owning my own place was my dream too, and quickly Liam's plans to travel were put aside and owning our own hotel became a dream we shared. It was all we talked about. Setting up a boutique where every guest felt seen.

Six months later, Liam swapped to work at a different hotel so we could match up our shifts. We moved in together into a room in a house share with strangers because it was cheap. And we started to save and plan and dream. Every time I worried we were stretching too far, or that we couldn't do it, that we'd never find the right location, Liam would list the reasons everything would be OK, ticking them off on his fingers.

'One, we've planned for every eventuality. Two, we're both going to work really hard, which makes us unstoppable. And three, I love you, and that's never going to change.'

A voice whispers in my head now. *You could forgive him. You could call him.*

The hurt is still too raw, but I wonder if maybe, if he calls again, I might answer. Just to say hello and hear his voice. For so long, the closure of the hotel and the end of our relationship have felt like one awful, terrible thing, but being back in Skelwick, getting distance from everything that happened, the two are starting to separate.

In the armchair, Mum sighs softly, eyes still closed. I stand silently, planning to leave her to sleep when she speaks. Her voice seems faraway. 'Your father knew the truth. We both did, but we kept it from Jess.'

I freeze then lean forward, holding my breath, waiting for Mum's next words. She never talks about Dad. It was like when he left, she deleted him from her thoughts, refused to talk about him or why he left.

I take her hand, keeping my voice gentle. 'What do you mean, Mum? What did Dad know? What did you keep from Jess?'

'He knew about the accident.' She sighs, opening her eyes, looking almost angry. 'He didn't want to admit it, but he knew.'

I let her words settle, trying to read between them and understand. 'The day on the *Calypso*? You mean about us taking the boat out when we weren't supposed to?'

It was something I'd only learned when I was in hospital recovering from hypothermia, Bryony crying at my bedside, telling me she was sorry. Dad had told her to wait for the weekend to sail and she hadn't wanted to. So she'd lied to me, knowing I'd refuse to go if we didn't have permission. There was something about a surprise, although I don't know what it was or if we never got that far, or if it's part of the memory that's locked away.

Did Dad know all along Bryony was planning for us to go sailing? Is that what Mum means? Coldness sweeps through me, icy talons stretching through my veins. I hear the roar of the wind in my ears. Feel a tightness in my chest.

Mum seems to shrink, drawing her hand out from under mine. 'I...' She looks at me, searching my face for something, a frown deepening the lines of her brow. 'I want to go home now.'

Her voice is shaky, and her gaze moves around the room like she can't place where she is.

'Sorry, Mum,' I say. 'Let's talk about something else. You could tell me about the lady in the room next to yours and her grandchildren.'

Mum opens her mouth to reply, but still no words come. She looks so frail and lost, I could cry. I want to reach forward and hug her, but it might upset her more. I've pushed too hard, asked too many questions. I've confused her.

We sit in silence for a while, and I turn over what she said about Dad. No one likes to talk about it. Maybe it's wearing Bryony's clothes, signing her name, pretending to be her, but I think for the first time how awful it must have been for her. She saved my life and risked her own to do it. And then, before anyone had time to process what happened, before I was even out of hospital, Dad was packing his bags and leaving. She'd always been closer to Dad than Mum, so I wasn't surprised she wanted to stay with him. It was her choice, but for the first time I think how hard it must have been to make. She left me and Mum and the town she loved and everything she'd ever known.

The side of my head starts to throb. The feeling returns that I'm missing something.

Mum is still unhappy when a staff member arrives at the door with a tray. 'Lunchtime, Andrea,' she chirps, smile wide. 'You said this morning that you'd rather eat in your room today, so I've brought you soup. It's chicken and mushroom. Your favourite.'

Mum nods, but her eyes are vacant, her expression still set somewhere between confusion and anger. 'Thank you.'

I stand. 'I'll come again tomorrow,' I say, and my voice wobbles. 'I love you, Mum.'

She looks up and it's like she's seeing me for the first time. She smiles, her face brightening. 'I love you too, Jess.'

The words make me sway. She knows it's me.

'Goodbye, Mrs Raffety,' the carer says, placing down the tray beside Mum's chair.

'That's Jess,' Mum corrects, tone impatient again.

The carer shoots me a sympathetic smile. 'My mistake,' she says, and I'm sure she's thinking Mum is the one who's confused.

The need to defend Mum, to tell her that I am Jess, pushes up, but I signed my name in the visitors' book as Bryony Raffety, and so I let her think she's right and Mum is wrong.

I lean down to kiss Mum's temple. Her hand snaps up and catches mine, squeezing me. 'Don't trust them,' she hisses under her breath.

A chill slides down my back. 'Who, Mum?'

Mum's eyes shoot to the carer, who offers another sugary-sweet smile. 'Come on now, Andrea. You can trust us.'

Tears fill her eyes, and she nods. 'Yes. Of course. Silly me.'

Outside, the wind has picked up. It pushes at me as I cross the car park, and by the time I slide into Bryony's car, my hands are shaking and tears are blurring my vision.

Guilt wrenches through me. I hate this. The pretending. The fear of being found out. The panic I feel thinking of Bryony and what she's planning to do. But I hate lying to Mum more than all of it. If everything goes to plan, Mum won't see Bryony again after this week. Will I tell her Bryony is dead? Will she understand? Is it a kindness or a cruelty to invent excuses, wrapping her in her own confusion? Neither feel right. The horror of what I've agreed to sits with me, heavy and cold. Two more days, I tell myself. And then Bry will return and I can go back to being me.

Except she won't – not really. She'll be home for less than twenty-four hours before she'll take the *Odysseus* out and let the town believe the sea took her. I rest my head on the steering wheel and breathe until my heartbeat stops racing. If I mess this up, if Alex sees through me, he won't believe Bryony is dead. He'll hunt her. He'll find her. And then he'll come for me.

Trouble is a wave I can feel rising fast. No time to swim out of its reach.

At the end of the road, a Land Rover is parked. Windows tinted. Engine running. My pulse jitters, and I think of Alex, think of the night I woke at Mum's house. The person at the door. The headlights on the road. The same car.

'He's in America,' I say aloud, putting the car into gear and forcing myself to drive away.

My gaze flicks to the mirrors every few seconds for the entire drive home, but the road remains empty.

I'm just paranoid and scared, I tell myself. It's only two more days. Reply to Alex's messages. Follow Bryony's routine. Be Bryony. I can do this.

TWENTY

Jess

The air in the house smells faintly of lemon cleaning products as I let myself in. The marble floors shine with a recent clean, but I'm relieved to find Paulina has left and there's no sign of Jimmy in the garden. Everything is too quiet. Too big. Too unfamiliar. I feel as out of place as I did this morning and last night.

I step into the living room. Its colours are muted greys and soft beige. Big fluffy white cushions. A splash of colour from the huge glass vases of purple gladioli either side of a white marble fireplace. It's all so Bryony, I can almost hear her voice in my head.

'Stop worrying, Jess. It's going to be fine.'

She said those words a thousand times in my childhood, coaxing me into games and fun I wasn't sure of. She'd said the same before hurrying away yesterday to set up a new life far away from here and from the abuse she's suffering. Far away from me too.

Her face stares at me from the photos on the wall, adding to the constant feeling scratching beneath my skin that I'm not alone in this house. Goosebumps rage across my skin, and I heave a sigh, feeling suddenly exhausted from the sleepless night and the pretence of being Bryony. I drop onto the plush cushions of the sofa and close my eyes, wishing I could block out my thoughts and the worries that won't stop circling as easily as I can block out this room.

Mum's words echo in my head. *Don't trust them.* Paranoia and anger are common signs of worsening dementia. But the comment sits uneasily in my thoughts alongside the mention of Dad.

Was she even talking about the accident? Or did I assume? *'Your father knew the truth. We both did, but we kept it from Jess.'* It could've been any day. About anything.

I heave another sigh and try counting down in my head from one hundred, like the nurse in the hospital suggested I try when I was thirteen and too cold and too scared to sleep because of the nightmares that dragged me back to that dark sea. Over the years, I've kept counting. Focusing my mind on the numbers instead of the worries and the thoughts I can't escape that block my head until I feel dizzy with them.

I must fall asleep because I wake with a jolt, eyes flying open into an unsettling darkness. My mouth is dry; my throat too. There's a fogginess to my thoughts. I'm cold, my neck stiff. Something moves in my mind – a flash of the sea, the wind, the boom swinging across the deck. The cold pressing in, crushing. Hands pulling me down. My lungs burn.

I jerk upright, gasping. I'm safe. I didn't die. Bryony saved me. It's just memories warped by time and distorted into a nightmare.

How long have I been asleep?

I pad into the kitchen, turning lights on as I go, wishing the light could chase away the unease as easily as it hides the ghostly darkness. Except the lights also turn every window into a vast black mirror. I stare at my reflection. Mascara-smudged eyes, hair a mess. I look more myself than I have done since sitting in the chair at the hair salon. For the first time, I realise there are no curtains or blinds downstairs. If anyone is standing on the driveway or in the garden, they could see everything and I'd have no idea.

I shiver, pulling the sleeves of Bryony's jumper over my hands, and switch the lights back off, preferring darkness over the thought of being watched. The red digits of the clock on the oven read midnight. I've slept for hours.

I gulp down a glass of water and think of making myself some toast. But then a noise filters into my thoughts – the humming I heard this morning and last night. At first, I think it's Bryony's phone ringing. I think of Alex's messages sitting unanswered for the hours I've been asleep and his anger and suspicion. But when I pull out her phone, the screen is blank.

I listen again, remembering the same hum I heard this morning. I thought it was the heating or hot water, but now I'm closer to it, I realise it's coming from below me, not above. Whatever it is, it's not a boiler.

I follow the sound, stepping from the kitchen into the hall that leads to the front door and the staircase. It sounds louder here. A steady vibration, faint but constant, like a machine running. The sound worms its way under my skin. I should ignore it. Make some food and go to bed. But I can't. Suddenly, the humming is all I can hear.

I turn to a door beneath the stairs. I didn't notice it yesterday in my search of the house. I grip the handle, and hinges creak, opening not into a storage cupboard like I assumed but to a staircase leading down. The basement – it has to be. The one Alex locked Bryony in when she tried to leave him.

Prickling fear has me wanting to slam the door shut, to back away, but the humming is louder, and something in me refuses to stop. From the moment I stepped into this house, I've felt a presence lurking out of sight. Like I'm being watched. Like I'm not alone. If there is a grain of truth to these feelings, the answer is down this staircase. It's the one place I haven't searched.

I step forward, drawn downward by a pull I can't explain.

It's cold on the staircase, like a window or door is open to the outside somewhere below. I find a light switch on the wall. At the bottom of the stairs, a bare bulb flickers before flaring to life, illuminating a narrow, steep staircase with no railing, just smooth walls on either side.

At the bottom of the stairs, the light fixing swings slightly on an invisible breeze, causing shadows to jump and twist on a closed door that must lead into the basement. And even though I feel foolish, my heart still hammers in my ears as I make my way carefully downward, sliding my hand along the rough wall to keep my balance.

I fight the urge to call out a 'hello'.

There won't be anyone. Nothing to find. I'm acting like a kid left home alone for the first time.

At the bottom of the staircase, the air smells of something chemical and metallic, like paint and rust. The hum is loud, and whatever is making the noise, it's behind this door.

I reach for the door handle, twist, and there's a click and the door moves a fraction, then stops. I try again, but it's the same. It's stuck. That's when I see the metal latch at the top. One on the door and one on the frame, and a padlock holding them in place.

I press my ear against the wood, unsure what I think I'll hear. Alex is in America and Bryony is safe, setting up her new life.

So what's behind the door? Why is it locked? And what's that noise?

I shift back, my feet suddenly unsteady, desperate to be away from this door and this basement and back in the comfort and warmth of the house.

I stumble, turning to the stairs, moving too fast. I've almost scrambled to the top when I trip. My foot catches on the final step, and I pitch forward, hitting the floorboards hard. Pain explodes behind my eyes – right at the spot where the boom struck me sixteen years ago. Then the world is tilting and I'm back there. The sea swallowing me, Bryony shouting my name. That laughter.

No air!

Can't breathe!

And something else – that fear again. The sense of danger, not from the storm but from something else. For years, I've thought that something was the water. The feeling of being pulled down. Drowning. But I'm starting to think the danger was on the boat with me and Bryony all along.

TWENTY-ONE

Jess

It's Wednesday afternoon and I'm driving back to Cliffview House from another visit with Mum, counting down the hours until Bryony returns tomorrow, when the Land Rover appears out of nowhere. One minute I'm staring at the bay shimmering with sunlight and the promise of summer, still feeling shaky from the fall and the prickling unease of the basement yesterday. The next minute, the rear-view mirror is blocked by black paintwork and a bonnet so close, I can't see the driver.

My hands tighten on the wheel. It's a common car, and yet my thoughts race back to the same vehicle I saw that night at Mum's house, then again when I left the care home yesterday. And yet it can't be Alex because his car is parked at the airport and he's not due home for two more days.

I pull to the side of the road and twist in my seat, desperate to see the driver, but the Land Rover is already speeding past, so fast I tell myself it's an impatient driver. How many Land Rovers are there in Skelwick? Dozens, I'm sure. *Don't overthink it.* Except, like always, I do.

It used to be Mum who calmed me down. '*See, no harm done.*' Then Bryony, reminding me I was being stupid. Then I met Liam, and he counted the reasons on his fingers why it would be OK.

'*And third of all, I love you.*'

I drive away pretending my legs aren't shaking, and a few minutes later, I pull into the driveway of Cliffview House and stare at the glass and chrome, not wanting to enter but knowing I have no choice.

My phone rings on the passenger seat, making me jump. Not Bryony's but mine. The withheld number. Again. Fear grabs me by the throat. I've not called, not answered, not even opened the letter that arrived by signed delivery that Kelly gave me.

'*I don't want to escalate this.*'

Trouble is closing in, and I can't keep avoiding it.

So I pick up my phone and force myself to answer. 'Hello?'

The gravelly voice sighs in my ear. 'Miss Waters,' he says, sounding relieved and impatient all at once. 'At last.'

I swallow hard, fighting the urge to hang up. 'I'm sorry for not calling back sooner. My mum hasn't been well.' It's not quite a lie, but it feels like one.

'I'm very sorry to hear that, but we do need to discuss the loan and your inability to pay. You're aware you've missed your first three repayments?'

I scrunch my eyes shut, wishing I could take it all back, rewind to that desperate moment when I was so hell-bent on saving the hotel, when I'd have said anything, promised anything, done anything, to keep our dreams alive.

The voice speaks in my ear. 'We understand your business has failed and you're having a difficult time, Miss Waters, but this is a personal loan that you've taken with the bank, and you must start making repayments.'

'I know.' I force my eyes open. No bank would give us another business loan. But they would give me a personal loan. One just in my name.

'As I explained last week, avoiding my calls isn't going to help you. If we don't arrange a satisfactory repayment plan, I'll be forced to escalate this. Which means moving your debt to the debt collections department. This can lead to bailiffs coming to your address and even personal bankruptcy.'

The word sends a jolt of fear through me. If I'm declared bankrupt, it will follow me for every new job application. I'll never be able to start again.

'I understand,' I whisper. 'I can make a repayment now over the phone.' I swallow back my disgust for myself as I think of the money I took from Bryony's purse and the sum I withdrew from her account at the bank in Merkshaw on Monday. Money I feel like I stole from my sister. She told me to use her account and the cash if I needed it. But not like this, I'm sure.

We go through the motions of taking a payment and set up a payment plan that I won't be able to keep paying without Bryony's life insurance. My heart is racing, and I feel sick. I let her convince me this was the only way. I told myself I owed her for saving my life. But it's not the only reason. And that truth is hard to swallow. Did I even try to think of another way out for her? Or did I see only how this helped me too?

By the time the call ends, I feel strung out and exhausted.

One more day. For Bryony. For myself.

As soon as I step into the hall of Cliffview House, the feeling returns – the same crawling unease I felt the first night here. But this time it's more than a feeling. There's a noise. A clatter from the kitchen.

I freeze. My breath catches. There's only one person it can be – Alex. Has he come home early like he said he would? If he finds me like this – if he sees me pretending to be Bryony, it's over for both of us. I suddenly wish I knew where she was. How far away is she? An hour? Five hours? Why didn't we talk about this more?

I have to get out of here.

TWENTY-TWO

Jess

I scramble for the door handle, rushing, trying to escape as my head spins with how I'll explain this to Alex – not just that I've walked freely into their home, but that I'm wearing his wife's clothes, her sunglasses, hair just like hers.

Then a voice calls out, 'Jess,' and relief floods me so fast my knees almost give way. Alex is still in America. I'm safe.

'Bryony.' I turn to see my sister in the kitchen doorway. A bottle of her favourite Pinot Noir in one hand, a corkscrew in the other. Her face breaks into a grin, and I can tell she's as relieved as I am in that moment. For a second, I look at her smiling face and I can almost believe it's an ordinary afternoon. Like she hasn't just spent the last few days hidden away in a secret location, setting up the bones of a new life. Like she isn't planning to take the *Odysseus* out on Friday afternoon before Alex returns and vanish. Pretend to the world that she's dead. Gone forever.

But then she steps into the hall and I see the brittleness to her smile and the worry in her eyes. Even so, she looks radiant.

'Oh my God,' I blurt. 'Bry – I thought you weren't coming back until tomorrow.'

We move at the same time and collide in the middle of the hall, arms wrapping tight. I breathe in her expensive perfume. 'You scared me half to death,' I say against her shoulder. 'I thought you were Alex.'

'Sorry. I was ready early,' she says, holding me tighter. 'And I told you, Alex always says he's going to come back early from these trips and he never does. He acts like he's this pure artist who just wants to create, but he secretly loves the attention from the art dealers.'

Bryony gestures towards the kitchen. 'Come on – let's catch up. I want to know everything that's happened.'

I follow her to the table and sit down as she uncorks the wine in seconds and the dark liquid glugs into two glasses. I'm still jittery from the call from the bank and the scare of coming home to someone in the house, and find myself gulping back the first two mouthfuls, searching for a release even as I know it won't be found in this glass.

'Are you... OK?' I ask. 'You're ready?' What I want to ask her is if she's still going through with her plan. If she's sure. I want to ask if there's still time for her to change her mind, choose another route that doesn't end with me no longer having a sister.

'I'm ready,' she says, and I can tell she means it from the brightness of her eyes. 'How's everything been? Has Alex been messaging you constantly?'

'Yes.' I sigh. 'He wanted photos too.'

Bryony's mouth drops open. 'I didn't think about that.'

Something hard knots in my chest. What else hasn't she thought about? On Friday, when she disappears, it's me who'll be left here to fake grief and answer questions from Alex. And I've never had Bryony's way of lying without thought or hesitation like I saw her do throughout my childhood and my early teens, when Mum or Dad would ask about homework or where she's been or if we were wearing our life jackets. A knack I know she still possesses after watching her lie so effortlessly to Alex at his exhibit when he'd caught us talking.

'What did you do?' she asks.

'I sent a photo in the gym of my feet and a dumbbell. After that, I sent shots of outfits or coffee without my face or anything identifiable. I was terrified he'd see something in the photo that would give me away.'

She rolls her eyes. 'He only wants to check I'm doing what I said I was. It's another way of controlling me.' Her voice falters.

I reach across the table and squeeze her hand. 'I know. It was awful this week. He wasn't even here and I felt constantly watched. You've had it far worse.'

'Thank you.' She wraps her fingers around mine, and this time it's her who offers reassurance. 'You handled it. And you'll handle anything else that comes your way. I know you will.'

I nod, wishing I felt a fraction of that confidence.

'Did anything else happen while I was away?' she asks.

I sip my wine, buying myself time. Should I mention the money I withdrew from her account? Does she already know and is prompting me to tell her? I want to. I should. But the humiliation burns me from the inside out and I can't find the words. And what good will it do now? She'll be gone in a few days. I don't want her to worry about me on top of everything else. I tell myself she was leaving that money behind anyway. I tell myself it won't do her any good to know, and wish the guilt didn't feel so spiky.

'Jimmy saw me. He was in the garden and I was in the kitchen,' I say at last, choosing that truth at least. 'He stared at me for a long time. I thought he might have guessed.'

'We'd know by now if he had,' she replies, pouring more wine into our glasses, and then we run through the plan again. What I'll say when Alex calls me to tell me she's missing. How

I'll react. What I'll do afterwards. 'The minute he realises I'm not at home and not answering my phone, he'll call you. I know he will.'

I nod. 'I'll tell him I haven't seen you, but I knew you were planning to go sailing.'

'You have to sound calm at first,' Bryony says, swirling the wine in her glass, the stem pinched between two fingers. 'Play the worried sister.'

'That's something I can do,' I say, and we both smile.

'Don't be hysterical though,' she continues. 'Let him be the one to panic.'

Suddenly, it's real. It's not a plan. Not hypothetical. It's happening. Nausea roils in my stomach. There are too many questions. Too many unknowns. Bryony has lined up the dominoes, but each one must fall before the next for it to work, and I don't know what will happen if they fall out of order and I'm the one left here with a man who has threatened to kill us both.

I think of the version of Alex I've seen since my return to Skelwick. The control he has over Bryony. The hint of threat in everything he says. Pouring away her wine without a word. Squeezing her knee too hard, telling her what to do, where to go.

Bryony is so much stronger than I have ever been. I pick at my worries like a scab I can't leave alone. If Alex presses me for answers, I will fold. I will crumble. I will not survive.

'When do we call the police?' I ask before the panic can dig its claws in too deep for me to escape from.

'Offer to call them, but Alex will want to do it. He'll want to mention that he's a big donor to the coastguard charity. He'll want to use his name.' She takes another sip of wine.

Outside, the darkness is closing in. The windows are becoming mirrors again. With Bryony taking control, it feels less intense. Less like I'm being watched. Less like there's someone or something else in this house with us. And still the hair on the back of my neck prickles.

Bryony keeps talking, running over and over the plans for weeks ahead. She talks about the funeral and the call to the life insurance company and when to do it.

The more she talks, the less pretend the grief feels. Bryony will be gone; any contact we have will be carefully orchestrated and illicit. Mum is slipping away day by day. Liam has stopped calling. I'll be completely alone.

'And you'll send me a message?' I push. 'You will let me know you're OK?'

Her face pales, and for the first time I see a hesitation, like a loose thread on a jumper I desperately want to pull but daren't. 'As soon as I get to shore. But Jess...' She hesitates, wrestling with her own realisation, I think. 'After that, it could be a while before you hear from me again. I have to make sure it's safe for both of us. You understand that, don't you?'

I want to ask what 'a while' means, but I'm not sure I want to know.

The silence wraps around us. There are no more plans to make. The clock in the hall ticks. Somewhere outside, the wind rattles against the garden furniture. Bryony stands, moving through the downstairs to turn on the lamps. For a moment, it feels almost cosy. For a moment, I let myself remember a different kitchen table, a different night. Mum laughing as Dad burned the pizzas on a Saturday night. Bry and I not caring about the crispy crusts as we planned what film we'd watch later.

I cook us pasta, and Bryony tops up our wine, neither of us wanting the evening to end. But soon it's late and there's nothing more to say.

I pack my belongings and change back into my own clothes. I've felt uncomfortable and exposed in Bryony's tight-fitting, expensive outfits. I've missed my loose jeans and jumpers.

Except they now feel unfamiliar too. Tears swim in my eyes when we stand in the hall to say goodbye. I hand her back her phone, grateful to be free of it and the pressure of Alex's WhatsApp messages.

I stare at my big sister. I have so much I want to say, but the words clog in my throat like the balls of rubber bands we'd make as kids.

She reaches for my arm, tugging me into another hug. 'It's always been me saving you,' she says in a soft voice, her eyes glassy too. 'Since—' She stops before mentioning the accident, like it's a note she can't quite hit, but I know anyway. 'This time it's the other way around. I'd be dead without you, Jess.'

'Don't say that.' My voice cracks. I can't tell her that however scared I am of all that's coming, a part of me needs this too – Bryony's death is my survival.

'What if I need to get in touch with you? What if I need to tell you something?' I say suddenly, drawing back to look at her face as we continue to hold each other. 'What if something happens with Mum?'

Bryony pales. I can see she's as scared and stricken as I am. 'I... I'll have the unregistered phone. The one I'll use to message you when I reach the shore on Friday. You'll have the number then. Keep it hidden. And only use it for emergencies.'

I nod and blink hard, relieved we'll have a way to contact each other, but the tears still threaten. 'I hate this,' I whisper. 'I hate all of it.'

'I know.' She leans in; presses her forehead to mine. We stay like that for a long breath.

When I open my eyes again, the kitchen blurs. Suddenly, I'm back in a hospital bed, the room too bright, the smell of bad food in the air, clinging to my gown and my unwashed hair, clumped and tanged with sea salt. My body cold to the marrow no matter how many blankets they give me. Dad sitting beside me with red rims to his eyes, telling me he and Mum are getting divorced, the word floating up to the ceiling like a balloon and bursting there. He's transferred from the office in Exeter to one in Norwich. Found a house in a village surrounded by hills and trees. No lake. No sea. No sailing. He tells me nothing would change when everything already has.

I can still feel the empty space that opened inside me when he and Bryony left. But this goodbye is different. Whatever contact we might scrape together at some unknown future time, it won't be the same. It will be snatched in times when it's safe.

'OK,' she says at last, pulling back. She wipes her eyes and makes an effort to be the brave one again. 'We've got this. By Friday night, it will all be over.'

We hug a final time, and it feels like both of us are stalling.

'Thank you,' she whispers into my hair.

I pull back, swipe a hand under my eyes and blurt out the question that's been worrying the edges of my mind. 'Bry, I forgot to ask, what's in the basement? I heard... there's a hum. And it's locked. Why?'

For a heartbeat, something shifts in her face. I watch the emotions play out. Surprise, then fear, then caution. Before she smooths them away. 'It's just Alex's stuff,' she says with a shrug. 'Art supplies. Power tools. Solvents. The hum you heard is probably the freezer he uses to store his ice for sculpting.'

I remember the same easy lift of her shoulders she gave to Alex at his exhibit when she lied. That too-bright smile at the house the day before. Small tells that she's holding something back. She's lying to me. I'm certain of it. But why? And what's down there?

Her phone buzzes, and she glances at it. 'It's a message from Alex. I should reply.' She squeezes my hand. 'I love you, Jess.'

And suddenly the basement is shoved far back in my thoughts. 'I love you too,' I say, no longer fighting back the tears.

Her words echo as I turn away. '*By Friday night, it will all be over.*'

But she's wrong. It's only the beginning for me.

TWENTY-THREE

Jess

'I wish there was another way,' I say to the walls of Mum's old bedroom on the morning of Bryony's sailing trip and her fake death. My voice sounds small and flat, the air thick with the smell of old clothes and old perfume.

There's an eerie quiet to the house. I keep pausing. Listening. Thinking I'll hear Mum's laughter at the front door as she chats over the fence to Kelly. The clink of tools as my dad fixes something. Mum teasing him.

'Watch out, girls, your dad is pottering again. Better tell him if you don't want another shelf in your bedroom.'

I've tried to keep busy. Sorting, folding, deciding what stays and what goes. Bags line the hallway: some for charity, some for the bin, others to keep for reasons I can't quite name. It feels cruel to throw away something treasured. My hands trail over the lace of the blue dress Mum bought for my art show in London. The tags still hang from the label. Never worn, never returned. I don't know why she kept it for all these years but never wore it, or why I'm finding it hard to place it on the donation pile. Beside it lies the yellow top with the butterflies Mum wore on Sundays for no reason other than she liked it. She liked looking nice. Like Bryony.

I've always been the opposite, throwing on whatever's nearest, hair scraped up, face make-up free. Most days, when I worked front of house at the Kilstern, greeting and helping guests, I'd make the effort to look professional – skirt, blouse, a touch of mascara and foundation and lipstick. Liam would do a comical double take as he'd jog down the huge wooden staircase, always on his way to place another order or check the kitchens were running smoothly or fix something.

'Have you seen my girlfriend?' he'd say with a wink and a grin. *'About your height, button nose, looks like she fell into a bush and got back up again.'*

I'd swat his arm, laughing. *'Hey, I do not.'* Then he'd pull me in and kiss me. If Bryony was visiting, she'd roll her eyes, saying we never stopped kissing. It was true. I loved his lips pressed to mine.

The memory tugs and twists, sharp and tender all at once. But it's not anger I feel this time. Not even betrayal. Just a hollow longing. I pick up my phone. The screen is black.

'Do I call him?' I whisper to the room, as though Mum is with me and can tell me what to do. My heart stutters as I picture that moment in the hotel bar when I walked in to find Liam kissing another woman. Then the moment when he'd sprung away, bewildered, horror-struck as he'd turned to see me, as though even drunk, he couldn't believe it either.

My thumb hovers. 'Fuck it,' I mutter and tap his name. I'm desperate to talk to someone. To hear his voice. It doesn't mean I've forgiven him, but it's been weeks since he tried to call me, and it feels like I miss him more each day.

The phone rings. Once. Twice. Three times. Then his voicemail. I hang up without leaving a message, disappointed not to hear his voice but a little relieved too. I want distraction, that's all. I want something else to think about that isn't Bryony and what she's doing today. My gaze drifts to the window. The sky is a pale, washed-out blue, the trees trembling under the wind. The perfect day for sailing.

My phone buzzes in my hand, a message lighting the screen. Bryony. *Heading out on the Odysseus at 2 p.m. if you change your mind x*

My breath catches. Right on time. The message I'll show Alex later. Proof of her plans.

I type my reply, the words already memorised, just as we rehearsed. *You know I won't. Call me when you're back x*

I hit send and stare at the screen until the two blue ticks tell me it's delivered. Then I sink onto the bed and press the heels of my hands into my eyes, as if I can block out the weight of what comes next.

I stare around at the walls and the furniture. The house feels haunted by memories, by the silence, by everything that's coming. Every tick of the clock sounds like a countdown. I can't sit waiting for Alex to call tonight when he gets back from America and realises Bryony's gone. I shove my feet into my trainers and grab my jacket.

The blustery cool wind hits my face the moment I step outside and start striding towards the town. The streets glisten faintly from last night's rain as I make my way to the care home, choosing a route that will keep me away from the harbour and the sailboats.

As I round a corner, a woman walks towards me on the opposite side of the road. She's in her mid-thirties, with black hair and a warm, open face. She waves at me, glancing both ways before crossing the road to meet me.

'It's Jess, right?' she says. 'Gosh, you look just like your sister. I'm Addie. I was your mum's carer before she went into the care home. We spoke on the phone a few times when Mrs Raffety wasn't available.'

'Addie, hi. Thank you for everything you did for Mum,' I say. 'I was so grateful knowing you were there every day – and Bryony too, of course.'

Something flickers across Addie's face. 'Speaking of Mrs Raffety, is she OK?'

My stomach drops. Nothing's happened yet. No one should suspect anything. 'She's fine,' I say too quickly. 'Why?'

'That's a relief.' Addie shifts her bag on her shoulder. 'It's just... I was driving past her house last month and there was a man on her doorstep, banging on the door. She opened it, and they seemed to be arguing. I only caught a glimpse, but when I looked back at my dashcam footage, it made me wish I'd stopped. But you know what life is like – it went clean out of my head until just now.'

Suddenly, I remember Kelly's cryptic question the day after I arrived in Skelwick. She'd mentioned some trouble. It must be this.

'You didn't recognise the man?' I ask.

She shakes her head. 'No, but I'm pretty sure the footage is saved on my dashcam app. I'll send it to you if you want.'

Before I can tell her it isn't necessary, she waves, already moving off down the pavement. 'Anyway, lovely to meet you in person, Jess. Give my love to your mum.'

I stand there a moment, cold in the shadows from the buildings. Bryony never mentioned an argument. It's nothing, I tell myself. It was probably Jimmy, their gardener, and maybe Addie saw it from the wrong angle and misunderstood. But the image Addie painted – a man, angry, banging on the door – feels likes something else to worry over.

It's still rolling around my mind as I sign my name in the visitors' book and make my way to the third floor. I check the time. Early afternoon already. Bryony will be heading to the harbour around now.

The sweetened air inside the care home hits me. It's so strong, I can taste the bitterness of it in the back of my throat. Mum's door is open and she's dozing in her armchair, a blanket tucked over her knees. Calm sweeps through me at the sight of her, looking so frail and old, but still Mum. When she's asleep, it's easy to convince myself she'll wake up and see me and know me and all will be well.

I move silently across the room and sink into the chair opposite, burying my head in my hands and letting my hair fall over my face. I still haven't gotten used to the length and the colour, but I've stopped styling it and its natural kink is back. No longer sleek and smooth, but not feeling quite like my own hair either.

'Bryony?'

I start at the sound of Mum's voice. I drop my hands and sit up, biting back the selfish desire to correct her. She's always more confused when she first wakes. I want to be me, and I want my mum. But it isn't fair after pretending all week to be Bryony to confuse her now and tell her the truth. Still, the disappointment stings.

'You're kind to visit.' She reaches and pats my hand. Her fingers are warm, her skin dry and paper-thin.

'Of course I visit,' I say softly.

Her eyes glisten, tears filling the corners. 'I know I'm forgetting things, but I haven't forgotten what I did to you, and I'm sorry.'

A fresh wave of grief and hurt wells up. Poor Mum. She's getting worse. Slipping further away from reality. 'You did nothing wrong,' I soothe.

'It was my decision to send you away,' she sighs, her gaze moving to the window, her voice barely above a whisper as though she's no longer talking to me or to Bryony, but to herself. 'Your dad didn't agree. He said if I wanted you to leave, he'd go with you. He said if I felt that strongly about it, it would be the end of our marriage. I didn't want the divorce or to destroy the family, but I didn't know what else to try. I honestly thought it was for the best,' she says.

No. That's not right. Bryony always said she chose to go with Dad. He left because their marriage fell apart. Mum must be confused.

'It's OK, Mum,' I reply. 'I wanted to go.' It hurts to pretend to be Bryony, today of all days, knowing that right at this moment, my sister is preparing to sail out of the harbour and never come back.

'I didn't know what else to do,' she says again, her fingers worrying at the blanket. 'I was so scared.'

'Why were you scared?' The question slips out before I can stop it.

She blinks rapidly, the threads of her thoughts unravelling at my push. 'You were so jealous.' Her tone sharpens. 'You always wanted what Jess had. Clothes and toys and her friends. The boys she liked. Even Alex.'

I shake my head. Bryony's never been jealous of me. It was always me looking up to her.

Mum tsks lightly. 'You were never the same after your sister was born. Everything became a competition. Any compliment for Jess was an insult to you.'

She reaches out, squeezing my hand. 'And then I almost lost you both,' she says with a shuddering breath.

She means the accident. She's never spoken about it. Not once in the years since I left the hospital. Like her divorce from Dad, it seemed she'd put it out of her mind. I have to ask her about it. It could be my one chance to get the truth no one will tell me. The parts I can almost remember, like they're on the tip of my tongue.

'That day we took the *Calypso* out,' I say. My tone is casual, but every muscle in my body is poised and alert. 'Who was with us, Mum?'

She looks up, startled. 'You and Jess.'

'But someone else...' Pain spikes through my temple before I can finish. The air shifts. The past rushes in – salt and wind and the feel of my feet on the deck. The sound of Bryony's scream. The memory takes me, dragging me down into the cold again.

I remember. I remember everything.

TWENTY-FOUR

THE DAY OF THE ACCIDENT

Jess, age 13

The worry feels like snakes in my belly, sliding over each other, desperate to reach the surface. The sky is too dark, the wind too fierce, the sea too violent. I can barely keep my balance on the deck as the *Calypso* bucks beneath us, the waves slapping at her hull.

'We should go home!' I shout, but the wind tears the words from my mouth, carrying them away before Bryony can hear. 'Bryony!' I yell again. 'We should go back!'

I look at my sister. Eyes bright. Smile wide and a little wild. She's laughing, and I have that uncomfortable feeling I get when it feels like I'm missing something. Like I'm not part of the joke.

'You wouldn't understand. You're too young.' I've heard Bryony say it so many times all she has to do is look at me a certain way and I hear it in my thoughts.

But I understand plenty. Like how we shouldn't be out on the sea right now. I understand the wind is too strong and the sky too heavy. I grip the side rail, my knuckles white. Another gust slams into us, bringing with it the sting of salt water.

'Bryony, please–'

There's a sound from the cabin. Something falling or moving. My gaze darts to the little window that looks inside. I start to move. I have to make Bryony understand this isn't fun anymore.

'Stay there,' she shouts, and the urgency in her voice freezes my feet. She's the better sailor.

She's the captain, and however much I want to go home, I do as I'm told.

'It's fine! Stop worrying!' she shouts. 'I have a surprise for you.'

My eyes drag to the horizon and the darkening sky, and I feel the boat shift under my feet. Out the corner of my eye, there's a flicker of movement on the deck. I start to turn, heart lurching, but Bryony's voice slices through the air.

'Jess!'

My breath catches. For a split second, I *swear* someone is standing beside her. My mind rushes to fill the space: the sound of movement in the cabin, Bryony's delighted laughter. Her mention of a surprise.

But as I turn fully towards her, the light shifts.

And there is no one. The shadow dissolves. The movement was nothing but the sail jerking. Only my sister, standing alone in the centre of the deck.

There's something dark in her features, but before I can process it, the boom swings across the deck in a blur of white metal. There's no time to duck, no chance to move. It slams into the side of my head with a sickening crack. Pain bursts behind my eyes, and the world spins.

My feet lift from the deck. For an awful second, I'm suspended, the air gone from my lungs. I'm flying, weightless, then falling. The roar of the wind fills my ears; the screech of gulls cuts through the chaos.

I'm going to die today.

The thought floods through me, cold and certain. Panic grips every part of me.

No!

I claw at the air, trying to catch hold of something – anything – as the waves reach for me, greedy hands pulling me down.

Grey sky. Screaming gulls. The white of our father's sailboat flashing above.

Then a scream.

Bryony.

It all happened so fast, but now I see the exact moment before the boom hit. The way the corner of Bryony's lips curled into a vicious smile. The way she shoved the tiller hard away from her body. A fast, deliberate movement, causing the boom to swing violently at me. Her mouth forming a word. 'Surprise.'

It was all Bryony's fault.

TWENTY-FIVE

NOW

Jess

My temple throbs, pulsing in time with my racing heart; a bone-deep tremor rattles my body. It feels like being thirteen again, lying in that hospital bed after the accident, when my body refused to warm up. They said it was hypothermia, that my organs had started to shut down, my temperature too low.

A hollow terror seeps into my chest as the truth starts to take shape. I remember standing on the boat. I remember Bryony moving the tiller. I remember everything that came before that too. It was no accident. Nothing like the explanation Bryony gave me when I was barely conscious. *'The wind caught the sail, wrenching the tiller from my hand,'* she said. *'And you'd moved, Jess. I told you not to, but you didn't listen.'* But that's not true. I was standing exactly where Bryony told me to stand. Exactly in the way of the boom should it shift suddenly.

As the fragments of that day have surfaced these past few weeks, I started to think there was someone else on the boat with us. Someone I'd forgotten. Someone dangerous. Someone who wanted to hurt us. But now I understand. There *was* someone else on the boat that day – just not a stranger. It was the other version of my sister. The one I never let myself look at too closely. The one I'd only caught in flashes over the years – sharp, cruel, vindictive. The version who smiled when other people stumbled, who held grudges like precious things, who knew exactly how to twist a moment to her advantage.

That was the person by the tiller. That was the darkness I kept sensing. It wasn't a shadow of someone else. It was her.

She was the one who wanted to hurt me that day. I was in that sea because Bryony put me there. It was no accident. My own sister – the one who was meant to protect me, look after me, love me – had let it happen. Had *made* it happen. We loved each other. We still do. How could she have done that to me?

Mum's voice breaks through my thoughts, sounding frail and far away. 'I always loved you, Bryony. But I couldn't have you in the house after what you did. You understand, don't you? I had to send you away with your father. For Jess's sake.'

'How... how did you know it wasn't an accident?' I ask as a voice whispers in my head. *She didn't mean to hurt you.* It was a joke. A mistake. She probably just meant to scare me. I want to believe that so badly.

'You were always so jealous,' Mum replies. 'And Jess had won the art competition. Your father and I were worried you'd try to sabotage it like you did sometimes with her art pieces. Always spilling something over her work or her... and you took her out without telling us.' Tears swim in Mum's eyes.

My heart pounds hard enough to burst. My head throbs; my mind is spinning. It all makes sense now. Why they left so suddenly. Bryony didn't go with Dad by choice. He took her away from me for my safety.

Mum's gaze locks on me, eyes still narrowed. 'But you did save her, didn't you?'

I nod, voice shaky. 'I jumped in the water after her. She's fine now, isn't she? We're both OK.'

The truth is like oil and water in my thoughts. Bryony is the reason I was in the sea. Bryony wanted to hurt me. But she is also the reason I'm alive. She risked her life to save me.

I have to talk to her. I need her to tell me why she did it.

I say goodbye to Mum and hurry out of the care home, blinking in the sudden brightness. The sunlight feels too sharp, slicing across the pavement, glinting on car roofs. My hands shake as I check the time on my phone. Nearly 2 p.m. Bryony will be setting sail any second.

It's not in the plan for me to be near the harbour, but I don't care. I have to talk to her. I have to stop her before she disappears for good. Before it's too late.

I start to run. The road curves past the row of cafés, and my lungs burn with exertion and urgency. Already I'm trying to make sense of it. Explain it away. My memory has to be wrong. Bryony wouldn't hurt me. Not like that. And yet I can't unsee that curve to her smile as she'd moved the tiller.

'Surprise.'

The road dips towards the town, the view opening out to the bay. The closer I get, the more the panic builds. My heart feels too big as it beats against my ribs.

I pass the surf shop and the sailing school, where the kids all gather in the summer, learning to sail in the bay on little red dinghies. I jump off the pavement, not slowing as an older man and a young boy round the corner, surfboards tucked under their arms, wetsuits still on, hair damp. A car horn beeps, but I don't slow down, don't wave an apology.

I have to stop Bryony, so I only run harder, ignoring the stitch biting at my side. It's no longer just about the accident and wanting to look into Bryony's eyes as I ask her what really happened that day. It's about stopping this madness. She can't fake her own death. She can't disappear.

I've been swept along in her pain, her fear, her desperation. Doing as I'm told, like always. Following orders. Allowing my own debts and fear to cloud my judgement. But there has to be another way.

When I reach the harbour wall, I'm gasping in air that smells of diesel and salt. The water glitters in the sunlight, beautiful and enticing, hiding the current and danger beneath those gently lapping waves that reach up to kiss the sea wall.

My gaze snaps to the *Odysseus*, already by the harbour walls, the mouth that leads to the open sea. I watch as the sail unfurls like the wing of a giant sea bird. Bryony is standing at the helm, hair catching the light. I shout her name, waving my arms in the air, not caring who sees, but I'm too far away. She doesn't hear. Doesn't turn back.

As the *Odysseus* moves through the walls, I see her crouch down towards the cabin like she's talking to someone out of sight. Then she straightens again, head high, facing towards the horizon. There's no fear in her posture. No furtive glance back. I squint into the glare, but the sail shifts, blocking my view, and then the boat is sliding further away.

Bryony's plan is simple: take the *Odysseus* out, use a spare dinghy to return to shore unseen, let the current carry the empty boat until the coastguard finds it. No other person. No accomplice.

And yet a chill seeps through me. That sense that, yet again, I'm missing something. If I just turn fast enough, look hard enough, I'll see the truth.

It feels like I've been blindfolded in a game, spun around and pushed into the unknown, walking myself into danger without even knowing.

TWENTY-SIX

Jess

I watch the *Odysseus* sail towards the horizon and fight the desire to scream at the top of my voice for Bryony to come back. I don't care that it's not in the plan – I call her phone again and again, but she doesn't answer. I look around, desperately searching for a way to stop her. My gaze lands on the small red hire boats sitting in their berths, waiting for the first tourists of the season to take them into the bay.

Those little engines won't go far or fast, but maybe it's enough to reach her. Enough to make her turn back. I rush down the stone steps, pulse juddering, breath ragged. But when I reach the final step, my body locks. I can't move. My feet root to the stone, unable to cross onto the wooden walkway over the water.

The burn of frustration is enough to make me cry out. I have to talk to Bryony. But I can't move. My eyes drag down to the dark-green water lapping against the wooden pillars, and it hits me all at once. The icy cold. The saltwater burning my throat. The drag of the sea, the weight of it pressing me down, the desperate fight to breathe.

My stomach twists – frustration and fear – and I turn away, scurrying back up the steps until I can breathe again. I don't know what to do, so I do the only thing I can – I go home.

Bryony will send me a message tonight from a new phone, telling me she's made it to shore. I'll call her then. I'll tell her our plan is crazy. I'll convince her to come back before it's too late. I can ask her what happened on the *Calypso* too. Why did she knock the boom into me? Why did she want to hurt me?

The minute I'm home, I don't know what to do with myself. The walls of the house seem to be holding their breath. The clock ticks too slowly. I sit on the edge of my childhood bed, the memory of the day on the *Calypso* playing over and over. But other memories replay too. Ones I hadn't forgotten but see now in a different light. Like the day Bryony stopped sharing this room with me, hearing her voice, a shrill shriek.

'You always take her side.'

Mum's sigh. *'That's not true, Bryony, but this is your mess, not your sister's, and I've already asked you twice to tidy it. You're not going to the cinema with your friends this afternoon unless it's done.'*

'Jess did it,' Bryony had hissed, flinging a hand in my direction, where I was sitting on the bed, pretending to read. My cheeks had flamed. How could she lie like that? She was the one who threw her clothes on the floor, complaining about having nothing to wear to the school's non-uniform day on Friday.

'Jess?' Mum had looked at me. Bryony had looked at me. The need to be honest warred with the desperate need to please my sister.

Tears had spilled onto my cheeks. My face had grown redder. I'd pinned my lips shut, dropped my gaze.

'That's it,' Mum had said. *'No cinema or pocket money this*

week, Bryony. Not only is this your mess, but you're trying to blame your sister. Tidy it up now.'

She'd turned away, footsteps heavy on the stairs. The murmur of Dad's voice had drifted up. Then Mum's. Both low and angry. I'd stared at the words of the Enid Blyton book I was reading, wishing it was me who was shipwrecked on an island with my friends.

'Thanks a lot,' Bryony had hissed under her breath, snatching at her clothes.

'I'm sorry,' I'd said, even if I wasn't sure what I was sorry for.

'I can't even look at you. In fact' – she'd scooped another pile of clothes into her arms, the venom in her voice like a bite – *'I'm not sharing with you anymore.'*

I'd sat up, tears spilling down my face. *'What do you mean?'*

She'd stormed out of the room without replying and gone to find Dad. By the time I was back from the cinema, they'd cleared the junk from the spare room and made it Bryony's space. There was barely room to stand with a single bed in there, but she was so happy with it, lips curling at the edges as she looked at me across the table at dinner that night, telling me since she was grounded she shouldn't watch a film with me, even though it was what we always did on Saturday nights.

I'd always told myself she wanted her own space. But now I see it for the punishment it was. She knew I hated sleeping alone. Knew I got scared. She squashed herself into that spare room anyway. She clung to her grudge for weeks afterwards, only talking to me if Mum made her.

Another thought slips in, uninvited: *And you gave up Alex for her.*

Is that true? Alex hadn't been mine to give up, and yet I'd been a sheltered and lonely eighteen-year-old. He'd been twenty-one and seemed so mature and clever, and he'd known himself in a way that had blown my mind. Of course, I'd ignored the heated silences and the electric shock every time his hand grazed mine. I wouldn't let myself believe that someone like Alex could ever be interested in me.

But I'd longed for it. I'd yearned for him to look at me the way I looked at him. To make the first move because I was too scared. Then Bryony had come home. Effortless, magnetic Bryony, and I'd watched his attention flick between us. Our faces so alike but everything else about us so different.

'Do you like Alex?' she'd asked me one night, a week after she came home, when we were both sitting on my bed, painting our toenails.

'I…' I'd known what she was asking. I'd wanted to say yes, that actually I thought I was a little bit in love with him, but instead I'd said, *'He's nice.'*

'But do you like him *like him, because I do. I really like him, Jess, and if you're just friends, then it's OK for me to go out with him, isn't it? You wouldn't mind?'*

I'd felt the weight of her stare on me, and when I'd looked up, I'd seen pleading eyes, eyebrows raised in question – and something else. Like she was reminding me without words that I owed her, that she'd saved my life.

How could I refuse her? So I'd squashed down my feelings and stepped aside and watched her flirt and giggle, and of course Alex had fallen in love with her. If Bryony set her mind to something, she always got her way. That's when I found a job at a hotel in London – moved away so I wouldn't have to see it every day.

Only now do I think she must have known how I really felt about Alex. My face went red every time we were together or I talked about him. She hardly gave me a chance to explain my feelings before she asked me to step aside. But does it matter now? I met Liam, and it felt like something solid. Something real. With Alex, I'd idolised him. Told myself I wasn't good enough, old enough, talented enough to be more than his friend. Liam was different. It felt like we were in sync from day one.

Our feelings for each other and our dreams. That was real love. A partnership.

I wander the house as the hours slip away; I try to sort through drawers and cupboards in the kitchen, but now thinking of strangers in Mum's home seems intrusive and all wrong.

I check my phone every few minutes, waiting for a message from Bryony that doesn't come. Why hasn't she contacted me yet?

Then my phone rings in my hand, and I yelp, jumping back, wincing as my elbow slams against the wall.

I stare at the screen.

Alex.

It's happening.

TWENTY-SEVEN

Jess

'Jess.' Alex's voice is a sharp blade cutting through the silent house. He sounds angry and far too close. 'Is Bryony with you?'

I tighten my grip on the phone, my mouth turning dry. 'With me? No.' I try to pitch my voice light, breezy, pushing a laugh I don't feel, trying to think of Alex as he wants to be seen – an old friend and a worried husband, and the artist loved by all. Not as the monster I now know he is.

'I haven't seen her today,' I continue.

It's a lie. My first already. I wasn't supposed to see Bryony today. I wasn't supposed to call her, but I did both. I rushed to the harbour and saw her steering the *Odysseus* out to sea. Someone could've seen me. I want to take it back, but already it feels too late.

'How was America?' I continue because it feels like that's what I should ask. 'Did the exhibit go well?'

There's silence before he replies, tone still clipped. 'It was fine. But I'm worried about Bryony. She was supposed to be here when I got home.'

I remember all those messages he sent. The demands. *Where are you? What are you doing? Message me when you're home. Send me a photo.* The control he exerted from thousands of miles away.

'She messaged to say she was taking the *Odysseus* out this afternoon.' The words sound too rehearsed.

'What time?' he asks.

My stomach feels tight. I imagine him in his house, striding from room to room, fists clenched. 'I think she said two p.m.'

'Damn it.' Something slams on his end; a door, a fist against wood – either way, it makes me jump. I swear the tension is vibrating out of my phone, wrapping itself around me in a stranglehold.

There's a long pause. My mind blanks. I know I'm supposed to say something else. Then I remember. 'Have you tried calling her?'

'Of course I have. She isn't answering.' There's the sound of movement. 'I'll call you back in a minute. I'm going to walk down to the end of the road where I can see the harbour. I'll check if I can see the *Odysseus*.'

The call ends, and I lower the phone, hands trembling. The rock-solid plan Bryony constructed feels flimsy now. Not enough. Already I feel in too deep.

My gaze drags to the kitchen window and the night closing in. If Bryony left the *Odysseus* an hour after sailing out of the bay – even two hours – she'd be ashore by now. Why hasn't she messaged me to tell me she's safe?

My phone vibrates again. Alex.

'Jess?' His voice bursts through the phone, ragged, breathless. There's wind in the background, or maybe it's just his panicked breath against the speaker. 'The *Odysseus* isn't back and it's getting dark.'

'Try not to worry,' I say, using the words Bryony gave me.

They come out wrong. Trembling and unsteady. 'Bryony's an experienced sailor. She'll be fine.'

But she should've messaged by now. I should be able to say those words and mean them, even just to myself. But I don't know if she's fine. I don't know anything.

'No.' His voice cracks. 'No, Jess, something's wrong. I can feel it. What should I do?'

For a heartbeat, my mind screams the truth: *Call the police. Call them now. Search the waters. Find her. Find the boat.* But my tongue sticks to the roof of my mouth.

There's another loud thwack-like noise in my ear. Alex is upset, but he's angry too. And all at once the need to protect my sister rushes through me. Even if Bryony moved the tiller on purpose that day on the *Calypso*, she might not have meant to hurt me. Maybe it was a joke. And no matter what else, she jumped in after me. She saved my life.

And it doesn't change what Alex has become. The nightmare Bryony has lived through all these months at Alex's hands. Those bruises were real. No matter what, she deserves a chance to live free of Alex. And that means sticking to the plan, buying her time to reach land unseen and disappear.

'Maybe give it another hour. If she still isn't back, then call the police and they'll contact the coastguard.'

There's a moment of tight silence and then—

'No, I'm calling them now,' he says. There's a strangled sound, like he's bitten back a sob. 'Will you come to the house?'

I freeze, breath catching in my lungs. The pause draws out, and it's Alex that fills it. 'Please,' he says. 'I need to talk to you about what happened while I was away.'

'What do you mean?' I ask, thinking of the obscure photos I sent. The gym. A coffee cup. The garden. A wine glass. Then there's Kelly's double take when she saw me driving. All she'd have to do is tell one person who'd tell another person.

'I saw Jess in Bryony's car. She's had her hair done like her sister now too. Like she's trying to be her.'

Did we really think we'd fool anyone? The question is chased away by another. What if Alex already knows everything and he's asking me to the house to confront me? To hurt me, like he'd planned to when he'd threatened Bryony. Goosebumps erupt over my skin.

'I mean, was Bry OK while I was away?'

'She was fine,' I lie.

'Jessie, please come. I need you.' His tone is pleading, but there's something else there too – a warning.

And what can I say other than *yes*? If Bryony was really missing, if I didn't know what Alex was capable of, of course I'd go. If I refuse, he'll know I'm hiding something and protecting Bryony.

'OK,' I hear myself say. 'I'll leave now.'

He ends the call without a goodbye, and I stare at my blank screen, willing Bryony to message me.

I never pictured what happens after: me here, alone, with Alex's temper and fury. I'd been so focused on Bryony's escape, on rehearsing the words I needed to say, that I hadn't let myself think about the aftermath.

I grab my coat and hurry through the darkening streets, unable to escape the feeling that I'm walking straight into danger – straight into the hands of the man who said he'd kill me if Bryony tried to leave him...

TWENTY-EIGHT

Jess

The walk up to the cliffside house feels like it takes forever and no time at all. I keep my coat wrapped tightly around myself against the biting wind and the cold knowledge of what I'm walking into. By the time I'm nearing the house, the last of the daylight is slipping below the horizon. It's too dark to still be out sailing.

I worry over all the reasons Bryony hasn't messaged me. Did she think it wouldn't be safe to reach out? Did the unregistered phone she bought get wet in the little dinghy as she made her way to shore? Or has something happened to her out at sea like it did to me? Is she really in danger and fighting for her life?

The questions leave me queasy as I approach the imposing windows of Cliffview House. I half expect the front door to swing open the second my feet touch the drive, for Alex to appear and drag me inside, shove me down the steps to the basement and lock me away with whatever else is down there.

My pulse hammers so hard I swear I can taste the bitter fear in my mouth. Would anyone even know if I disappeared?

Mum's dementia is getting worse week on week. Maybe she'd notice I wasn't there, but who would believe a woman in a care home who can't trust her own memory?

There's Liam. At one time, he was everything. I wish he was still calling, but clearly he's moved on faster than I have. The realisation is a prod to a fresh wound I can't look at yet.

Maybe Bryony would realise eventually. She's promised she'll find a way for us to see each other when it's safe, but how long will that be?

The truth is, Alex could lock me up forever or kill me like he told Bryony he would, and no one would know – not quickly enough anyway. My mind churns over the locked basement. The strange humming. Why does it bother me so much?

I feel the vibration of my phone in my pocket and pull it free, hoping it's Bryony or Liam. Instead, it's Addie, Mum's old carer. I scan the message preview, remembering the fight she saw between Bryony and a man on her doorstep: *I've just remembered I said I'd send you the dashcam footage of Bryony. Here it is.*

The front door flies open before I have a chance to tap play. Alex stands in the doorway, raking a hand through his hair. His eyes are red-rimmed, his shirt untucked. He looks wrecked. For a heartbeat, I almost forget he's not the victim but the monster.

'Jessie,' he says, rushing across the drive and wrapping me in a hug I'm not ready for. It's only as he draws back without a word that I remember my hair is shorter and cut the same as Bryony's. I was worried how I'd explain it to him, but he hasn't noticed.

He gestures for me to come inside, stepping back to let me pass. Inside, the house is too warm, the air stuffy with heat. The canvases of Bryony seem to loom over me. Watching. Reminding me of our plan, which I'm suddenly terrified might already be falling apart.

'I've called the police,' Alex says as we walk into the

kitchen. He moves automatically, putting the kettle on, opening cupboards with frantic, jerky precision. 'They've contacted the coastguard.' His voice cracks again.

'That's good,' I manage. 'They'll... they'll find her, Alex.' I swallow hard. 'Maybe something went wrong with the boat,' I add, but this time my voice trembles, and not because I'm acting, but because the fear is real now. 'Maybe she couldn't radio in. Maybe she had to anchor and wait.'

I'm babbling, desperate to sound like a sister clinging to hope, but the truth is I *am* clinging. Because I don't know where Bryony is. I don't know if she made it ashore. And the horrible possibility that something genuinely happened feels like cold fingers trailing up my spine.

I take a shaky breath, forcing myself to meet Alex's frantic gaze.

'We'll find her,' I whisper, wrapping my hands around the steaming mug he gives me.

'She never listens,' he says almost to himself, slumping onto one of the stools at the long marble breakfast bar. The tone is the same I heard on the phone. Short and bitter, but with his appearance and the wide, wild look in his eyes, it feels less like anger and more like fear.

'What do you mean?' I ask, leaning against the counter, still wanting to keep my distance in case he lashes out.

Alex exhales hard. 'I told her the sea was still too rough. I thought she should've waited another month before sailing alone. But she wouldn't listen. It's always been like that with her. The same with her drinking.' He glances up, his eyes finding mine. 'You must have seen the way she goes through that damn Pinot Noir. She promised me she'd cut down. It's not good to drink as much as she does.'

A knock at the door startles us both. Alex pushes his mug to the worksurface and crosses the hall in long, urgent strides, calling over his shoulder, 'That'll be the police.'

I follow him to the door, and it opens to a man and a woman in black uniform, padded vests and hats tucked under their arms. The man is broad-shouldered and looks to be in his forties, his cheeks ruddy from a life spent by the sea. The woman looks barely out of school, her uniform still new-looking, her notebook clutched tight to her chest.

'Mr Raffety? I'm Sergeant Miller; this is PC Hughes. May we come in?'

Alex steps back quickly, urging them to come in. 'Has the coastguard found the *Odysseus*?' His gaze darts between them.

'Not yet, sir,' Miller replies. 'They've launched a search, but with the light fading, it's possible they'll need to call it off soon and resume at first light.'

Alex introduces me, and I nod a wordless greeting, not trusting myself to speak. I'm all too aware that one wrong word could see Bryony's plan falling apart.

Alex leads the officers into the kitchen, and we settle around the table. Them on one side, Alex and I on the other.

PC Hughes flips open her notebook. 'The first thing we're trying to do is narrow down the search area. Do either of you know the route Mrs Raffety was planning to take today?'

Alex shakes his head then looks at me. Do I imagine the accusation in his gaze?

'No,' I say. 'Sorry.'

Hughes nods. 'What about sharing locations through an app? If her phone's active and we can see where it is, we can pass that information to the coastguard.'

Alex shakes his head immediately. 'No. We don't do any of that stuff.' He gives a short, humourless laugh. 'The last thing we need in this world is more tracking.'

I blink, startled. He reaches into his pocket and pulls out a phone so small and cheap-looking it could be a child's toy. 'We don't have any cameras here – or CCTV. I don't even have a smartphone,' he adds.

My heart lurches. He's lying. He has to be. There's no escaping the AirTag hidden in Bryony's car. No denying the constant WhatsApp messages he sent to her phone while I was living in this house, pretending to be my sister.

Miller's radio crackles to life, static filling the room. He presses the radio to his ear. 'Go ahead.'

I hold my breath. Then a voice cuts through the static, faint but clear: 'The *Odysseus* has been located, drifting approximately five miles off the coast. No one on board.'

The words fall heavy in the silence. Alex gasps, the sound breaking in his throat. 'Bryony must have gone overboard.'

The sentence hits like a physical blow. They're almost the exact words I was supposed to say. The line Bryony made me rehearse three times.

'No. Please, no.' Alex slumps into a chair, face in his hands.

Miller lowers his radio. 'The coastguard is beginning a sea search now with lifeboats and drones.'

'But it's getting dark,' I say, glancing to the windows and the sky beyond. It's almost black now, the glass reflecting the lights in the kitchen and my own fearful-looking face.

'They'll continue until the point they decide it's too dangerous,' Miller explains. 'Then they'll pick up again at first light.'

Alex drops his hands, still staring at the floor, lost to his thoughts and his... grief, I think. 'I should never have gone to America.'

'When did you get back?' Miller asks, his tone casual, but the question is clear. Where was Alex when Bryony disappeared? I wonder if they sense something is wrong. That this is more than an accident.

'Only a few hours ago. I called Jess when Bryony didn't answer her phone.'

Miller's next question is asked in a gentle tone. 'Did she leave a note? Or seem upset about anything?'

Alex straightens, his voice raw. 'She wouldn't kill herself, if that's what you're asking. She's happy. We both are.'

The officers exchange a look. Their gaze shifts to me. I nod quickly. 'She would never take her own life.' It's the truth at least. Maybe the last piece of honesty I can give – even in the darkest moments she shared with me over the last weeks, she never mentioned once that she had considered ending things.

The officers ask more questions, building a picture of Bryony's life. The more I say, the tighter my chest feels. At some point, they'll learn I called her just as she was sailing out the harbour. Not once, but four, maybe five times. How will I explain that? I'm sure my face must be burning with the lies I'm telling.

I wish I could tell these officers the truth. That Alex has an iPhone. He tracks Bryony's every move. He's the reason she's disappeared. I want to tell them the plan Bryony made and how I went along with it because Alex threatened to kill us both.

The knowledge tightens around me; a chokehold I can barely breathe through. I'm lying to Alex, but I'm lying to the police too. It's not just that it's a criminal offence. That I could be arrested and charged for what I'm saying and what I'm holding back. It's that I'm helping Alex walk away from his abuse. By keeping quiet, it isn't just Bryony who's escaped and is free. It's Alex too. There's no justice here.

Realisation dawns slow, sweeping through me like an icy wave. It's too late to rewind these last ten minutes and tell these officers everything. The plan is already in motion. The lies already spiralling, multiplying, swallowing me whole. Somewhere out there, in the dark water, the coastguard is searching for a body that won't ever be found.

Bryony has escaped. She's free.

But I'm trapped in the lies we've told.

TWENTY-NINE

Jess

Afternoon sunlight slants through the kitchen window, too bright in my state of exhaustion. It lies over me like a blanket, leaving my skin clammy. I can't stop staring at the big station clock as the hands inch around to 2 p.m. It's been twenty-four hours since Bryony sailed out of the harbour. I still don't feel like I'm standing on solid ground.

The coastguard searched long into the night before breaking and returning again at dawn.

All night, Alex and I have moved around each other like ghosts, making cups of tea neither of us drank, pacing the same paths across the kitchen tiles. He paused at the windows as though he was searching for her in the pitch-black. He was waiting for dawn and the search to resume. I was waiting for Bryony's message. My phone has barely left my hand all night. She promised she'd tell me when she was safe. But I've heard nothing.

Alex sighs and looks at me from where he's standing by the

sink, a mug of coffee clutched in his hand. His T-shirt is creased, and his eyes are even more bloodshot than yesterday. He looks wrecked. I try to offer a smile, though my throat feels tight. Every time he draws near, my pulse jolts in my throat and fear freezes my limbs. Thank goodness he's too distracted to notice. I can't stop thinking about what he'll do to me if he learns what Bryony has done.

'She's strong,' he says, for what feels like the tenth time today. 'Bryony's always been a fighter. She'll be OK.'

'They'll find her,' I reply, hating the lie, even if it is to Alex. 'The police will be here soon, won't they? They said they'd come with an update.'

A dark shadow of tension seems to linger around us. Around the entire house. The constant humming from the basement is a reminder of the padlocked door and what Alex is capable of. It doesn't matter how many times I tell myself it's just Alex's ice freezer, I can't stop myself fixating on the sound.

Alex rakes a hand through his already tangled hair, leaving dark strands sticking out at the sides. He looks more and more like the younger, windswept version I first met.

His face pales before me. 'What if—'

Before he can finish his question, there's a knock at the front door.

Alex moves so fast it's like he expects Bryony to be standing on the doorstep. He throws open the door, seeming to deflate at the sight of Sergeant Miller and PC Hughes, both looking sombre, like they'd rather be anywhere else than here with us. The feeling is mutual, but I manage a smile.

'Mr Raffety. Miss Waters,' Miller says by way of greeting. 'May we come in?'

'Have you found her?' Alex asks, already stepping back to let them into the hallway.

Miller doesn't answer straight away. He waits until we're

seated at the kitchen table, his notebook resting unopened in front of him.

'The *Odysseus* has been recovered and towed back to the harbour,' he says. 'The coastguard deployed a helicopter, two lifeboats and a drone. They searched through the night and again from first light this morning.'

'And?' Alex cuts in.

'The search was conducted based on tidal movements and projected drift patterns from the point of where the *Odysseus* was recovered,' Miller continues. 'And unfortunately, there was no sign of Mrs Raffety. I'm very sorry.'

'So she's missing.' Alex's voice is desperate. 'You're saying she's a missing person. You're not here to tell me she's gone. You can't—' He swallows then continues. 'This only happened yesterday. She could still be out there.'

'I understand your feelings,' Miller says quickly. 'But witnesses saw Mrs Raffety leaving the harbour. With the abandoned sailboat and no evidence of anyone else involved, no signs of a struggle and no indication that the vessel was interfered with, we are ruling your wife's case as an accidental drowning. Again, I'm very sorry for your loss.'

Silence presses in around us.

'Given the time that's passed,' Hughes says, her voice gentle compared to Miller's matter-of-fact tone, 'the sea temperature and the strength of the currents overnight, the coastguard has determined that continuing the search is extremely unlikely to change the outcome.'

'You're giving up on her.' Alex's voice cracks.

Miller's gaze doesn't waver. 'At this stage, with the information we have, we have to follow protocol and treat this as an accidental drowning.'

Even though I was expecting this, I still gasp. It isn't fake either, but the damning realisation that she's done it. She's gone.

I cover my face with my hands, hiding my expression. I'm too tired to know if it's guilt I feel, or relief or grief, but I don't want the police officers or Alex to see something I don't want them to. I've helped my sister fake her death. The plan worked. It's done. But there is no sense of victory or relief.

Alex's eyes are glassy with tears. 'No, that's not possible. Bryony is too strong to drown.'

'I'm very sorry, Mr Raffety,' Miller replies. 'The coastguard's report will be made available once it's finalised.'

The sound that escapes Alex is raw and broken. Hughes talks in a gentle voice about next of kin and what to do in cases of presumed death, but I barely hear her.

'We'll stay in touch if there are any updates,' Miller says quietly when he and Hughes stand a little while later. 'We're so sorry for your loss.'

I walk them to the door, murmuring gratitude that feels hollow. The cool air from outside hits my face as they step out, a welcome relief before I close the door, trapping myself back in the heat and Alex's grief.

When I return to the kitchen, Alex is exactly where I left him, slumped in the chair at the table, his finger tracing the knot in the wood like he's trying to smooth it away.

'I can't believe she's gone,' he whispers, looking up with red-rimmed eyes.

'I'm so sorry,' I say because it feels like I should. I grit my teeth. It's not just fear I feel now towards Alex but anger. How can he play the grieving widower when he's the reason she had to leave? He drove her to this. He was hurting her, controlling her. Watching her every move. And now he has the audacity to cry.

'You've lost her too,' he says in a faraway voice. 'I'm sorry.'

I search his face for the smallest slip – a sign of the monster beneath – but he's too good. All I see is his grief.

'I... I'll go see Mum,' I say, desperate now to leave this house and this man. Take a moment to breathe away from this smothering tension. Be out in the open and not feel darts of terror every time Alex looks at me.

Bryony has done exactly what she planned. She's faked her death. Tricked Alex so he won't come searching for her. Tricked the coastguard and the police. She's escaped, and now all I want is to do the same.

He scrubs a hand over his face, looking utterly broken. 'Will you tell her? If you do, I can go with you if it will help.'

'I don't think I can,' I reply honestly. 'I'm not sure she'd understand, and it would only upset her if she did.'

He exhales shakily then blurts out, 'Will you come back later? Can you stay here for a few days? I can't be alone right now, Jessie.' Tears swim in his eyes, and instead of the monster I know he is, I see the twenty-one-year-old artist with no money to his name, not even a place to live except his van. The man whose parents died when he was a little boy, meaning he grew up in foster care, living in six different homes before the care system aged him out and he was left to fend for himself. He worked as a labourer for a year to save up enough money to buy his campervan, with some savings left over to live on. Then he drove from Leeds to Devon to live by the sea. I see him dragging driftwood back to his campervan, so excited about the art he was going to create, he could barely contain his words. I'd trailed behind with pockets full of shells.

'Please,' Alex adds, and once more I know I must say yes. Staying here is the very last thing I want to do, but what possible excuse could I give? Alex is my old friend and my brother-in-law. If I say no, he could guess something is amiss. However much I hate this, I have to think about how I'd behave if this was real and I didn't know the truth.

'Of course I will.'

He gives a tired smile. 'Thank you.'

As soon as I'm outside, I draw in a deep breath, allowing the last twenty-four hours to crash over me.

As I make my way down towards the bay, cars pass, going about their days. In the sea, surfers are bobbing in the waves. It feels like the world has kept turning for everyone but me.

I reach for my phone, wanting to call Liam. I don't care how our relationship ended anymore. I don't care about the woman in the bar. Liam was drunk and hurt because I'd taken out a huge personal loan when he'd begged me not to. He'd seen what I couldn't – there was no saving our dream. It was a decision I made when I was stone-cold sober. He made his mistake in one awful moment, half a bottle of whisky in.

I need to hear his voice and know he still cares. But when I open my phone, I see the message reminder from Addie still sitting unopened. The dashcam footage she caught of Bryony arguing with someone on her doorstep. I hesitate. What difference does it make now? And yet, whatever Addie saw, it was enough for her to send it to me.

I tap the screen, and the video starts to play. I see the red front bonnet of Addie's car as it winds around the curve of the cliff road. Up and up, slowing down and pulling over by Bryony's house to allow another car to pass. It's the perfect angle. A man banging on Bryony's front door. Then it opening. The unmistakable image of Bryony in the doorway, wearing dark jeans and a white knit jumper. Even from the angle of the camera and the distance, I can see she's frowning at the man standing before her, shaking her head as he talks. He's leaning forward, towering over her, menacing. She says something to him, her face contorting in anger. I'm about to close the screen, too exhausted to care about whatever disagreement Bryony is having with this man, when the figure turns. Addie's car has already started to pull away, but in the last second, it catches the face of the man on Bryony's doorstep. Just a split second where he glances around before his hand is on her arm and he's stepping into the house. The gesture isn't just angry but familiar.

My heart lurches.

I know that face.

I know that man.

Liam.

THIRTY

Jess

Two hours later, I'm showered and in clean clothes but no less exhausted as I sit in the armchair across from my mum, watching her sleep, my thoughts still spiralling. Before she drifted off, she shared memories from her childhood as we looked through an old photo album together. Telling me stories of collecting conkers and a trip on the big ferry to France one summer.

And all I can think about is that Liam went to see Bryony. Why? Why go to see her but not me? What were they arguing about? And when was this? I rake over the conversation with Addie. '*I was driving past her house last month...*'

I stare at my phone, thumb hovering over his name. I press call, but it doesn't even ring. Just goes straight to voicemail as though his phone is off. Except Liam's phone is never off. Even at dinner, when I begged him to put it down, he'd be scrolling through supplier emails with one hand. Neither of us were good at switching off. Neither of us ever did. It's why we worked.

But his phone is off now.

There has to be a reason he went to see Bryony. They knew each other well. She used to visit us at the hotel once a month or so, breezing in with that air of chic beauty that made everyone stop and look. She'd laugh too loudly at the guests' jokes, charm the staff and vanish again before I could tell her how stressed I was. But she and Liam always got along.

A memory rises uninvited: Bryony leaning over the reception desk, her hand on Liam's arm, eyes bright with mischief.

'*Should I be jealous?*' I'd asked him later that night in our cramped attic room, knees tangled under the thin duvet.

He'd laughed. '*Come off it, Jess. You know what your sister's like. She has to be adored by everyone.*'

'*She does, doesn't she?*' I'd replied, realising he was right.

'*There's only one woman I adore,*' he'd whispered, pulling me close.

And if it hadn't been for the night I saw him with another woman at the end of our relationship and the end of our dreams, I would have sworn I could still trust him. But now I'm not so sure.

I replay the dashcam footage and watch again as Liam takes Bryony's arm and steps into her house. Addie is right. They're arguing. There's a heat between them. Even from the video, I can see Liam's shoulders are locked with tension. But the way he takes her arm seems possessive and familiar.

My hands start to tremble as I open my voicemail. Adrenaline shoots through me, pushing aside the heavy layer of exhaustion from my thoughts. I deleted so many of Liam's messages without listening, but not all of them. I scroll to the last message I have saved. His voice fills the quiet room, low and urgent: 'Jess, call me back. It's important. There's something I really need to tell you.'

The message ends with a click, leaving only the sound of Mum's soft breathing beside me. Was he calling to say he was sorry for how our relationship ended or to confess something else? Something about my sister.

I stare at Mum's peaceful face, willing her to wake and see me. Hug me. Tell me it's all going to be OK. The comment she made when she thought I was Bryony flits through my mind. *'You always wanted what Jess had.'*

Mum thought Bryony had taken Alex from me. Maybe there's a small truth in that thought, but I won't pretend I didn't willingly step aside when she asked me to. But Liam? He was the love of my life. He made me feel seen in a way no one ever had.

Is it so much of a stretch to think he could've been dazzled by her glamour and beauty and the fun she brought to every room. So different from my worries and the constant need for reassurance. And Bryony? She was unhappy with Alex, looking for an escape. When I think about it like that, it seems more than plausible.

I sit forward, elbows on my knees, head in my hands, breath coming fast. Liam and Bryony. My boyfriend and my sister. Would they? My mind scrambles, and I feel sick. I hate this feeling, like standing in a pitch-black room while everyone else has night vision goggles. It's like the truth is right there – I just can't see it.

A soft knock at the door makes me jump. A woman in a black suit and white blouse steps in.

'You must be Jess,' she says.

I nod. 'Hi.'

She glances towards Mum before looking back at me, speaking in a quiet voice. 'I'm Rebecca Church, the manager here. One of the staff let me know you were visiting. Could we have a quick word in private?'

'Of course.' I stand quietly, careful not to wake Mum, and follow her into the corridor.

'I've just heard about your sister,' she says. 'I'm so very sorry.'

I'm not surprised the news has made its way around Skelwick already. It's a small community, and Bryony is well known because of Alex.

My throat tightens as I glance back through the open door at Mum, asleep in her chair. 'Thank you,' I manage. 'I don't want Mum to know yet. It'll only confuse her more.'

'I think that's sensible,' Rebecca says softly. 'Mrs Raffety didn't visit often, so it shouldn't be a change for Andrea. I'll make sure the staff know not to mention it.'

'Thank you,' I whisper. 'Actually, I should go now. I'll be back tomorrow.'

At the front desk, I sign out of the visitors' book as Rebecca's words loop in my head. *'Mrs Raffety didn't visit often...'*

She must be mistaken. Bryony told me she came most days. That she'd sit with Mum for hours, reading to her, holding her hand. It was one of the only places Alex would let her go.

I shoot a look around me, checking there's no staff member nearby before flicking back through the pages and dates, eyes scanning the names. Alex's neat handwriting appears once or twice in the weeks before I returned to Skelwick, but not Bryony's. I keep turning back over the months searching for her familiar looping handwriting, but it doesn't appear. All the months Mum's been in this care home and Bryony didn't visit.

Poor Mum. Hurt cuts to the bone. Followed by a sour guilt that sits in the pit of my stomach. I should've been here.

Bryony lied to me.

There is no sharp surprise, no sting of shock, just an awful realisation. My sister always had a casual relationship with the truth growing up. Lying to our parents about homework. Lying to her friends at school sometimes when she wanted our life to seem more exciting than it really was. Lying to Helen – our friend and neighbour – about boys she said liked her. *'It's a laugh, Jess,'* she'd say when I asked why she did it.

And then the accident happened, changing our lives forever. When I lay in that hospital bed with no memory of anything except being in the water, Bryony told me I'd been standing in the wrong place on the deck. I still can't believe she'd have tried to hurt me on purpose. I still think what happened was a joke gone wrong, but she said it was my fault I was hit with the boom and fell in the water, and that's a lie because she moved the tiller on purpose.

I don't know why Bryony told me she visited Mum nearly every day. Did Alex not let her go? Was she too embarrassed to tell me how little freedom she had? If that was the reason, I'd have understood.

And she never mentioned Liam visiting her either.

I think of how she lied to Alex at the exhibit when he caught us talking about her plan to escape him. That casual shrug, like it was so easy for her.

She lied as a child. She lied as a teen. She's lying now. To Alex and to me.

I double over, fighting against the spots of black pushing at the edges of my vision. My thoughts stumble and drag, pulling me somewhere I don't want to go. Somewhere dark and too awful to comprehend, and yet still the question comes – what other lies has she told me?

THIRTY-ONE

SIXTEEN YEARS EARLIER – THE PLAN

Bryony

I'm so bored I could drop dead as Jess and I trudge up the hill home after school. I'm bored of lessons, bored of being told that I have to focus and revise and do well in my exams or my entire life will be ruined. I'm bored of this walk and the same chicken casserole and mash potato Mum will give us for dinner again because it's Jess's favourite. Why do we only get chips one night a week? It's so stupid!

I can't wait for school to be over so I can go to college and get out of this place, meet someone who sees how amazing I am. Jess wants to go to an art college in London when she's older. It sounds tedious and a bit stuck up, but I like the idea of sharing a flat with her in London. I've got friends, but it's easier with Jess. She doesn't get annoyed when I speak my mind. She knows that's just my way. Sometimes, I feel like I have to walk on eggshells when I'm around other people. Not Jess though. She gets me. It's just one more thing she's good at.

'Are you OK, Bry?' Jess asks from beside me.

I give her my most dazzling smile. 'Yeah, I'm good. Are you?'

Jess tightens her hold on the art sketchbook that never leaves her side. 'I'm a bit nervous about tomorrow. What if all the other artists they selected are ten times better than me? I bet they are. I bet everyone will laugh at my display.'

I bite back a groan. Is no one capable of talking about anything else? It's always *'Jess this'* and *'Jess that'* and art and this stupid, boring award.

At least today will be exciting.

'Stop worrying. It will be fine. You wouldn't have won if you were rubbish.' My tone is sharp, but Jess needs bluntness sometimes. She worries about everything; overthinks everything. It's so draining. Why can't she be happy she's won?

'I just keep thinking maybe the judges were being nice,' Jess says, kicking a pebble along the pavement.

'Or maybe you're actually good,' I say with a long sigh. 'Seriously, Jess. You're driving yourself mad. And me.'

She gives a small laugh. 'Sorry.'

We turn the corner onto our street and see our boring end-of-terrace house. Another thing I can't wait to leave. I don't care if the teachers can't see it. I don't even care if Mum and Dad don't see it. But I'm destined for more. I know I am. Maybe I don't know what that means yet, but my future is going to be so much better than this. One day, I'm going to live in one of the big houses on the cliff and look down on everyone else with their boring, small lives.

By our front door, Jess digs out her key from her bag, knowing without asking that I've lost mine. I know it's in my room somewhere. And it's not like I ever need it when Jess always has hers.

Next door, Helen's bike lies abandoned on the grass in their front garden, one wheel still spinning slowly. I feel a prick of annoyance staring at the bike. We used to ride home together, dumping out our schoolbags in the hall and heading straight to the kitchen for a snack. Helen's house always had the best snacks. Wagon Wheels and KitKats and packets of Hula Hoops. All Jess and I get is a plate of sliced carrot and peppers and a few crackers to snack on. So gross!

Helen and I were best friends. We had been since pre-school. We even had those matching necklaces with two halves of a heart. Our bikes were our freedom. We used to spend entire summers cycling down to the beach every day. We sat together in every class, slept over at each other's houses every weekend, taking over the living room and watching horror movies and eating chocolate.

Then Helen changed. She didn't like it when I wanted to do things my way and not hers. We started to bicker and hang out less. She started spending more time with Jess just to annoy me. But even I couldn't believe it when she accused me of copying her on a test. Like all the years of our friendship meant nothing. Five months later, her accusation still stings.

Of course, the teachers believed Helen over me. She's always a suck-up at school. Now I have to sit at the front of every class with all the losers. And I didn't even make prefect. What's the point of being the oldest in the school if you can't tell everyone else what to do? It isn't fair that she gets to be prefect and not me. I reach into my schoolbag for my pencil case, pulling out the compass Mr Larson insists we need to learn how to use, even though they're so dumb. There is no way I will ever need to use a compass when I'm older.

Anger flares. Hot as lava, rich as treacle. I lean into it. Dive deep. Drink it all up. Smile as the metal glints wickedly in the autumn light. Then I step onto the grass, lean down fast and stab the point of the compass into the rubber tyre of Helen's bike. A hiss of air escapes, the sound so satisfying. One wheel, then the other.

'Bry!' Jess's voice is a whisper of horror. 'What are you doing?'

I straighten, move back to her side, shove the compass back into my bag and push Jess through the front door of our house. 'If anyone asks, we saw a group of year nine boys hanging around.'

Jess shakes her head, paling at the thought of a tiny little lie. 'You shouldn't have done that.'

'Have you forgotten what she did to me?' I reply.

'That was months ago.'

I shrug. 'So? I should've been head girl. I didn't even make prefect. And now she's the one wearing that stupid badge in assembly. You should've seen her face. She's a smug bitch.'

'Bryony,' Jess whispers a warning, eyes shooting to the kitchen.

I roll my eyes. 'Mum's in Merkshaw, remember? She's gone dress shopping for your thing tomorrow. And we need to hurry if we're going to take the *Calypso* out before it gets dark.'

Jess frowns. 'Sailing? Now? Did Dad say it's OK?'

I nod without hesitation, the lie too easy. 'Of course. He said the weather's fine.'

Jess hesitates of course. Honestly! What good is a surprise if everyone knows? And I've got a big surprise for Jess planned. 'We haven't done anything together for ages,' I plead, shooting Jess the pitiful look I know she can't resist.

'I don't know.' Jess bites her lip, hugging her sketchbook tighter. 'I want to, but I should probably—'

'You never want to spend time with me anymore,' I sigh. First Helen ditches me and now Jess is trying to do the same. 'It's always about your art,' I add.

Jess shakes her head. 'I... I'm sorry. I've just had so much to do with the exhibit. But I've finished everything.'

'Exactly.' I smile, victory curling through my chest. 'So we can go. It'll probably be our last chance until spring, and I have a surprise for you.'

Jess hesitates only a moment longer before nodding. 'OK. Let's get changed.'

Upstairs, we throw off our uniforms and scramble to pull on our sailing clothes. The worry is still evident in Jess's face, but I don't mind anymore. I've won.

I smile to myself as we grab our bikes, cycling hard then pulling back as we hit the downhill stretch to the harbour. People give up too easily. But not me. Never me. When I want something, nothing stands in my way. And right now, I want an afternoon with Jess and a reminder of the days before everything became about the stupid trip to London tomorrow. I want to forget the looks the teachers give me and the fight I overheard Mum and Dad have last night.

So what if Dad didn't exactly give permission to take out the *Calypso*? I left a note in the kitchen. That counts.

Ahead, the bright white of the *Calypso*'s stern comes into view, and I feel a surge of excitement. This is the best thing about living in Skelwick – the sailing. Most of the locals have boats. We might not have the money and fancy clothes of the summer tourists, but we grew up learning to sail like most kids learn to ride bikes.

Ten minutes later, the *Calypso*'s bow noses out from the shelter of the moorings. Overhead, the gulls spiral and swoop, their cries distant against the put-put of the *Calypso*'s little petrol engine, which we'll use until the open sea is ahead of us and we can release the sails. The early October air feels cool and fresh, the sea waking up after a late, hot summer where the surfers bobbed on still waves.

Jess stands beside me, glancing to the sky. I follow her gaze, taking in the heavy grey clouds on the horizon.

'Are you sure we've got time before it gets dark?' she asks, biting on her lower lip.

I ignore the pinch of annoyance in my belly and widen my smile. 'Of course. We've got hours of light left, and we won't be out for long.'

'But that looks a lot like bad weather coming, doesn't it?' Jess pushes, nodding to the horizon.

'Stop worrying. I thought you wanted to spend time with me.'

'I do,' she replies. 'It's just—'

I move my lips into a playful pout. 'If you've changed your mind, we can go back.' I let the words hang just long enough to sting then soften them with a light laugh. 'I'm teasing you. Come on, Jess. Don't you want your surprise?'

Jess nods, zipping up her sailing jacket and turning to me with a smile that feels like the first one she's given me in weeks. 'Come on then, Captain – let's set sail. Where are the life jackets?'

'Don't be boring, Jess. We don't need them.'

The *Calypso* slips past the end of the outer wall, and the world grows. As soon as we're clear, I kill the engine, loving the sounds of the creaking mast and the lap of water against the hull.

'Ready?' I ask.

Jess nods.

We throw ourselves into the work. We've done this so many times now that I don't have to tell Jess what to do anymore. In no time at all, the main sail is up and flapping in the wind. The boom lifts, and the *Calypso* leans, finding her feet.

The heaviness leaves my chest, replaced with something light and fizzing. This is exactly what we need. No parents, no teachers, no talk of award ceremonies and London train times.

'When do I get my surprise?' Jess asks as I shift the tiller and steer the *Calypso* into the wind. The sailboat surges, like she's as eager as we are.

'Soon,' I tell her. Very soon. 'You won't know what's hit

you.' I point to one of the rope tie-down points on the starboard side. 'Can you tighten that cleat for me?'

Jess nods and starts to move, inspecting the rope tied to one of the fittings. Right where I want her.

One day, I'll be rich. I'll be admired. I'll be the one Mum and Dad can't stop talking about. I'm going to make sure of it.

THIRTY-TWO

NOW

Jess

An entire week passes before I realise I have to call my dad and tell him Bryony is gone. I feel awful for not thinking of him sooner. Bryony and I only talked about Mum. I don't know why she didn't mention Dad. They were always close. Maybe because Dad's in Spain and living his own life, so far away, and the plan was so rushed. Again, I worry about what else we've forgotten.

I make the call sitting in Bryony's Mercedes, which still carries the lingering scent of her perfume. But even this is better than the stifling warmth of the house and feeling as though I'm walking on eggshells, scared to say the wrong thing in case I let something slip. Scared of igniting Alex's anger too.

Every day I've continued to play the part of the grieving sister. The good sister. The helper. I've continued Bryony's lie and accepted casseroles and bouquets of flowers from well-meaning neighbours and friends who knocked on the door of Cliffview House. The people of Skelwick have come in a steady stream, Alex refusing to see any of them. My only escape has been the visits to Mum each day.

It's been impossible to think straight. Impossible to sort through the mess of questions and worries and lies twisting me in knots. But whenever I suggest going back to Mum's house, Alex begs me to stay one more day. I don't know how to tell him I want to leave.

Dad answers on the fifth ring with a sleepy, 'Hello.'

'Dad, it's Jess,' I say, glancing to the clock on the dash of Bryony's Mercedes. It's lunchtime, which makes it early afternoon in Spain.

'Jess! Hiya, love,' Dad says. 'How's it going with the hotel, and how's Liam?'

I bite my lip, realising how long it's been since I spoke to Dad. He's always been a kind and loving father when we've seen each other, but he's not one to reach out. Over the years, I got sick of always being the one to make the effort. I think a part of me never forgave him for what felt like abandonment, of me and of Mum. For leaving so suddenly and taking my sister away from me.

Those events are painted in a whole new light now I know the truth about the accident. Dad didn't leave me. He took Bryony away to protect me. And yet chose Bryony over me and Mum.

Dad is waiting for me to reply. The enormity of what I have to do crashes down on me. 'Dad, Bryony had a sailing accident. She's...' My chest tightens. The words don't want to come. I'm telling a father his daughter is dead. It feels like the worst thing I've ever done. Suddenly, I'm grateful for Mum's dementia. That she's shielded from this. 'It's been a week,' I admit. 'They're saying she drowned.'

'What?' Dad's voice is hollow in my ear. Shock and hurt and grief echoing in that one word.

'She's gone,' I whisper.

'No. That's not possible. Bryony... she's fine. She's always fine.' The next sound is a keening sob. 'Oh God.'

Tears streak down my face. Every breath feels like it's been dragged over broken glass. I don't think I'll ever forgive myself for causing Dad this pain and grief. But even as his hurt wrenches through me like it's my own, I wonder if this is the reason Bryony didn't mention him. Would I have agreed to do this if I'd thought about this call and the hurt I was inflicting? I'd like to think I wouldn't, but looking back on those days between Bryony telling me about Alex's abuse and forming a plan, it feels so rushed and panicked. All I could think about was Bryony being safe, and how her safety was the answer to my financial problems.

She's a liar. The thought hits me again, like it has every day since she left. Again, I try to ignore it. I'm not ready to face what exactly she's lied about.

'I'm sorry, Dad.' My words seem to pull him out of his crying.

He sniffs. 'Are you OK, Jess? Are you and Alex holding up?'

'Yes,' I reply in a faltering voice.

He focuses on the practical details then, and it seems to help. He asks me to tell him what happened and what the coast-guard said. He asks if there will be a funeral to which I reply, 'I don't know.' Alex hasn't talked about it. Is it even called a funeral if there's no body?

We start to wrap up the call. Dad promises we'll speak in a few days, but he doesn't mean it. I think about that day on the *Calypso* and the fierce jerking of Bryony's hand as she'd moved the tiller. And yes, it's the worst time to ask him this, but if I don't do it now, I might never find the courage, and I'm so sick of feeling like I'm in the dark.

I talk before I can change my mind. 'Dad, I need to ask you something.'

'What is it?'

'The accident on the *Calypso* – did Bryony cause it? Is that why you took her away?'

'Jess—' I can tell by the pleading way he says my name that he doesn't want to answer. Just like I can tell I'm right.

I close my eyes as the world presses in. 'Why didn't you tell me?' I whisper.

'You didn't remember what happened, and your mum and I thought it would be better if you didn't know. We only suspected, Jess. We didn't know for sure what Bryony meant to do. She always denied it, but her jealousy had been building up. I didn't think she'd meant for it to turn out so badly. But your mum insisted Bryony be sent away from you. She thought the space would help Bryony too. So I took her to Norwich. I made her see a therapist, and she worked through her jealousy. She changed in those years it was just me and her.'

'But—' I don't even know what I'm going to ask or say, only that I want to know everything. How could they keep this from me? They might have thought they were protecting me, but they have no idea how much the accident has haunted my life. It's woven itself into me. It's not just the nightmares of being in the dark, cold water. It's Bryony. I thought she'd risked her life to save me. I've lived with that knowledge for sixteen years. I've always felt a debt. As though I owe her. I could refuse her nothing.

'Please, Jess,' Dad cuts in, his voice breaking. 'Can't we just remember her for the good she did. She loved you. That's all that matters.'

We say our goodbyes and both make false promises to call. His words ring through my head.

'She loved you. That's all that matters.'

Except it isn't. Because what matters is the truth. I've been avoiding the question for a week, but I can't avoid it any longer. I have to know how much of what Bryony told me since I returned to Skelwick is true. I need to know if Alex is the monster Bryony told me he was. I want to know why Liam was on her doorstep. What were they arguing about? And why did it look like there was something more than anger between them?

I wipe the tears from my face, eyes darting around the car, then throw myself into motion, fingers digging between the leather of Bryony's driver's seat.

'Where are you?' I say aloud, shifting position, running my fingers along the leather sides, searching for hidden pockets.

'Damn it,' I whisper into the silent car. I know it's here.

I sit back in the seat, resting my head on the seat rest. I reach for my phone and pull up Liam's number. I've stopped trying to call. Every time, it goes straight to voicemail. Instead, I skip through the messages he left me, one after another.

The first is his voice, uncertain but soft. *'Jess, it's me. Call me back. Please. I miss you. I need to talk to you.'*

The next message came only hours later: *'I hope if you won't pick up, you'll at least listen. I'm sorry, Jess. I know what I did is unforgivable, but it wasn't planned. It was five stupid seconds of my life, and I hate myself for it. But. Jess, don't let that ruin what we had.'*

Another message followed a few days later, his tone strained. *'I can't stop thinking about the Kilstern, Jess. Can we talk? Just about the business. There are things I have to tell you.'*

The final message I've not deleted is quieter but desperate: *'Please call me. It's important.'*

I shove the phone back into my pocket, frustration burning under my skin. It's another dead end. I shift forward, resuming my search. I check under the passenger seat, fingers stretching, brushing something hard. Plastic, round. I pull it free. A white disc gleaming in the light. An AirTag.

My heart kicks up. Bryony showed me the alert. She told me Alex planted the tracker in her car. I close my fist around it and walk back into the house. The scent of coffee and something stale hits me with that warmth again. I want to throw open windows, craving air and freshness.

Alex is at the kitchen counter, a half-drunk mug of coffee beside him. He's sketching a landscape in his notebook. Trees, hills, a river. His pencil moves fast.

'Alex,' I say, placing the AirTag on the counter.

He glances up, blinking. Dark circles surround his eyes. Instinctively, I want to step back, keep some distance between us, but I can't keep being scared.

'What's that?' he asks.

'It's an AirTag,' I reply. 'A tracking device that connects to Apple phones. You put it in a bag or car so you can track where it is.'

He picks it up between his fingers, turning it like it's an alien coin. 'The world's gone mad,' he mutters. 'Why do you have it?'

'It's Bryony's,' I say carefully.

He shakes his head, baffled. 'Why does she have one?'

I study his face, searching for deceit, but all I see is confusion and grief and exhaustion.

'I don't know,' I reply honestly.

I unlock my own phone, a chill crawling up my spine. I open WhatsApp, type his name and find nothing. Just a prompt to invite him to join the app. And yet all those messages he sent Bryony the week I pretended to be her came on WhatsApp to her phone. I didn't check it was the same number as Alex's contact in my phone. Why would I? Bryony gave me her phone. The name on the messages said Alex.

'I just tried to send you a WhatsApp,' I say slowly. 'But you don't have the app.'

He shrugs. 'You know I hate all that tech stuff. People are obsessed with staying in touch. If I want to see someone, I'll see them. Otherwise, I'd rather be left alone.'

For a moment, all I can do is stare at him. Alex said the

same thing to the police last week. I'd assumed he was lying and had a second phone he used to track Bryony. But in the long, quiet days we've shared in this house, I've only ever seen him with the basic model he showed the police. Then I think about how there's no CCTV at the house. Inside or out. If Alex had really been obsessed with knowing Bryony's every move, wouldn't he have installed cameras?

My mouth is dry. I've been desperate for some scrap of truth, and here it is. If Alex doesn't have WhatsApp, then it wasn't him messaging me from Bryony's phone. And if he didn't plant this AirTag, then he hasn't been tracking Bryony.

I look at Alex again. He has his dark moments, flashes of grief and frustration. He's intense, yes, but suddenly he doesn't seem the monster Bryony painted him to be. Is anything she told me about him true?

'Alex, that day I came to the house and we all had coffee... Why couldn't Bryony come with me to visit Mum?' I ask, remembering the way Bryony had asked me to '*play along*' and the strange tension in the house; Alex's insistence she went with him to the studio.

Alex frowns. I hold my breath as I wait for his answer.

'Wasn't that a few weeks before the exhibit?' he says, not waiting for my reply. 'I had a journalist writing a feature on me. He was with me at the studio all that week. Bryony was part of the feature – the artist and his muse – and so she had to be there too.'

I let out a breath as Alex's explanation settles over me. It sounds perfectly reasonable.

'And the wine?' I add quickly before I can change my mind. 'You poured her glass away when you came to Mum's.'

He shrugs. 'She drank too much. She promised me she'd cut down and she was driving that day. I probably shouldn't have tipped it away, but I knew she'd drink it in one go if I didn't.'

I find myself nodding slowly. I'd noticed Bryony's drinking too. I put it down to stress.

My mind races back over every interaction with Alex since I've been back in Skelwick. I saw the intensity I remembered from our earlier friendship. I saw his adoration for Bryony, his obsession with his work. But Bryony showed me bruises, told me stories of control and anger, and I saw everything Alex did through that lens.

She's a liar. The voice again. And this time, I listen.

Alex rubs a hand over his face before looking up. 'Why are you asking?'

I stare at the broken man slumped at the breakfast bar and realise I have two choices. I can brush my questions away as nothing. Or I can give him some honesty. Not all of it but some. 'I just... sorry if this sounds crazy, but it seemed like over the last few weeks, you've been a bit... controlling over Bryony.'

He makes a noise that almost sounds like an exhale of amusement. But then he nods. 'The exhibit and the trip to Long Island. I was stressed. Maybe I haven't been as attentive a husband as I should've been. But controlling?' He gives a small smile. 'Jess, come on.'

Inside, my world shatters. 'Sorry. It sounds stupid now I say it out loud.' Because he's right. All this time, I had struggled to believe Alex was the kind of man who'd hurt Bryony, and maybe I was right.

Oh God.

It was Bryony. It was all lies.

Everything she told me.

It's the only explanation that fits. She didn't just lie to me, she tricked me. The bruises, the tears, the AirTag, the messages. The threats. To Mum. To her. To me.

Those awful days I pretended to be her, alone in this house, constantly terrified that I'd be found out by Alex or someone else. Deceiving Mum.

I feel sick. I hurry from the kitchen, hand trailing the wall for support as I make my way to the living room and drop down onto one of the sofas. The full scale of everything she's done these past weeks feels like a hand closing around my throat.

If Alex wasn't the monster she said he was, then why did she lie to me? And if she wasn't running from an abusive marriage, if neither of our lives were really in danger, then why has she faked her own death?

THIRTY-THREE

Jess

'I'm cooking dinner,' I call later that evening as Alex steps into the kitchen. He's fresh from a shower, smelling of limes and soap. There's more colour in his face than I've seen in days. 'I can't stand another casserole.'

He smiles faintly. 'Me neither. Why does everyone assume I'm a vegetarian?'

'It's art-arian-ism,' I reply, stirring the pasta. For the first time in days – weeks – I feel the tension and the fear loosen its hold on me, and I like it. I need it.

'That's not a word,' he replies, amused, pulling open a cupboard.

'It should be,' I reply. 'The ability to look like an artist and a vegetarian.'

'Right now, I look like a man who needs a drink.' He takes out a bottle of wine and holds it up. 'You'll join me?'

I nod. The truth is I'm grateful to be cooking. To be doing something more than walking from room to room, catching the soft incessant hum from the basement, unable to escape it any more than I can escape my thoughts and the questions I can't answer about Bryony and Liam.

I feel almost certain that Bryony lied about the abuse. All along, I couldn't wrap my head around it. Around the idea that Alex, who loved Bryony so much, could ever hurt her. And maybe the reason I found it so hard to stomach was because it wasn't true. I was wrong about Alex. Which means I have nothing to fear. Except for whatever Bryony has in store for me. Because now I have to question why she's done all this. Why she's lied to me about everything. Why she's gone to such lengths. And worse... what she plans to do next.

When the dinner is ready and the wine is poured and Alex has softened the lights, we sit at the table together. It feels strangely intimate. Even with its wide spaces and high ceilings, the house feels cocooned from the world and the wind and rain lashing against the glass.

'God knows why she loved this stuff so much,' Alex says, taking a long sip. 'She wouldn't drink anything else. Even had it shipped on holiday with us.'

I take a sip and it's as smooth and fruity as I remember. By the second sip, I swear it's gone to my head. 'I'm not much of a drinker,' I say. 'Liam would order the wine at the hotel.'

A shadow crosses Alex's face. The devastation that has clung to him all week returns like a dark cloud. 'I'm sorry it didn't work out for you.' His voice cracks, and I'm sure he must be thinking of Bryony.

Something tells me Alex doesn't want to be sad tonight. Or maybe it's me. Maybe I need a break from playing the grieving sister. I hold the wine up to the light, the colour a pale red. 'It's a lot better than that cider you used to buy and try to get me to drink in your campervan.'

Alex huffs a laugh. 'That stuff was the only thing that kept me warm at night.'

He sits across from me, elbows on the table. 'I still

remember how surreal it was meeting you on the beach that first time. The rain was practically horizontal. I didn't think anyone else would be crazy enough to be out.'

'The tide had just gone out. Best time for—'

'Shells,' he finishes. 'And collecting driftwood. I thought you were taking my wood when I first saw you.'

I smile. 'I wouldn't dare.'

The wine loosens something inside me. Alex seems lighter too, the lines around his eyes softening. We talk about those early days – his first art pieces, the long walks, the freezing nights by the van. It feels almost normal, like we've shaken off our grief and the awfulness of what's happening as easy as a coat, left hung on a hook to collect later.

'I'll admit something,' he says, swirling his glass. 'I was falling for you back then.'

My pulse quickens, mouth dropping open, and I mask it with another gulp of wine, finishing my glass. 'You never said.'

Alex stands to fetch another bottle. I can't believe we've drunk one between us already. 'We were friends, Jess,' he says over his shoulder. 'I didn't think you wanted to be anything more. Then Bryony appeared.'

'She was hard to ignore,' I say.

He sighs as he sits down once more, topping up both our glasses. I should stop drinking, but I like the fuzziness and the lightness it brings to my thoughts.

'It was like I was under a spell in those early months,' he says. 'I couldn't separate my sudden success with this beautiful woman who seemed to love me. It felt... inevitable. I couldn't believe *she* wanted *me*.'

'She wasn't the only one,' I say quietly before I can stop myself, pushed on by the wine fuzzy in my mind and Alex's honesty.

He looks up, his dark eyes filled with something I can't read. Sadness and maybe hope. 'You don't mean that,' he says.

'I do,' I whisper. 'I mean, I did have feelings for you back then.'

A silence closes around us, the air suddenly charged and fragile. It feels like we're both waiting to see what the other will do.

I'm not sure what I want to happen. This entire situation is messy enough. I'm tangled so tightly in the lies Bryony told me, I can barely move. And then there's Liam. We're no longer together, but I still love him. He's still the first person I want to tell things to.

But those thoughts all feel so distant, dulled by the wine swimming in my veins. And sitting here with Alex, just the two of us, without Bryony shining so bright, feels nice. More than that, it feels right. For once, I'm the one Alex is looking at like I'm the whole world. The exact look I yearned to see in his eyes all those years ago before Bryony came home. He could've fallen for me back then. Would've done, I bet, if we'd had a little more time, like Mum said. But Bryony had to take my happiness from me. Always lying. Always getting exactly what she wants.

No more.

I'm here with Alex now, and Bryony isn't. Why should I hold back when she never did? And so I smile softly and reach my hand to cover his.

'Bryony and I… it wasn't easy living with her,' he says then. 'I was thinking of leaving her. Did she tell you?'

I shake my head, and Alex threads his fingers through mine. My heart starts to race, head spinning a little more. I know I should pull back, go to bed and sleep off this wine before we both cross a line we won't come back from, but a whispered voice is urging me to stay. Bryony lied to me about everything. She's lied to me my whole life. Our entire relationship since the accident has been her in control, me subservient, knowing I was only alive because of her.

She took Alex from me. She was meeting Liam behind my

back. She takes everything that's mine, and now it's my turn to take it back, and so I lean a little closer and continue to drink my wine.

'How did she take it?' I ask, wondering in the back of my mind if Alex wanting to leave her had anything to do with why she really faked her death. But I've had too much wine to think clearly.

'She called me crazy,' Alex replies. 'I told her I didn't want this life anymore. The parties, the exhibits, this house,' he says, waving a hand to the floor-to-ceiling windows. She called it a midlife crisis and told me to explore ice sculpting. Even had a huge freezer put in the basement to store the ice.'

The thought of the basement sobers me for a moment. I study Alex's face, still searching for any flash of the man who would lock my sister in a basement and threaten to never let her leave. I see nothing and hate myself that a part of me still trusts Bryony after everything I now know. This man before me wants to give up his wealth and his lifestyle and live in a campervan, focusing solely on his art.

He is kind and thoughtful, and when he was told his wife had been declared dead, one of his first thoughts was of me and if I needed support telling Mum. And he doesn't deserve to be treated like this – to grieve for a woman who isn't really dead.

He stands and carries the plates to the sink.

'Alex—' I falter, following him with the empty wine glasses. I place them on the side. 'I have to tell you something.'

He turns to face me, close enough that I can feel the warmth of his body and catch the woody scent of his aftershave. He deserves to know what she's done. But when he reaches to brush my hair away from my face, my stomach dips.

'Sometimes,' Alex says, before I can continue, 'I wonder what my life would've been like if I'd told you how I felt back then.'

The air between us feels suddenly heated and dangerous.

My breath catches with the pull of something I don't want to name. I look at Alex and see the boy from the beach – the one who made driftwood beautiful. The one I was falling in love with a decade ago.

Before I know what I'm doing, I'm leaning in, pressing my lips to his. For the smallest moment, he hesitates, then he's kissing me, his tongue in my mouth, mine in his – hot and electric. His hands slide around my waist then roam up my back, drawing me closer, pressing my body to his. My core ignites, fire rushing through me, and I push myself even closer, desperate for more, for the feeling of being wanted by this man at last.

We stumble towards the bedroom, kissing between gasps for breath, tugging at clothes as we go. Dropping them on the stairs and in the hall. Alex's hands slide over my bare skin, lips kissing my neck, and suddenly there's nothing else in my head but how much I want this.

THIRTY-FOUR

Jess

I wake in the dark, mouth dry, head pounding. I blink, taking in the bedroom and the shape in the bed beside me, remembering the dinner, the laughter, the wine, the heat of Alex's skin against mine. My stomach twists with guilt. I think of Liam, and hurt slices through me.

We're not together. We haven't spoken for months, but I know now that I still love him. I feel sick. From a hangover as much as what happened between me and Alex. Without the cosiness of the kitchen and the fuzziness of the wine, what happened between us feels more about trying to recapture our past than it does about any real connection now. And maybe a part of me wanted to get back at Bryony too.

Stupid!

Regret lies heavy in my stomach. I don't know how I'll face Alex in the morning or where we go from here. I slide out from beneath the sheets and collect my clothes, moving quietly through the half dark. I'm searching for my underwear when I see something metal glinting on the floor beside Alex's bunched-up jeans. It's a set of keys. The small, silver kind that fit a padlock.

My heart lurches. The basement.

That humming. The strange sense that I wasn't alone in the house. The feeling of unease as I'd stood by that door at the bottom of the stairs. Alex's explanation of the ice freezer makes sense. I'm certain Bryony was never locked down there now, but something still calls to me. That feeling of being in the dark and wanting to throw on the lights. I have to know for sure what's down there.

I glance back at the bed. Alex is motionless, his breathing deep and even. I hesitate, pulse thudding in my throat. Then, slowly, I reach for the keys and close my fingers around them before tiptoeing out of the room, easing the door shut behind me. The click of the latch sounds deafening. I hold my breath, listening for the rustle of bed covers or a heavy sigh, but only silence rings in my ears.

I pull on my clothes; my bare feet move soundlessly across the hall as I clutch the keys in my hand. Goosebumps prickle my skin, and it has nothing to do with the chill in the air. I hurry down the stairs and down the hall to the door that leads to the basement. For a long moment, I just stand there, heart hammering, trying to work out what I think I'm doing. I don't know what I'll say if Alex finds me here – what excuse could possibly make sense? But I can't stop. I need to know.

I open the door and turn on the light. Just as before, the single bare bulb sways slightly at the bottom of the steep staircase. The air is colder and carries a slight chemical tang. *Alex's art supplies*, a voice whispers in my mind. The same voice that wants me to turn off the light, creep back upstairs and return the keys.

But even now, a wrongness prickles at the back of my neck. I can't explain it, can't name it, but it crawls through me all the same. All I can hear in the silence is that humming. It's enough to make me edge forward, one hesitant step at a time, until I'm standing before the padlocked door.

Then I fit one of the keys into the lock and turn. The click is loud, making me freeze. I hold my breath again. Listen. Nothing. I pull the padlock free of the latches and twist the handle, pushing the door open an inch at a time. The hinges creak.

The bare bulb swings a little more, throwing long, trembling shadows across the concrete floor. I swallow, throat dry. I half expect something to leap out, but instead, I find myself staring into an ordinary-looking basement. I turn on another light and see shelves lined with jars of paint, boxes of brushes, and tools. Nothing sinister. Nothing hidden. Relief rushes through me so fast I almost laugh. I've terrified myself for weeks over nothing.

Then my gaze falls to the source of the humming. The huge, white chest freezer in the corner of the room. The exact kind of freezer a person would need for storing ice. And still, I move towards it, like something is pulling me in. My hand reaches out. There's a spot of something on the lid.

Dark red.

I step closer. Hand hovering.

Another spot.

Then a third.

Paint. It's paint. Of course. There are tins lining the shelves behind me. This is where Alex keeps his supplies. I tell myself that, whispering it like a prayer, but my body doesn't believe me. My nerves are stretched thin, heart banging against my ribs. The air feels thick, slow to draw into my lungs. The hum from the freezer is louder now, vibrating through the soles of my feet. My hand shakes as I reach for the lid. The metal is cold, slick with condensation as my fingers curl around the edge of the handle.

Then there's movement behind me. Feet hitting the cement. A hand grabbing me, yanking me backward. I scream, the sound ripped from somewhere deep in my chest. For a second, the world tilts; saltwater fills my mouth, and I'm back in that freezing sea, the rush of waves slamming into me, the weight dragging me down.

'Jess!' Alex's voice. 'It's me.'

I blink and he's there in front of me, his expression unreadable. I can't tell if he's annoyed or concerned. The grip of his hand on my arm is tight enough to make me wince in pain. When I glance down, his knuckles are white. He follows my gaze and releases me, stepping back.

'What are you doing in here?' he asks.

'I—' My voice catches. 'I thought I heard a noise. I thought maybe an animal got trapped down here.'

He stares at me, and I know he doesn't believe my lie. He must know I took the padlock keys. His eyes darken. 'In the freezer?'

I force a shaky laugh. 'No, I just wanted to look at the ice sculptures.'

'It's empty right now.' There's something final in his tone. 'Come on. It's late. Let's go to bed.'

I nod, letting him take my arm. He guides me out of the basement, and I watch as he turns back to relock the padlocks, sliding them into place with a metallic snap. The sound echoes in the stillness.

His expression is unreadable as he leads me back up the stairs. My arm still throbs where he grabbed me.

As we reach the top, I glance back. Through the door, I can still hear the hum of the freezer.

If it's empty, why is it still running?

THIRTY-FIVE

Jess

Alex barely looks at me when I come downstairs the next morning. He's standing at the counter, hair messy, a mug clutched in both hands. The tension in the air feels brittle and lacks any of the heat of last night. We move around each other as I fix myself a coffee and some breakfast. It's awkward. Neither of us mentions the wine, the kiss, the way it spiralled. We don't talk about the basement either.

'I think I'll go to my studio today,' he says, eyes fixed on an invisible point beyond the window. His tone is casual, but I swear I catch an undercurrent of anger. 'I don't know if I'll be able to work,' he adds, pushing a hand through his hair. 'But what else can I do? I'll probably stay there late.'

I nod. The message is clear. I'm no longer needed here. I don't know if it's because of what we did or that he found me in the basement, or if this moment was always coming, and sleeping together was marking an end.

Beyond the confusion is relief. Last night was a mistake. I'm grateful it's Alex that's drawn the line so I don't have to. One thing I am certain of is that I want to find Liam. Sleeping with Alex has made me realise I'm still connected to Liam and our relationship. I long to talk to him. I want to ask why he visited Bryony. And if there's any way back for us.

I've got the number for his parents in my contacts. I'll call them later.

'I'm going to see Mum today,' I say. 'And then I'll carry on sorting the house. Call me if you need me.'

He glances at me for the first time. 'I spoke to our solicitor this morning. You and I are both executors of Bryony's will. He wants to meet with both of us. Is next Monday OK?'

'Fine,' I say.

I make my way upstairs and gather my belongings from the spare room. By the time I'm shrugging on my coat, Alex's Land Rover is already nosing out of the driveway, saving both of us an awkward goodbye. Outside, the morning air is sharp and cold, the sky grey and promising rain. The walk to the care home feels longer than usual.

My mind replays the moment we kissed in the kitchen and the one just before it when I was going to tell Alex that Bryony had faked her death, that she was alive, that we'd tricked him. Tricked everyone. I could've told him this morning, but something about the way he gripped my arm in the basement, the darkness in his eyes, stopped me. Now I'm away from the house and him, a niggling uncertainty is starting to drum in my thoughts.

I thought I'd found answers, but away from the house and away from Alex, I worry I've allowed Alex to manipulate me as easily as Bryony did. Tears prick at my eyes. If I could just speak to Bryony, I know I could make sense of what's happening. But she never contacted me to tell me she'd made it ashore. Did something go wrong on the *Odysseus*? I remember the moment I thought I saw her talking to someone. Did I imagine it?

By the time I reach the care home, my mind is a storm of questions. Mum is sitting by the window when I arrive, bright and cheerful. She pours me tea from a floral pot, gossiping about the other residents, her hands fluttering like birds, not letting me get a question in. It almost feels normal, until her gaze slides over me when she thinks I'm not looking and I see the flicker of confusion, and I realise she has no idea who I am and is trying to mask it.

Only when I'm walking up the road to the house does something pull me out of my head. A feeling of unease settles over me. I turn around, glancing behind me, certain I'll find someone there, but the pavement is empty. Still, the unease remains. Two more steps and I stop again, scanning the empty street, looking between the parked cars, feeling stupid when still there's no one.

When I reach the front door, Kelly is leaving her house, a chocolate spaniel tugging at the lead. She stops when she sees me. 'Jess,' she says softly, 'I heard about Bryony. I'm so sorry.'

'Thank you,' I murmur.

Kelly shakes her head. 'I can't say I always agreed with her actions, especially after what she did to the Bartletts, but she was one of a kind, that's for sure.'

I remember Bryony mentioning the community turning against the Bartletts. How everyone in the town had boycotted the fishing and gift shop, Tackle and Tat, and Damon's sister's bakery too. 'What Bryony did?' I ask.

'Surely you know.' She searches my face before she continues. 'Damon criticized Alex's driftwood collecting. He said it was ruining the shoreline and affecting fishing.'

'I knew that bit. I thought there was a boycott in support of Alex.'

She nods. 'There was, but only after Bryony made it her personal mission to turn everyone against him and his sister. Within weeks, they couldn't sell a loaf of bread or a spool of wire. They were forced out. But it never would've happened without Bryony rallying people.'

Bryony never mentioned her own involvement in ruining the Bartletts. Another lie. Another manipulation. I'm no longer surprised.

Kelly sighs, tugging her dog closer. 'Anyway, it's water under the bridge now, I suppose. And I'm sorry she's gone. No one deserves to die like that.'

She studies me, hesitating. 'Are you still planning to turn your mum's place into a holiday rental?'

I hesitate. The truth is, I don't know what I'm doing anymore. I've been so caught up in Bryony and this awful game she's dragged me into that I haven't stopped to think much about myself and what my future looks like. The money I withdrew from Bryony's account has bought me some breathing room. For the first time in months, I don't feel the pressure of the debt breathing down my neck. And I no longer feel guilty for taking the money from Bryony either.

But it will run out, and I don't know what I'll do then. I could get a job locally. Find some summer work in a hotel. Live in Mum's house myself for a while. Wait for Bryony's life insurance payout. Except, after all the lies she's told, do I believe her?

'I... I don't know,' I say eventually. 'I'm not sure what I'm going to do.' Tears fall onto my cheeks. I'm tired and I'm hungover, and there is so much I still don't know or understand, and the only person I really want to talk to right now is Liam.

'No rush to decide anything, love,' Kelly says, stepping over the lead of her dog to draw me into a hug. Her body is soft and reminds me of Mum, and that just makes me cry even more.

Eventually, her dog tugs the lead, and I draw back and wipe my eyes. 'Thank you,' I whisper.

'Any time, Jess,' she says, giving my hand a final squeeze before stepping away. 'It's good to have you back in Skelwick,' she calls over her shoulder.

Inside, Mum's house feels small and tired after the week I've spent in the luxury of Cliffview House. And still, I'm happy to be home. I lose the afternoon sorting through Mum's things, choosing photos and trinkets to take to her room at the care home. When I finally collapse into bed, the exhaustion is a smothering blanket, making sleep impossible.

I reach for my phone and try Liam's number. It's still switched off, cutting straight to voicemail. *Where are you, Liam?*

This time I leave a message. 'Hi. It's Jess. I... want to talk. Can you call me when you get this?'

I end the call, frustrated and empty. Why isn't he answering? I remember my earlier decision to contact his parents. It's not late, and they're always up at this time. I scroll through my contacts, finding their number. It rings four times before his mum, Evelyn, answers with a hopeful, 'Hello?'

'Evelyn, it's Jess. I'm sorry to—'

'Jess,' Evelyn says, voice brightening. 'It's so good to hear from you. We've been wanting to get in touch, but I couldn't find your number. We're very worried about Liam. Is he with you?'

An awful feeling starts to worm its way into the pit of my stomach. 'No, he's not. That's why I'm calling. He isn't answering my calls.'

'Or ours,' Evelyn says. 'You know how Liam always called on Sundays, but we haven't heard from him for over a month now. The last time he called, he told us he was going to Skelwick to see you. We know the break-up and the hotel failure hit him hard. We hoped he was taking some time with you to regroup.'

'I'm sorry. I've not seen him since he left Oxfordshire.'

'And you haven't spoken since?' she asks, voice rushed with worry.

'He was leaving me messages and calling,' I reply. 'But not for weeks either.'

'I just don't know where he is,' Evelyn says, sounding near tears.

'Could he have gone travelling?' I ask. 'Liam talked of travelling a lot before we found the Kilstern.' Maybe whatever Bryony said to him convinced him to pick up and go.

'I honestly don't know,' she replies, but there's a hope in her voice that wasn't there before. 'I know he was restless and sad. Maybe that's it. Maybe he's taking some time away from it all. I just hoped he was doing that with you. But I think we'll pop down to the police station tomorrow and see what they say. He's an adult, of course, but it's not like him not to call.'

I agree that it's not, and we chat for a few more minutes before promising to stay in touch. I end the call and stare at the blank screen as a thought strikes me. I tap through my settings until I find the deleted messages folder. I should've thought of it earlier. I tap on the icon and there are all the voicemails from Liam I deleted without listening to. I tap on the last one he sent me.

His voice fills the room, low and rough. 'Jess, it's me. I'm in Skelwick. I'm coming to see you. I have something to tell you. It's going to be hard to hear, but I can't keep this to myself. Please open the door and hear me out. I'll be there about five.'

I stare at the date. The message was sent the day I arrived. I pull up Addie's dashcam video of Liam arguing with Bryony. There's a date and time stamp in the corner. It reads 3 p.m. The date is the same. He came to Skelwick to see me. He went to Bryony's house first, and something made him change his mind about visiting. He kept calling me after that, but I never picked up and he stopped leaving messages.

I grit my teeth, frustration still burning through my body. I can't take this anymore. I've had enough of the lies and the second-guessing, the guilt. I should never have agreed to Bryony's plan.

First thing tomorrow, I'm going to tell Alex everything.

What Bryony told me and everything we did, and how she's still alive. I chickened out last night, but he deserves to know. And after that, I'm going to go to the police station in Merkshaw and tell Sergeant Miller and PC Hughes everything too. I'm complicit in this crime. I might be arrested and charged, but all I can do is hope for leniency, hope they see that I've been manipulated by my sister since the day she moved the tiller and the boom swung across the *Calypso* and knocked me into the sea, and maybe since before that too.

Whatever happens, I'm done being a pawn in whatever game my sister has dragged me into.

THIRTY-SIX

Jess

I wake in the dead of night to a hand grabbing my arm, feeling the cold of the basement floor on bare feet, Liam's voicemails whispering in my ear, the curve of Bryony's smile in my thoughts.

I bolt upright, heaving in a breath as I take in the familiar shapes of my childhood bedroom. But the silence I expect to wrap around me isn't there. Instead, I catch the urgent wail of sirens. I throw off the covers and move to the window. The flashing blue lights of the emergency vehicles are tracking their way through the streets of the town below, making their way towards the bay where the unmistakable orange glow of a fire is staining the night sky.

I know exactly where that fire is.

It's by the car park with the toilet and shower block, the surfboard hire shop and the beach café. It'll be a kitchen fire in the café, I tell myself. Because otherwise, those orange flames can be from only one other place – Alex's studio.

I dress quickly, scrambling to pull on my jeans and a

jumper, fingers fumbling to tie my trainers. Then I'm out the door, coat half on, racing through the streets towards the promenade. The night air is sharp and cold, but there's the distinct taste of smoke and I haven't even reached the bottom of the hill yet. My lungs burn, my pulse roaring in my ears as the sirens grow louder.

I run through the town and around the corner to the bay, and then I reach the promenade and it's chaos. Thick black smoke billows out over the water, turning the bay into a churning fog of fire and ash. The smell hits me – burning resin, charred wood, salt and heat so fierce it scalds the back of my throat. I gag, pulling my sleeve over my mouth as I push through the crowd. Even from this distance, the heat feels like it burns my cheeks and singes the wisps of my hair.

I know before I even reach the front of the gathering crowd what I'll see, and yet nothing prepares me. I gasp. Alex's studio is engulfed. Flames leap from the roof like greedy orange tongues, tearing through the timber frame. The windows have burst, leaving shards of glass scattered across the ground. The sound is a monstrous roar of fire and splitting wood, like it's a living thing.

'Stand back please, Miss.' The voice is commanding, and I turn to find a tall police officer, arms out, moving the crowd. 'We need everyone to move across the road,' he continues, shouting over the noise of the fire as another officer unravels blue tape.

'Is anyone inside?' I ask.

'I don't have that information,' he replies, shuffling me back.

My eyes sting, throat raw with smoke and emotion as I watch men and women in thick padded uniforms unravel hoses and spray the tops of the flames. The water arcs through the air, hitting the fire with a hiss. It's not enough. The heat surges. There's a loud bang from inside the building, like a tin can exploding.

'Alex could be in there!' I choke out. The words are raw with panic. The smoke burns my eyes, tears streaking my cheeks as I cough. 'Please tell them Alex Raffety could be inside!'

The officer's face softens, but he doesn't move. 'We're doing everything we can.'

Another section of roof collapses inward with a crash, sparks spraying high into the sky. The voices of the crowd rise.

'No one could survive that.'

'Do you think Alex was inside?'

Another voice replies: 'His car is there.'

I scan the car park, squinting to look beyond the smoke stinging my eyes and the bright orange flames. They're right. Tucked beside the building being swallowed up by the fire is the unmistakable mound of Alex's Land Rover.

'No,' I whisper.

Then I'm coughing again, the smoke catching in my lungs as I struggle to draw in each breath. This can't be happening. Alex was fine this morning. I saw him leave. He told me he was going to try to work. *'I'll probably stay there late.'*

I thought it was an excuse. A way to let us both off the hook for spending another night together. Maybe he walked home. That's possible, isn't it?

He could be at the house right now. He could be OK.

I have to know.

I glance back at the blaze. It will be hours before the fire crew can get inside, so I turn and run again, this time uphill, lungs burning, praying I'll find Alex safe in bed, unaware his studio is burning down. My trainers slip on the damp pavement as I climb the narrow road towards Cliffview House. I'm breathless by the time I reach the driveway. Just ahead, a car is pulling away, headlights bright against the night sky, but I barely notice as I sprint to the front door.

Every light is off, the house black and still. I fumble with the key Alex gave me, hands shaking. My voice hoarse from the smoke as I step into the hall and call out, 'Alex?'

Nothing. The only sound is the echo of my footsteps as I hurry from room to room.

'Alex?' I shout again.

In the kitchen, his coffee cup still sits on the counter where he left it this morning, like he hasn't been back since. His sketchbook lies open on the table, a half-finished drawing of a valley. But there's no sign of him.

He's not here.

Which means...

I can't bring myself to think the next words. Instead, I step outside and hurry back to the town. The night air feels cold against my hot cheeks. There's nothing I can do, no reason to go back to the fire, but I can't be anywhere else either.

The crowd has doubled since I left, voices high with shock and excitement.

'Poor man.'

'He was devastated after Bryony's accident.'

'Do you think he set the fire on purpose?'

'It wouldn't surprise me.'

Alex wouldn't kill himself. No way. He was sad. Grieving, yes. But he wouldn't have done this.

Hours pass in a blur of smoke and shouted orders. The firefighters move in and out of the cordon. Someone presses a takeaway cup of sugary tea into my hands.

I stare into the dark where the studio once stood, the fire finally dying down to a glow. The fire has to be an accident. He would never burn the studio down and destroy something he'd built from nothing. Except...

My thoughts jump ahead. I want to pull them back, but it's too late. Alex would never set a fire like this. But Bryony would.

From the moment I realised the extent of Bryony's lie, I've been trying to understand why she'd go to such lengths to manipulate me and fake her death. There was no abuse, no reason to need to escape Alex. I'd wondered over dinner with Alex, in the haze of wine, if Bryony had faked her death out of spite. I'd wondered if she'd wanted to hurt Alex by leaving him in the most awful, definitive way because he'd told her he was thinking of leaving her.

It had sounded crazy. Extreme, even for Bryony with her vindictive streak. But what if there was more to it? What if she wanted to do more to Alex than hurt him? What if she faked her death because she wanted to kill him and make sure she got away with it?

The thought comes hard and fast, and the more I think about it, the more it makes sense. Bryony set the fire. She planned this from the start. She would've been humiliated if Alex left her. It would've destroyed her status in Skelwick. She'd no longer be the wife of the famous artist. So she acted first.

She faked her death. Not to run. Not to escape him. But to come back and kill him. She must've known they'd suspect Alex's death would be suicide after the loss of his muse. And even if they landed on foul play, she could never be a suspect.

You can't be a murderer if you're already dead...

THIRTY-SEVEN

SIXTEEN YEARS EARLIER – THE RESCUE

Bryony

The second the bright white spotlight lands on my face and the orange boat moves alongside us – as soon as strong arms are hauling us out of the water and into the coastguard dinghy – the words fall out through chattering teeth and frozen relief. 'I tried to save her.'

The crew are distracted. Working fast. A foil blanket is wrapped around my shoulders, another over my legs. But the attention is on Jess's limp body lying near my feet. Of course it is. Jess is always stealing the attention. It's what she does.

'Is my sister OK?' I blurt, voice lost to the rumble of the engine. The smell of diesel fills the air.

No one replies. No one listens.

The boat moves with a jerk, and then we're cutting through the sea, bouncing across the waves as spray needles my already ice-cold face. I wiggle my toes. They hurt but respond. For a long time, I sit on the bench of the dinghy, staring into the pitch-black sea. Then the bay comes into view. A scattering of distant lights around the harbour and the flashing siren of an ambulance waiting on the shore.

Beside me, Jess isn't moving. Her hair is slicked across her cheeks, eyelashes spiked with salt, and even in the darkness, her lips look a strange shade of blue. One of the crew is kneeling over her.

The moment we reach land, one of the men scoops Jess into his arms and rushes her to the ambulance. The other crew members cut the engine and moor the boat. Frustration burns through me as I climb out of the boat myself and stand on the shore. No one cares that I'm here too. That Jess wouldn't be alive if it wasn't for me.

'My little sister moved,' I say, voice loud. I add a choked sob for effect. 'I told her not to, but she didn't listen. The wind caught the sail, and the boom swung at her. She fell overboard, and I... I didn't know what to do, so I jumped in after her. I held her up. I stopped her from sinking. I tried to save her.' Emotions choke my throat for real this time. That burn of frustration. Why is no one listening to me?

Then a gloved hand lands heavy on my shoulder. 'You did really well, Bryony,' one of the coastguards says. 'Most adults wouldn't have done what you did. You're a brave girl. Your sister wouldn't be here if it wasn't for you.'

'Will she be OK?' I ask in a faltering voice.

'I don't know, love. But she's alive right now. And that's because of you.'

I let my eyes grow wide and the tears fall. Real tears. Crying for the hours in the sea. I cry for how scared I was. And I cry with relief that I'm alive. And then I wipe my cheeks and wrap the foil tighter so it rustles with each shiver, and I let the relief settle into victory.

It worked.

For a moment earlier, when I'd stood on the deck of the

Calypso and watched Jess's body sink beneath the waves, I'd thought about leaving her to sink. The indecision had pulled and tugged. But then I'd always have been the person who took my sister sailing and didn't bring her back. Jumping in was a risk. One that almost cost me my life. But now things have worked out better than ever. Tomorrow, there will be no stupid art exhibition. No trip to London with the whole world patting Jess on the head for her birds or whatever else she painted. Tomorrow, there will be nurses and doctors, and everyone will see me as a hero. I'll probably be given an award, and Mum can wear a new dress for me.

One of the ambulance crew finally steps towards me, checking I'm not hurt, guiding me to the vehicle to sit on the bench next to where Jess is lying.

'I'm OK,' I say. 'It was Jess that fell in. I had to jump in after her.'

'Best to get you checked out anyway. You were both in the water for a long time.'

'I couldn't leave her to die.'

'You were incredibly brave. We'll look after you both from here. Your parents will meet us at the hospital.'

I sit back on the bench and close my eyes as the ambulance pulls away. The thought of our parents and the hospital steadies me. My body shakes with cold, and my mind hums with certainty. I saved Jess's life. And now Jess will owe me for the rest of hers.

I wanted to hurt her today. To make sure she knocked her head and got a scare. Just enough to make it hard for her tomorrow on the trip and during the exhibit. I didn't think she'd fall overboard, but it's all worked out. Better than I could've expected in fact. Finally, Jess has got what she deserves. She's stolen our parents' attention for as long as I can remember. Always playing the worried little girl in need of comfort, always tugging on Mum's hand, always soaking up the praise. Every tear, every anxious frown ensured there was never any time left for me. Dad isn't so bad. He takes my side when Mum tells me off for nothing. But Jess isn't stupid. She's been playing the part of the sweet, innocent sister from the day she was born. I'm tired of being the forgotten one.

And I've never been one to forgive and forget. If someone crosses me, they pay. Always.

THIRTY-EIGHT

Jess

The knock on Mum's front door comes the following morning just as I finish getting dressed. My hair is still damp, clinging to my neck, and I can't seem to scrub away the smell of smoke that clings to my skin. The shower has done little to help, as though the smoke has seeped inside my bones. I can still taste the ashy scratch in the back of my throat and hear the shouts of the fire crew and the crowd.

'No one could survive that.'

When I open the door, Sergeant Miller and PC Hughes are standing on the step. They look like they haven't slept either. Miller's face is grey, lined deeper like he's aged five years in a week. Hughes doesn't look much better. Both have eyes rimmed with red, and like me they still smell of the lingering smoke.

'Good morning, Miss Waters. May we come in?' Miller asks.

'Call me Jess,' I say automatically, stepping aside.

It feels like a lifetime ago that they came to Cliffview House to tell Alex that Bryony was presumed drowned. Was that really less than two weeks ago?

I lead them into the living room, unable to bring myself to ask why they're here. The answer feels inevitable, and I'm not ready to hear it.

It's hard not to compare the living room to Cliffview House. The room looks bare without the family photos and Mum's trinkets. Home but not home. Familiar but missing something.

They decline my offer of coffee and we sit – them on one sofa, me on the other.

Miller clears his throat. 'We're trying to track down the next of kin for Mr Raffety. Are you aware of any family members? Parents or a brother or sister?'

'He was orphaned as a child and grew up in foster care. Bryony was his only family.' I swallow, unable to stop the question from forming. 'Is he OK?'

Tears build in my eyes. I know the answer. If Alex was OK, these officers wouldn't be sitting in my living room asking about next of kin.

Miller shares a look with Hughes before setting his gaze on me. 'Even though you're not technically next of kin, Jess, I believe you may be the closest Mr Raffety has to it, and so I'm here to inform you that unfortunately a body was found at the scene of the fire, and the deceased is believed to be Alex Raffety—'

'No.' My throat closes. Alex is dead. I knew this was coming, I knew the odds, and yet the truth hits like a physical blow.

Miller continues gently, in that steady, professional tone that only makes the words worse. 'A formal identification has not yet taken place. An investigation is underway to confirm the identity using dental records and DNA. This process may take some time, particularly due to the chemicals present in the studio, which acted as an accelerant in the fire. That level of heat means fingerprint analysis isn't possible.'

He reaches into a sealed evidence bag and holds it up. 'We did recover this ring from the body.'

He passes me a small evidence bag. Inside is a band of gold. The metal is tarnished, but the inscription inside is still visible: *Yours forever B x*

The sight of it cracks something inside my chest. I remember the day Bryony slid it onto Alex's finger – the way she smiled at him, that glitter of triumph in her eyes; how happy he'd looked. Barely able to stop taking photos of her to say his vows.

The tears come fast. Whatever the truth is to his or Bryony's versions of their relationship, he was still my friend first. The man who saw beauty in broken things and debris.

I grit my teeth, fighting the swell of emotions. I can't make sense of a world where he doesn't exist anymore. 'Do you know how the fire started?' I manage to ask.

'Not at this time,' Miller replies. 'There will be a full investigation. But given the circumstances, and after the tragic nature of Mrs Raffety's own death last week...' He pauses, choosing his words. 'We are considering the possibility of suicide.'

My chest tightens. I shake my head before I can stop myself. 'No. No, Alex wouldn't – he wouldn't do that.'

Miller gives me the kind of look reserved for people too fragile to argue with. 'We'll wait for the fire report before drawing any conclusions. And we would like to arrange a convenient time with you to collect some personal items of Mr Raffety's from his home to test them for DNA. A toothbrush often works best.'

I nod. 'Paulina, their housekeeper, will be at the house this morning. She can let you in.'

'Thank you,' Miller replies.

Hughes leans forward slightly. 'Can you tell us the last time you saw Mr Raffety?' she asks.

'Yesterday morning,' I reply. 'I'd been staying at the house, helping him after... after Bryony. He said he wanted to try to work. I told him I was going to visit my mum. She has dementia and is in the care home in town. He said he'd probably stay late at the studio.'

Miller nods, jotting something in his notebook. Hughes avoids my eyes. I can almost see their minds turning over what I've told them and drawing their conclusions. Alex wanted to be alone. He'd been devastated after Bryony's death.

They stand in unison.

'Thank you, Jess,' Miller says. 'We'll keep you informed once we have more information.'

I walk them to the door, pulse drumming in my ears. I should tell them everything. They need to know Bryony is still alive. But the shock of Alex's death is still clinging to every breath, and I let them leave with the same soft words and tired faces they arrived with. I close the door behind them and press my back to it, the quiet ringing in my ears. I catch my reflection in the hall mirror. I'm pale and hollow-eyed. My throat feels sore, like I've swallowed glass as well as smoke.

Alex didn't kill himself. I don't care what those officers think. I'm almost certain now that my sister did this, but I didn't tell them because... because if I helped her fake her own death, am I also complicit in his murder?

Did I do this too?

My legs feel weak beneath me, and I move to sink down on the bottom stair, my head in my hands, feeling sick and adrift from my life. I'd planned to tell Alex the truth, but now he's dead and I can't. I'd planned to tell the police, but I can't risk being arrested for murder, not yet anyway.

I have to find Bryony first. She's out there somewhere, alive, watching this unfold, still controlling everything. I helped her get away with her own death, and now Alex's too. I will tell the police everything, but only after I can also tell them where to find Bryony. Because if I'm going to be arrested, then so is she.

I won't let her get away with this. The more I think about it, the more certain I am that Bryony faked her death so she could kill Alex without anyone suspecting her. He was planning to leave her, but she got there first.

I take a steadying breath and wipe the tears from my face. It's time to stop letting her control me. And suddenly I know exactly where to start searching for her – the last place she was seen.

THIRTY-NINE

Jess

Despite my resolve, it takes me three days to find the courage to step onto the wooden gangplanks over the water. I've walked down to the harbour each morning since the fire and the police at my door. I make it to the bottom stone step, staring at the *Odysseus* as she rocks gently in the water, willing myself to move. Telling myself that if Bryony hid anything – any clue to where she's gone – it would be on that boat. The one place that was truly hers. I've already searched Cliffview House top to bottom, except for the basement. The keys to the padlocks are nowhere, tucked inside Alex's pocket when he left the house that morning and now lost to the fire, I guess.

If there's anything to find, it will be on the *Odysseus*. And yet, every time I try to reach the boat, crippling fear grips me. My gaze drags down to the water and I'm frozen in place. Ice floods my body, a cold that lives in my chest, dragging me back to that day. The slap of waves against the wooden beams. It feels like the sea is waiting for me, ready to swallow me whole all over again.

In the last three days, the world has kept turning, just like after Bryony left. Wreaths have filled the car park beside the charred remains of Alex's studio – lilies, roses, handwritten cards, the town's grief displayed for all to see. A solicitor called me yesterday – the same one I was supposed to meet with Alex. His voice calm and professional, telling me I'm the executor and sole beneficiary of the Raffety estate. Just like that, I'm the owner of Cliffview House, of everything that once belonged to Alex and Bryony. It should feel like freedom. I thought money would save me. Wipe the debt I owe the bank, pay for Mum's care home indefinitely. A chance for me to start again. To rebuild the life I lost when the hotel went under. But I can't stop thinking of the cost.

I've lied to the police, withheld evidence and crossed so many lines I've lost sight of where the truth even lies. And when the life insurance payout comes through, I'll be committing fraud on top of everything else. It feels like every decision I've made has tied me tighter to Bryony's deceit. And that's just half of it. Because I no longer have a sister. I no longer have Alex. Liam still isn't answering his phone. His parents reported him missing. I hope he's OK. Maybe he's finally gone travelling, like he always wanted to.

Bryony's shadow still stretches over everything. I'm certain now that when the legalities are over, when Alex's death is settled and the insurance is paid, she'll reach out. She'll expect me to hand that money over. To be the obedient sister I've always been.

Bryony has won. Again.

The wind picks up, warmer now than it has been since I arrived. The cafés along the promenade hum with life again – their ice cream machines carried onto the pavements. Buckets and spades hang from the awnings, waiting for children to beg their parents to buy them. Life, relentless and normal, pushes on.

And all I can think is if I don't do something – if I don't take control – I'll always be trapped in Bryony's game. Which is why I have to find her. Confront her. About her lies to me. About Alex's death. And about Liam. What did she say to him that made him change his mind about visiting me and stop calling his parents?

That thought is what finally pushes me forward. My heart rattles against my ribs, my fear screams in my thoughts, but I take the first step from stone to wood, and stand over the water.

Then I'm walking fast, head high, refusing to look down. The keys to the *Odysseus* bite into my palm where I'm gripping them too tightly.

I reach the berth and freeze again. Every nerve in my body screams at me not to step aboard. My right temple throbs with pain. The last time I was on a boat, I nearly died. I grit my teeth, fighting the nausea and the dread clawing up through me. Because that thought isn't true. The last time I set foot on a boat, Bryony almost killed me. That's the truth. Not an accident. Not the boat. Bryony. My sister.

I take a breath and climb aboard.

The *Odysseus* rocks beneath my weight. My stomach lurches, memories colliding with the present. A flash of white metal swinging, the crack against my temple, cold water. I grip the railing, whispering to myself, 'This isn't the *Calypso*.'

And then I unlock the hatch and move carefully down the narrow steps into the cabin. My body is shaking, legs barely holding me upright. I swear I can feel the sea rising, its claws hitting the hull, swaying the boat and wanting to grab at me, drag me under. Nausea swills in my belly, but I refuse to let the fear take over.

The cabin is compact, everything in its place. Shelves lined with books on sailing and Greek mythology, bottles of Bryony's favourite wine tucked into the secured racks. I open one of the seat benches and find neatly folded clothes inside – spare shorts, a soft jumper, a sailing jacket, life vests.

I search the few storage spaces, and hope dies. There's nothing here. Suddenly, I wonder what I really expected to find. A letter confessing everything she's done? A map with a red circle showing me exactly where to find her?

I turn towards the last narrow locker. At first, there's nothing. Just a coil of rope, a waterproof bag. I pull it out and beneath it a jacket catches my eye. Crumpled fabric in a familiar dark green.

I tug it free. Shake it out. For a moment, my mind refuses to see what's right in front of me. Then the sunlight streaks through the small window at the right angle and hits the frayed cuff where the stitching is loose after it was caught on a door handle. My stomach drops. This is Liam's jacket. The one he wore every day, no matter the weather. The one I teased him about. How he needed an entire wardrobe of just this jacket because he loved it so much.

What is it doing here?

I search the pockets. In one, I find a thick white business card with gold lettering. The kind of business card that radiates money.

Goldman & Holt PR. There's a London address, and a name and contact details – Dan Jenkins. I trace the embossed letters, wondering why Liam would have this. Was he thinking of rebranding the Kilstern? Did he think there was a way to salvage what we'd lost? It doesn't fit. We both put everything into the business and came out with nothing. He wouldn't have had the money for an expensive PR campaign. And what would be the point when we'd sold the manor building and everything inside?

I shove the card into my pocket to look at again later. In the next pocket, my fingers brush the hard plastic of a phone. It's scuffed around the edges, familiar in its weight and shape. I'd know it anywhere. Liam's phone. The same one that was always in his hand. Always. There's no reason it should be here, unless—

I stop breathing, lungs frozen as my legs give way beneath me. My mind races, reaching back to that moment on the harbour wall, when I watched Bryony sail out to sea, remembering the way she was smiling. The way it seemed like she was talking to someone in the cabin.

I told myself it was a trick of the light. That I was imagining it, like I did the day of the accident all those years ago when my nightmares made me believe there was someone else on the boat with us. In a way, there was. Me and the sister I loved, and the sister who wanted to hurt me. Maybe even kill me.

For a moment last week, I even tried to convince myself that Alex was on the *Odysseus* with Bryony. That he'd killed her and come back to shore to go through with a plan of his own. But it wasn't Alex. And it wasn't my imagination. It was Liam. And now he's gone. His phone and jacket left behind.

The last voicemail he left me replays in my mind. His voice, urgent, desperate: '... *I'm coming to see you. I have something to tell you. It's going to be hard to hear, but I can't keep this to myself.*'

The blood drains from my face. I'd thought he and Bryony might have had an affair, but it's so much more than that.

I tuck his phone into my pocket and move the jacket. Something else falls free, hitting the floor with a jingle of metal. It's a set of keys. Not for the boat. And not ones I've ever seen Liam carry. But I have seen a set just like this. I took them from the floor beside Alex's jeans and used them to enter the basement. Padlock keys. If these are a second set of keys to the basement, then that's where I'll search next.

The thought should propel me forward. The urge to get off

this boat rises up, but still I stay sitting. Bitterness burns the back of my throat. Grief, rage, disbelief all tangled together. Liam was with Bryony the day she left. It wasn't her new life Bryony was setting up. It was *their* new life. Hers and Liam's. He was on the boat with her that day. He has gone with her.

FORTY

Jess

My grief and shock shift to anger as I stride up the hill to Cliffview House. The sun is sinking fast in the sky, taking the warmth with it, leaving the wind to whip at my face. I barely notice. My thoughts consume me. I'm no closer to finding Bryony, but I am closer to answers.

Bryony didn't just leave me here, complicit and alone, tangled in her games and her lies. She also took from me. She stole Liam. Every visit to the hotel, every overnight stay. I thought it was for me. I thought she understood that I couldn't get away to Skelwick as often as I wanted, that she came because she missed me.

Stupid!

Bryony never lifted a finger for anyone unless it benefited her. My love and gratitude for what I thought she'd done that day sixteen years ago blinded me to the truth. Mum's words to me when she thought I was Bryony ring in my head like a curse. '*You always wanted what Jess had.*'

But it was more than that. Yes, she wanted what I had. But

she also wanted to physically take it from me. It wasn't enough that she took Alex. She wanted Liam too. That's why she kept visiting. I can't wrap my head around the details of their affair. I can't make it fit with the man I loved, but before I saw him drunk and kissing a complete stranger in our hotel bar, I'd have thought him incapable of that too.

Somehow, Bryony convinced him to leave his life behind and run away with her. Did they both come back to kill Alex, or was that all Bryony's doing? I grit my teeth so hard the pain stretches across my jaw. My breath comes hard and uneven. My pace quickens. The betrayal twists inside me like barbed wire as I remember how suddenly Bryony reappeared in Skelwick at twenty-one. For the five years she'd lived with Dad on the other side of the country, she'd never mentioned plans to return. I remember we'd spoken on the phone the previous week. I'd finally told her about Alex. I'd kept our friendship secret for months, not wanting to burst the bubble of happiness I'd found. For the first time in years, I was no longer lonely or sad. But I couldn't keep it to myself any longer. I had to tell her how happy I was.

She came home the following week, and within a month, Alex was in love with her. No longer my friend but Bryony's boyfriend. She took Alex. And now she's taken Liam. My throat closes. Tears spill onto my cheeks. How could I have been so stupid? So clueless? How could I have not seen this?

I'm lost in thought, anger and hurt still pounding through my veins as I walk faster. The sun has sunk lower, a smear of dusty pink over the horizon. I don't see the car until it's too late. An engine roars. Headlights flare.

I freeze, one foot off the kerb as a black Land Rover swerves around the corner, bearing down on me. The horn blares, and I stumble back, close enough to feel the heat of the engine beneath the bonnet. I hit the ground, palms scraping the tarmac, looking up to see the Land Rover speeding away, taillights disappearing into the falling dark. I catch only a flash through the windscreen – a blur of hair caught in the last of the light.

A woman.

Bryony?

Tears sting my eyes as I shout after the car, my voice hoarse, swallowed by the wind, 'Haven't you taken enough?'

FORTY-ONE

Jess

My heart is still racing as I step into the house. The skin on my palms stings where I hit the tarmac, tiny stones digging in. I imagined Bryony watching from afar the fallout of her presumed drowning and the fire that killed Alex. Now I wonder if she's stayed closer all along. My mind races back to the night of the fire. My sprint to Cliffview House to search for Alex. The headlights of a car pulling away, and the Land Rover that I've caught following me or watching me since my return to Skelwick.

I close the front door quietly behind me, though there's no one left here to hear it. The air feels cold, the heating no longer turned on. It's only been four days since Alex walked out the front door and never returned, but already there's an empty feel to the place.

At the door under the stairs, I hesitate, fear spiking in my blood, before forcing myself forward. There's no one to stop me. No one to say I'm snooping. No one down there to hurt me.

This house belongs to me now, and I'm going to find out

what's in that freezer once and for all. If these keys don't work, I'll dig through the old tools Dad left behind when he moved away and find a pair of bolt cutters.

I ignore the unease prickling the back of my neck as I slide one of the keys into the padlock and release the catch. 'It's just a basement,' I whisper, but the words bounce back to me, sounding small and shaky.

The hinges creak as I push the door open, the sound loud in the silence. I flick the light switch, and a single bulb flickers to life, casting the cement floor and the room in a dim yellow glow, then I force myself to step inside.

Instantly, something feels different. I scan the room, trying to remember what I saw when I was here the other night. The shelves look the same. Rows of paint pots, tools and brushes lined neatly in place. A wine rack sits below, every bottle identical: Bryony's favourite Pinot Noir.

I turn slowly, my gaze fixing on the huge white chest freezer. And that's when it hits me. The hum. The low mechanical buzz that filled the room and the entire house, that niggled and annoyed me for weeks, is gone. The freezer is silent, the wall plug discarded on the floor beside it.

At some point after the night I crept down here and Alex caught me, someone else entered the basement and turned it off. I've been in and out of this house all week, hunting for clues, for anything that might lead me to Bryony. But I can't remember hearing the sound again. Not once. Why was it on when Alex said it was empty? And why go to the trouble to come back down here to turn it off?

I take a few steps closer. The smell hits me before I reach it. The sharp tang of bleach scraping at the back of my throat. I draw closer. The drops I told myself were paint are gone. The white surround and chrome handle shine from a recent clean. My heart starts to beat harder as I reach for the freezer handle. I hesitate, bracing myself, but not sure why.

The lid sticks at first then finally lifts with a whoosh. The smell of bleach floods out, choking me. My eyes sting, and I turn away, trying to breathe in air not clogged with fumes. Then I turn back and stare inside. At nothing.

The freezer is empty. A huge empty space. No ice. No shelves. Just a gleaming white interior, streaked faintly where it's been wiped down. My pulse refuses to slow. What was in here before?

The bleach scent hits me again, my head spinning with it. I step back, stumbling a little, my hip knocking the shelf behind me. The wine bottles clink. One sways, but I catch it before it can tumble to the floor and smash.

I pick it up, running my finger over the label, tracing the curve of the lettering. My throat tightens.

'She wouldn't drink anything else.'

I straighten slowly, clutching the bottle in my hand, fighting through the dizziness to grab at the realisation skirting the edges of my mind. Maybe I don't know what was in that freezer. Maybe I don't have all the answers. But I do know exactly how to find my sister.

FORTY-TWO

Jess

I'm back in Bryony's clothes: tailored cream trousers and a soft cashmere jumper the colour of bone, Gucci sunglasses perched on my styled hair, stepping out of her house and over to her car.

It took two minutes on Google to find the wine supplier who stocks Bryony's favourite Pinot Noir, and another ten minutes to charm them over the phone. I pretended to be a hotelier looking for a new supplier, the sort who uses words like exclusive partnership and long-term arrangement. The man on the other end had been eager to talk business. But what I need from him is more delicate. I can't just ask over the phone for a list of clients he's supplying wine to and expect him to hand it over. Better to try in person. Which is why I'm dressed in Bryony's clothes, the keys for her Mercedes gripped in my hand, stepping into a fresh spring morning that promises to be warm.

The last few days have crawled by while I waited for this meeting. I sorted through the last of Mum's things, took boxes to the charity shop, sat with her at the care home with an open packet of our favourite chocolate biscuits. I spoke to the police again about Alex. The fire investigation team have ruled the fire intentional. The police are set on suicide. Then I spoke to the coroner. They're waiting on the DNA analysis from his toothbrush before formally identifying the body as Alex. Until then, I can't arrange the funeral. Bryony's case is different. A presumed drowning is a legal mess. The life insurance company have started their own investigation, and a declaration of death is still likely to be months away.

I wonder if Bryony realised it would be so complicated. If she thought faking her death would be as easy as vanishing and the insurer paying out. But I no longer care about her plans. I'm making my own now.

I'm going to find Bryony and Liam. I'm going to look them in the eye and demand the truth.

Then I'm going to call Sergeant Miller and tell him my sister is alive, and she's been lying to everyone. She'll be charged with perverting the course of justice and wasting police time, then Alex's murder. I could be implicated too, but that's a risk I'm willing to take. I'm done lying for her. Done covering for her. Done being her pawn. This time, Bryony will pay for what she's done.

I unlock the car, about to climb in, when the low growl of an engine swells behind me. I turn, catching the flash of black paintwork glinting in the sunlight. Instinct takes over, and I'm running into the road before I can think. It's felt like this car has been following me for weeks, scaring me, almost mowing me down. If Bryony's behind that wheel, then our reckoning has come early. I'm done hiding. I step straight into its path, and the car screeches to a stop as I slam both palms onto the bonnet, barely breathing, heart stuttering.

The driver climbs out, shouting, 'What the hell?' at me.

It's not Bryony. Or Liam. It's a woman a few years older than me. Long blonde hair. A woman who behind the thick eyelashes and shimmering make-up, I recognise instantly. 'Helen?' I narrow my eyes at Kelly's daughter.

'Jess, I almost hit you! What were you doing?'

I shake my head. 'What am I doing? What are you doing? Is this your car? Have you been following me?'

Guilt creases the lines of her face. Her eyes widen. I have my answer. 'I… I'm sorry.' There's something suddenly fragile in the way she apologises.

My anger softens. 'Look, why don't you pull over? You're blocking the road, and I think we need to talk. I'd like to understand why you've been trying to scare me.'

Her mouth drops open. She's about to speak, but another car has appeared from the bend. She nods and hurries back to her car, manoeuvring it to the side of the road and killing the engine before stepping onto the driveway.

'I wasn't trying to scare you,' she says.

'You parked outside Mum's house in the middle of the night and tried to get in the front door.'

She shakes her head, blonde hair swishing, looking aghast. 'I wasn't trying to get in. I was…' She sighs, cringing a little. 'Look, I can see how you might've thought I was trying to scare you, and I'm really sorry about that, but honestly, that's not what I was trying to do.'

'What were you doing then?'

'That night, I'd written you a letter. I was parked outside trying to find the courage to post it through the letter box. I almost went through with it, even opening the letter box, which I guess is what you heard. The truth is, I'm getting divorced. I don't know if Mum told you.'

'No,' I reply. 'She only said you wanted to move back to Skelwick.'

Helen nods. 'I do, but it's because of the divorce. I want to be close to Mum and have some childcare help when I need it. I have two young children, and I don't think my ex is going to stay involved in their lives.'

'I'm sorry, but what's this got to do with me? Why have you been following me?'

'I've been trying to pluck up the courage to talk to you. I always thought you were nice, but I didn't know if you'd become more like Bryony over the years. She made my life a living hell after a teacher caught her cheating from one of my test papers. Like it was my fault. I used to let her copy me all the time. I didn't care. Did you know she wrote a letter of complaint to my last employer? This was before I had children. I was working as a sales rep, and she found out and tried to pretend I was selling illegal drugs on the side. It was insane. HR knew it was rubbish, but that didn't mean people didn't look at me differently.'

I'm not even surprised anymore that Helen's version of what happened is different to Bryony's, or that Bryony can hold a grudge for so long.

'Anyway,' Helen continues, 'I want to move back to Skelwick and rent a place, but with all the Airbnbs, there are hardly any houses to rent. Mum said we can live with her, but her house is small, and the kids and the toys, well... I think we need our own space. I've been trying to find the courage to talk to you and your sister. I followed Bryony the week she had her accident. I wanted to plead with her to forgive me. I knew even if I found a place in Skelwick, she wouldn't make it easy for me to be back. But I chickened out anyway.'

I remember the Land Rover tailing Bryony's car after I left the care home. I thought they were following me, but of course, I was pretending to be Bryony then.

'The truth is I wanted to plead with you both to let me rent your mum's house. I know I can't pay as much as a holiday let, but I'd rent all year round, and I'd be a good tenant.'

I almost laugh with how wrong I've been. All along, the Land Rover driver was Helen. A desperate woman who wants to live near her mum. Kelly's questions about my plans for the house and her disapproval make sense now too.

'It's OK if you don't want to,' Helen says quietly.

I think for a moment. Turning Mum's house into a holiday rental had been my plan when I'd returned to Skelwick. A way to earn money for her care. As the weeks have passed, the idea has felt harder to stomach, especially when it felt like moving into Bryony's guesthouse wasn't an option. But a family living in Mum's house – Helen and her children – feels good. It won't be the same money, but it will be less admin, and with Cliffview House soon to be mine, it makes sense to rent Mum's house to Helen.

The thought of living in Bryony's house with that unsettling shadow of tension turns my stomach, but there's still the small guesthouse in the garden for now. I don't need much space, and after everything I've done for Bryony and all the lies she's thrown at me, the thought of helping Helen feels good.

'When do you need to move in?' I ask.

Helen's face lights up. 'Whenever we can. I don't want to rush you.'

'It's a bit tired in places still,' I warn her. 'But you're welcome to move in any time. Just give me a few days to move the last of our things out.'

'Thank you,' Helen says, the words coming on an exhale of relief.

We talk through the logistics of a move for a few more minutes before Helen jogs back to her car and I check the time, realising I'm going to be late for the meeting with the wine-seller if I don't hurry. I've told Helen she can move in after the weekend. It's two days away. No time at all, and yet by then I hope to have found Bryony and Liam and gone to the police.

But as I climb into the Mercedes and start the engine, a thought gnaws at me – I was wrong about the Land Rover. What else have I been wrong about?

FORTY-THREE

Jess

I sit in the driver's seat of the Mercedes, heart racing, stomach knotted tight, and stare at the open Maps app on my phone and the location the wine merchant gave me. It was easier than I could've hoped for. All I had to do was paint the right picture. *'I'm planning to launch a boutique hotel, and I want exclusive use of a particular vintage of Pinot Noir...'*

The merchant was a stocky man in his mid-twenties, with slicked-back hair and a rugby player's build. His eagerness for the business made him chatty.

'This particular vintage comes from a vineyard in Kent,' he'd said proudly, pouring a small measure for me to taste, unaware I'd been drinking the same wine for weeks. *'It's not well known, but as you'll notice, it's easy on the palate, light with blackberry undertones. We currently only supply a handful of regular clients, so giving you exclusive sale of this wine wouldn't be a problem.'*

'Won't the private clients mind?' I'd asked, pretending to

hesitate, biting my lip as though I cared. *'There are other merchants I can try if it's a problem.'*

He'd laughed, quick to placate me. *'We'll offer them a similar vintage. They'll barely notice.'*

'Still, to deprive them of the wine they love...' I'd trailed off, pretending to look thoughtful. *'How local are these private clients? If they were in Scotland, for instance, I wouldn't have a problem sharing.'*

'Let me check,' he'd said, tapping on the computer, eager to appease me. *'One's local and lives in the Skelwick Bay area. And we've just had another customer buy a case for delivery to'* – he'd paused, glancing at the computer – *'a village inland called Little Morton. Other than that, we've got two London-based clients and one in Leeds.'*

The minute he said the name of the village, I knew it had to be Bryony. Just as I realised the merchant had given me enough. I didn't need to find a way to see his computer screen; I didn't need an exact address. I'd wound up the meeting, thanked him and hurried to the car, adrenaline pumping as I drove a mile down the road before finding a lay-by to stop in.

Little Morton.

I stare at the icon on the map. It's an hour from Skelwick. A rural location. Just a collection of houses and farm buildings. No shop or pub. Nowhere for people to gather and gossip. Remote but close enough for Bryony to slip back to Skelwick when she needed to. Close enough to return to Skelwick, set a fire and vanish again. It has to be her.

But it suddenly feels too easy. Like I'm missing something.

I scramble for my coat, dumped on the back seat, pull out the business card I found in Liam's jacket and stare at the heavy gold lettering. Goldman & Holt PR. I turn it over, tracing the embossed name: Dan Jenkins. I don't even hesitate.

The phone rings twice before a clipped voice answers. 'Goldman and Holt PR. How may I help you?'

'I'd like to speak to Dan Jenkins please.'

'Hold please.'

Another three rings, and then a wary female voice. 'Hello?'

'Hi,' I say quickly. 'I'm trying to speak to Dan Jenkins.'

'May I ask what it's regarding, and your name?'

'My name is Jess Waters. My business partner, Liam—'

The woman cuts me off. 'Miss Waters, as I explained to your business partner, Dan Jenkins no longer works for Goldman and Holt. Our brand is about building businesses up, not destroying others in the process. I left several messages last week with your business partner to explain that we will no longer run campaigns designed to ruin the reputations of businesses and ask him to stop calling. If you speak to your business partner, please share this information with him and apologise on our behalf.'

'Ruin the reputations of businesses?' I repeat, but it's not really a question. An awful, sick clarity settles over me as I end the call without another word.

We could never understand it. The review in *The Times* had put us on the map. We'd been fully booked for months ahead. We even started talking about expanding, adding a spa in the grounds. We thought we'd made it. And then overnight, it had all collapsed. Cancellations, angry calls, a wave of online reviews accusing us of food poisoning, unclean rooms, rats in the corridors. It was all lies. But they came faster than we could fight them, flooding every review site, even our own website. Our suppliers pulled out. Our chef quit. Within weeks, every booking had cancelled and the dream was gone.

It never made sense, how it could fall apart so quickly. Except now it does. We were targeted.

'We will no longer run campaigns designed to ruin the reputations of businesses.'

It's so vicious. So personal. So... Bryony. And Liam knew. Pain burns in my chest. Sixteen years ago, she sabotaged my trip to London for the art exhibit and award I'd won, almost killing me in the process. And all these years later, she's done it again. Destroyed the one good thing I'd built. She's kept me close, so she can take every good thing I ever had and make it hers.

My right temple is aching. I'm exhausted, thirsty, strung out. My body is crying out for sleep and food and a moment to stop and think. But I need answers. I need to know why Bryony has done all this – hurt me, killed Alex, disappeared. I need to stare into Liam's eyes and ask him how he could betray me – betray both of us. Because he knew about this PR agency. He knew what Bryony was doing. Maybe he even helped her. He destroyed us. He kissed the woman in the bar because he knew I'd never forgive him. He ended our relationship. Then he left with Bryony. Not saying goodbye to me or even to his parents.

I remember the easy way they had with each other on Bryony's visits to the hotel. Always so friendly. Almost flirty. A hand resting on an arm. A lingering look. A smile. A wink. I told myself it was harmless. But however much it hurts, I have to admit the truth. There was nothing harmless about it. Because it's all too easy to imagine Liam falling for Bryony. After all, I'd seen it happen with Alex. Seen his attention turn from me to her without a backward glance.

And yet, even as all the pieces click into place, a small voice is asking me why Liam kept calling after our break-up. Why did he leave those pleading messages begging for forgiveness? Was it all just a game to him?

'I will find you,' I say in the stillness of the car as I tap in a quick search for holiday listings in Little Morton. There are only two.

The first is a selection of cottages on a farm where children can feed the chickens each morning and collect the eggs. The second is a six-bedroom house at the end of a lane, surrounded by fields, that's hired out to big families and hen parties. There's something oddly familiar about the pictures on the website, something that makes me tap the postcode into my phone and start to drive.

The sun is setting as the car's headlights pick up the sign for Little Morton, and the sense of familiarity returns even though I'm certain I've never been here before.

I park on the lane a hundred metres from the house and cut the engine. Worry rises, pinning me to the seat. I have no idea what Bryony will say or do when she sees me. She's dangerous. Last week, she set a fire that killed her husband. I don't know what else she's capable of, but even with the sting of Liam's betrayal, I know he'd never let her hurt me. I grip the steering wheel, wishing I'd gone home to change. Thought it through. Contacted the police.

I check my phone. No signal. I think of turning back, but there's still a part of me that wonders if I'm wrong, like I was about the Land Rover.

I have to see if this is the right house. I have to see Bryony and Liam for myself.

I climb out of the car to wind that carries the smell of damp earth and sweetened woodsmoke. Cautiously, I step towards the house. The sun has slipped below the horizon, and a dark gloom wraps around the trees and the house. There are no lights on at the front. No sign anyone is inside.

I creep along the edge of the drive, every crunch of my shoes too loud. At the side of the house, I press myself to the wall beneath a window that looks into a cosy living room with worn sofas and an open fire. There's movement. A male figure in shadow. I duck down and continue making my way round to the back of the house where a faint light glows onto the garden. My pulse drums, every breath faster than the last. Adrenaline makes my legs tremble.

I edge closer. Through the glass, I can make out a farmhouse-style kitchen with a slate-grey flagstone floor, pale oak cabinets and a dark-green Aga in the corner. A bottle of Pinot

Noir sits unopened on the table. Bryony's wine. I've found her.

My pulse pounds in my ears as I move to the back door. It's slightly ajar. I hesitate for a final second before stepping into a tidy mudroom with an open door into the kitchen. I hear footsteps. Movement. Someone has just walked in.

I hold my breath and take the final step and freeze. Standing by the sink is a familiar figure.

Not Bryony.

Not Liam.

All the air leaves my body in a whoosh. The world feels like it's crumbling beneath me. I manage to whisper, the name leaving my lips in a strangled cry.

'Alex.'

FORTY-FOUR

Jess

'Alex?' I say his name again. The shock is like slamming into the cold sea.

Alex is dead. He died in the fire. The police believed it was him. They're just waiting for DNA evidence to confirm it, but it was his car parked outside. His wedding ring found on the charred remains. Everyone knew it was him.

A sob catches in my throat. I don't know how to feel. Relieved he's not dead? Furious I was deceived again? Both. I clench my jaw and bunch my fists and force myself to stand frozen in the doorway, staring at the man I thought was gone forever.

Outside, the night closes in, pressing against the glass, as though trapping us in this impossible moment. But suddenly I know why Little Morton seemed familiar. I'd seen it in the landscape sketch Alex was working on the week Bryony disappeared.

'Jessie.' Alex's voice trembles with the same disbelief that knots inside me. 'How did you—'

'I thought you were dead,' I blurt.

Alex looks down at his feet, fingers fidgeting, reaching for the wedding ring that's no longer there. I picture it in the sealed bag Sergeant Miller showed me the day he and Hughes came to Mum's house, smelling of the fire, eyes sore from smoke.

Alex's voice is quiet, almost detached. There's something unreadable flickering in his eyes. 'Art is about what the viewer sees as much as what the artist creates.'

'You burned down your studio as art?' My voice shakes with a sudden fury. 'That's bullshit, Alex.'

'I told you I wanted to start again.'

'No,' I snap. 'You told me you didn't want the fame anymore. You didn't tell me you were going to fake your death and burn down your studio.'

He doesn't answer. His expression is a mixture of shame and weariness. A white-hot rage hisses beneath my skin. This was not a decision made on a whim. He planned this. He lied to me. Manipulated me. Convinced me he was dead.

'I watched your studio burn to the ground,' I say, my voice breaking. 'I stood there while firefighters risked their lives to save what was left. To try and save you. It wasn't art, Alex.'

He looks up, eyes glassy. 'I didn't want you to see that. You were supposed to be at home.'

'Hard to sleep through all the sirens.'

He takes a step closer, hands raised like he's approaching a wild animal. 'You don't understand.'

'Then explain it to me!' I reply.

My head feels light, dizzy, like I'm standing by that open freezer, inhaling the bleach fumes. I was so sure I'd find Bryony here with Liam. Cosying in that living room by the open fire, drinking their bloody wine and laughing at me.

Alex's eyes flash with something like pain. He stops approaching and sinks into one of the kitchen chairs, rubbing his face. 'It wasn't supposed to be this way,' he murmurs.

I stay standing, nails digging into my palms hard enough to sting. 'Then what way was it supposed to be?'

The shock of seeing Alex loosens its hold on me. My heart starts to beat so hard it feels like it's going to crack my ribs. From somewhere in the house, a door bangs.

'They found a body,' I whisper.

Alex's head snaps up. 'Jessie—'

'In your studio,' I push on. 'The chemicals you use to seal the wood acted as an accelerant.' I speak fast, needing to get the words out. 'They couldn't get fingerprints, but they took your toothbrush from the house for DNA and they're checking dental records.'

'There aren't any dental records,' he says quietly. 'I've always had good teeth. Never bothered with anything but regular check-ups.'

'But the toothbrush – they'll find out it's not you eventually.'

Alex's face shifts again, and I think I catch a flicker of guilt or fear or sorrow. I can't tell which. Bile scratches the back of my throat. 'I thought they'd take it,' he says, 'I... I swapped mine for another one.'

'Alex,' I hiss. 'Who died in that fire?'

'No one,' he says sharply, the word cracking in the air between us.

'Someone is dead.'

'They didn't die in the fire,' he replies in a low voice.

I almost cry out. Alex's cryptic reply barely makes sense. 'Who?' I ask again.

I'm so focused on Alex that it takes me a moment to notice the figure stepping into the kitchen from the living room.

'You always were slow to catch on.'

I turn, and my mouth drops open, and it feels like everything I thought I knew has turned to dust.

FORTY-FIVE

Jess

'Hello, by the way. How are you, Jess?'

For a moment, I don't breathe. Bryony stands in the doorway, utterly composed, hair now an icy blonde. Her skin looks luminous, no sign of the fear or the bruises she faked. The scent of her perfume reaches me, reminding me of our last desperate hug and everything I've done for her. I thought she loved me.

She raises an eyebrow, lips curving into that familiar, taunting smile. The one that used to mean *I know something you don't.*

'Nice outfit,' she says, tone light, playful, but there's an edge there, a glint of mockery as familiar as the perfume. 'Seems like you quite enjoyed pretending to be me.'

'What the hell is going on?' I reach to steady myself, gripping the door frame, trying to make sense of what I'm seeing. Bryony and Alex. Together. They faked their deaths. Together.

My head spins, thoughts scattering. Only one question remains. Why?

All my assumptions, everything I got wrong, feels like being kicked in the stomach. I thought Bryony wanted to disappear to escape Alex's abuse. Then to hurt him because he was leaving her. Then to come back and kill him. But I was wrong. So very wrong. Because Alex is here with her.

'I told you she'd work it out,' Alex says, looking up at Bryony from where he's sitting at the table. And despite everything that's happened and my world falling apart, I still catch the look of adoration in his eyes as he gazes at my sister. 'She knew you'd lied about us.'

Bryony sighs. Impatient but not angry. 'Well, I can't be right all the time. I underestimated our little Jess. I thought she'd be so happy with our money and our life that she wouldn't bother to look too closely. Especially after she'd failed so badly with her little hotel.' Her words are mocking and cruel. Still my sister but an ugly, horrid version. The real Bryony, I think. No more pretending.

'You hired a PR company to destroy the Kilstern.' I force the words out. Not a question but a statement. 'We didn't fail. You destroyed us.'

Glee dances in Bryony's eyes. She raises her hands and gives three slow claps. 'Oh goody,' she says. 'I'm so happy you know. I've honestly been bursting to tell you. It really did crush you, didn't it?'

I nod. There's no point pretending it didn't. And I'm too sick of all the lies to add another. 'Why?'

'Because you don't deserve to be happy, Jess,' she replies simply. 'You always got everything you ever wanted. It wasn't fair.'

I frown, not understanding. 'What are you talking about?'

'Don't act all innocent,' she spits, angry suddenly, like a mask has been pulled away. 'You stole Mum and Dad's attention from me the day you were born. You've always done it. Always playing the helpless little victim.'

Her voice twists into a cruel, childish whine: '*I'm scared of the dark.*' Another mocking lilt, sharper this time: '*Oh, I'm so worried all the time.*'

'I was a child,' I reply, choking back a sob. This is what she's thought for all these years?

'So was I,' she fires back. 'A happy child until you came along. Mum and Dad didn't care about me after that. You were always the favourite.'

She doesn't even realise how insane she sounds.

'I was banished. Five years I spent in therapy, being treated like I was a criminal. Then having to endure Dad looking at me with pity and suspicion every time I walked into a room, pretending he didn't resent the hell out of me for making him leave you and Mum. All for what? Because I saved your life.'

'Saved me?' I cry. 'The only reason I was in the water was because of you! I remember everything, Bry. You moved that tiller on purpose. You wanted to hurt me.'

'Someone had to knock the smug out of you,' she replies. 'If I'd heard one more person mention your pathetic art award, I was going to lose it.'

'Why didn't you just kill me then?' I shout. My breathing is fast. The anger and hurt feels overwhelming. This is unreal. But the devastating, pathetic truth seeps through the hurt. Everything Bryony has done. All the years of manipulation. The lies. The accident on the *Calypso*. The faked death. It all circles back to this: a childhood grudge she never outgrew. Jealousy twisted into something monstrous.

I want to leave. Run out the door and never come back. But there's more here than childhood jealousy and trying to hurt me.

'Why didn't you just let me drown that day?' I ask.

Bryony laughs. 'Believe me, I thought about it.'

Alex keeps his gaze on Bryony. 'Please, this isn't helping.'

'You're right, darling. It's all in the past now anyway.'

'What are we going to do about Jess?' he asks.

'Good question,' Bryony replies lightly, plucking the wine bottle from the table. The movement is effortless – the casual grace of someone fully in control. She crosses to the counter, opens a drawer and retrieves a corkscrew.

They're talking about me like I'm not here. Like they haven't made me as much a part of this as they are.

'Who is dead?' I ask again, my voice raw, cracking in the space between us. 'Who was in the studio when the fire started?'

Neither of them answer. Alex looks away. Bryony doesn't. The expression on her face is one I remember from our childhood. The one where she's asking if I'm really that stupid.

Pieces of truth start to snap into place in my head. My throat tightens until every breath is a rasping struggle. My stomach twists, bile rising again.

There's only one other person it could be.

FORTY-SIX

Jess

'No,' I whisper, shaking my head before the word even forms.

The dashcam footage flashes behind my eyes – Liam on her doorstep, his voice sharp, his shoulders rigid. The jacket I found on the *Odysseus*, the one with the frayed cuff. And his phone that never left his hand. That day in Skelwick, he was planning to visit me, after he'd been to see Bryony. But he never made it.

My hands begin to shake, vision tunnelling. I see it all again: the speck of red on Bryony's coat the day she turned up at my door, eyes wide and terrified. The same day Liam went to see her. I'd told myself it was paint, like the dark droplets on the freezer lid in the basement. The freezer Alex said was empty. The one that was still on.

The truth crashes over me. Goosebumps prickle my skin. All this time I've been thinking of Bryony. Stealing Liam from me, destroying our hotel – they're exactly the kinds of things she would do. But in the hurt of our break-up, I didn't stop to consider Liam. I imagined him falling madly in love with Bryony, like Alex did. How could I have been so wrong?

Liam would never destroy the Kilstern. He worked as hard as I did to make our dreams come true. He wasn't calling the London PR agency because he'd hired them. He was calling because he'd discovered the campaign and had confronted them about it. Liam, who called his parents every Sunday without fail. Who always knew exactly what to say to smooth out my worry. '*And third of all, I love you.*'

The man who promised, '*I'll never stop fighting for us.*' And meant it.

A wave of guilt hits me. Not just for how wrong I was about Liam. But for my own actions and the part I played in our break-up. I should've listened to him. Trusted him. Should never have taken that loan. That was the first step to the end for us, and it was me who took it.

Bryony waves a lazy hand in my direction, her expression almost bored. 'I'm guessing, from your little freak-out, that you've figured it out.'

'Liam.' His name is a whisper, a plea. Even as I say it, I'm praying I'm wrong. Begging the universe, *Please, not him. Please, not this.* But then Alex exhales, a ragged, broken sound, and I know.

He slumps against the table, rubbing his hands over his face. 'We're so sorry, Jess. It was an accident.'

But my eyes are locked on Bryony. The faint smile playing on her lips tells me everything I need to know. There was no accident. Not with her.

'What happened?' My voice cracks.

She doesn't look at me. She's busy stabbing the corkscrew into the wine bottle, twisting it with sharp, impatient turns. 'Do you really want to know? Fine. Liam was another one who couldn't let things go. He figured out your little hotel failure wasn't bad luck but the result of a smear campaign.' Her tone is a mocking sing-song. 'He tracked down the agency, and the idiot account manager gave him my name.'

I close my eyes, feeling the walls close in. The last voicemail he left me plays in my head: *'I have something to tell you. It's going to be hard to hear, but I can't keep this to myself.'*

He went to confront her, and then he was going to tell me everything.

'Why did he come to see you?' I ask.

Bryony smirks, pulling the cork free with a dull pop. 'He wanted to know if I'd paid a woman to get him drunk.'

The words hit like a slap. A sob tears through me. 'You did, didn't you? It wasn't enough to ruin our hotel – to destroy everything we'd built together – you had to destroy *us* too!'

She shrugs, and her calm almost makes me scream.

'What happened? What did you do to him?'

'I was opening a bottle of wine when he grabbed me.' She lifts the corkscrew as though it explains everything. 'It was self-defence.'

'Liar!' I scream at her. 'You killed him. He had nothing to do with this, and you killed him.'

'He would've ruined everything between us, Jess.' Her voice softens, almost wistful. 'And I couldn't have that. Not when I was having such a lovely time ruining your life over and over again.'

My chest tightens. 'But you planned to leave! You were going to start a new life – you didn't need to kill him.'

Bryony gives an incredulous little laugh, like I'm missing the obvious. 'Seriously, Jess. Wake up. I only planned our deaths – all of this' – she waves a hand around us, her expression still so gleeful – '*after* I killed Liam.'

'But—' I start to reply, but she continues.

'Liam came to the house on the day you returned to Skelwick,' she continues lightly. 'We had a fight and, afterwards, I called Alex. He was at the studio. I knew he'd help me. That's what love is, isn't it? Doing whatever the other person needs.'

Her smile chills me to the bone. 'We talked for hours,

figuring out what to do with Liam's body, how to explain his disappearance. And then Alex said he wanted a fresh start. He'd been talking about it for a while. Dying was the ultimate fresh start. Rising from the ashes, so to speak.' Her smile widens, sickly sweet. 'And I realised he was right. If we were smart, we could both disappear, let the world think we were dead, cover up Liam's death and start again. It really isn't hard to buy decent fake IDs online if you look hard enough. We could be whoever we wanted.'

She shrugs, as if it truly was that simple. 'And as for leaving you behind, don't worry, Jess. I'd never forget you. I'm always going to keep an eye on you. Even from afar.' Her smile sharpens into something vicious. 'I wouldn't want you getting too happy now, would I?'

The truth sinks in, ugly and cruel. This is never going to end. She's never going to stop destroying my life.

My eyes snap to Alex. He flinches, guilt flashing across his face before he forces himself still. 'How could you go along with this?'

He pushes a hand through his hair. 'The kind of love we have, Jess... it's complicated. Bryony is everything to me. My muse. My art.' He shoots her a look of pure love before dragging his gaze back to me. 'She didn't mean to kill Liam. What kind of husband would I be if I'd called the police? She's my wife, and she needed my help.'

I cover my face with both hands, wishing I could block them out, even for a minute, just one second where the room stops spinning long enough for me to breathe.

'Except you got something out of this too,' I reply, forcing myself to look at him. 'So don't pretend you did this all for Bryony.'

He nods. 'You're right. I meant what I said to you. I'm tired. Of the studio, of the people, of being famous. I want to start again. Work anonymously. Find true art from scratch. And now, to the world, we're dead. We're free. It's like Bryony said. We can be anyone. Go far away from here. Europe even. I can have my campervan again, Jessie.' His eyes plead with me. 'You understand that, don't you?'

'You're murderers.'

I think back to the night he'd cried when the police said Bryony was dead – the grief I'd thought was real. It wasn't grief at all. It was guilt. Guilt for helping to cover up Liam's death, and maybe guilt for tricking me right alongside Bryony. He's as crazy as she is.

The sound of wine pouring into a glass breaks the silence. I blink, allowing the tears to fall. Liam is gone. Truly gone. My chest feels caved in, hollow. How do I tell his parents that the son they adored is lying in ashes because of my sister?

'The DNA the police took from your toothbrush...' I start to ask.

'Liam's,' Alex replies quietly. 'So there'll be no question it's me.'

Even through the storm of grief, something still nags. 'You killed Liam the day I came back to Skelwick,' I whisper. 'But that was six weeks ago. How—'

The words die in my throat. I feel sick, knowing what Alex is going to say before he opens his mouth.

'By the time I got home,' he says softly, 'Liam was already dead. There was nothing I could do. So we... we put him in the freezer in the basement. And then we started to make a plan.'

A sob tears through me. The freezer. The hum that wouldn't stop. All those hours I was in that house alone, pretending to be Bryony, then afterwards with Alex. All that time I felt a dark shadow – a tension – and Liam was dead in the freezer below my feet.

I sob, hand covering my mouth.

Bryony's voice cuts in, light and impossibly casual. 'It was my idea to use his phone to keep calling you, so you'd think he was still alive. I guess you found it. That was a stupid mistake. I'd meant to throw it overboard, but with everything else going on, it slipped my mind. Although I never thought scared little Jess would ever set foot on my boat.

'We did think about taking his body out on the *Odysseus*,' she says, sipping her wine like she's recounting a minor inconvenience. 'Throwing him into the sea, letting the tide take him.'

For a moment, I can't move. Can't speak. My body feels locked in place, every nerve thrumming.

'But then,' she continues, 'we realised that if we wanted to fake our deaths, we couldn't both very well go overboard and be presumed drowned. One person sailing alone and falling overboard is tragic. Two people going over together leads to too many questions. We couldn't have them thinking it was suicide. Not when I had a life insurance policy in place. And there's something so poetic about a husband dying so soon after his wife. It'll be a bigger story for the art collectors and increase the sale prices. That's when we thought about using Liam's body to be Alex.'

'Bryony, you don't mean—' Alex begins.

'Not now, darling,' Bryony cuts him off, and I don't give either of them a chance to continue.

'But you could've just left. Packed up and gone,' I say. It's a fight to keep myself upright. Not to sink to the floor. If I didn't want to keep as much distance from these people as possible, I'd step into the room and sink into one of the chairs.

She shakes her head. 'Oh, Jess, where's the fun in that? Besides, do you know what happens to the price of art when the artist dies tragically? And how lucky that so many of Alex's pieces are still in storage after his trip to America.'

'That's why you needed me,' I whisper. 'For your life insurance and Alex's art money. You need me to collect it, and what? Hand it over as cash in a suitcase when the time is right?'

'Something like that,' Bryony replies. 'Of course, I'd make

sure you had enough for Mum's care home costs. I'm not a monster, Jess.'

I would laugh if the world wasn't being torn down around me. Because my sister *is* a monster, and now she's standing before me, unmasked, I wonder how I ever saw her as anything else.

'But why did you make me pretend to be you? Sending me messages as though you were Alex. You didn't have to go that far,' I reply, my voice suddenly high.

Bryony shrugs, taking a long sip of wine as she leans against the counter.

'Jessie, she—' Alex starts to say.

'Don't,' I cut in. 'Don't you dare try to make excuses or explain anything on her behalf, Alex.'

He falls silent, and I catch Bryony rolling her eyes at him or me, I'm not sure which. Just what the hell is their relationship? He said last week over dinner that being with Bryony was like being under a spell. I stare at the man at the table and that's what I see. She's worn him down, manipulated and twisted him so much, he's lost himself somewhere, playing along to her games, jumping over the edge of sanity right alongside her.

We both look to Bryony, waiting for an answer.

'For the fun of it,' she says after a pause.

Alex makes a strained noise. 'You told me it was to make Jess believe it. That we had to pretend our relationship was in trouble.'

'Darling,' Bryony says with exasperation. 'Two things can be true at the same time. We needed Jess distracted and stressed so she wouldn't look too closely at what we were doing. And I did it because I thought it would be fun. And it was.'

I open my mouth to reply, but Bryony shakes her head at me. 'Let's not pretend you haven't gained from this too, Jess. You've inherited all our money and our house. You're a millionaire. And you're correct, when the time is right, we'll take our cut. But rest assured our precious mother will be well cared for,' she adds, almost spitting out the words. 'You were always her favourite.'

'She loves you, Bryony,' I reply. 'She told me when I went to visit and she thought I was you. If you'd spent time with her, you'd have seen that.'

Bryony's eyes narrow. 'It wasn't love. It was guilt. She loved you more, and we all knew it.'

Even with everything falling apart, I see a truth to her words. Mum did favour me. I was the easier child to love. But nothing can excuse what Bryony has done.

'See. No harm done,' she sing-songs.

Hurt slices through me. 'No harm done?' I cry. 'Liam is dead.'

She shrugs. 'You broke up with him. He cheated on you.'

'You set him up,' I say, cold fury threading through me.

There's a spark of something inside me. That hate I feel knotting into a malice in my stomach I don't recognise but don't shy away from either.

'And what about Alex cheating on you?' I cry.

The silence that follows is deafening.

I force myself to smile, to act like Bryony. 'Oh, he didn't tell you we slept together?'

The fury in her eyes is a blaze as fierce as the studio fire.

FORTY-SEVEN

Jess

Alex's face twists from guilt to desperation. 'Bryony, it meant nothing. We were both drunk. She was going to tell me what you'd done. I could tell. I only kissed her to stop her from ruining everything.'

She ignores Alex and keeps her eyes fixed on me. 'That's all in the past now. It's like Alex said: we're starting again.' She smiles. 'And since you've already figured it all out, I won't have to lie anymore and pretend to be the pathetic, lost sister who needs your help,' she says in a mock-woeful voice. 'You can just hand over all our money when it comes in.'

Alex groans. 'No, Bryony. Please. I'm sorry I slept with Jess, but we agreed we would start again. Live free of the constraints of wealth.'

'Constraints? Alex, you've not thought it through. You're talking about living without the basics. It's inhumane.' She sips her wine. 'Being free of our old lives doesn't mean we can't also have some home comforts.' She raises her glass and takes another sip.

A strangled sound escapes Alex. 'That wasn't the plan,' he says. 'And don't tell me "not now". I have a right to speak out.'

Bryony sets her glass down on the counter and smiles at Alex. When she speaks, her tone is syrupy sweet. 'You're right, darling,' she purrs.

He opens his arms without question, and she slips in, his face buried into her body as she stands over his chair.

'But sleeping with my sister wasn't part of the plan either.'

The world seems to pause. Just a fraction of a second where I stop breathing and the air shifts around us all. Bryony's fingers curling around something metal at her waist, arm moving up and up and up.

I scream. Shock and warning. 'Alex.'

She wouldn't—

He starts to draw back, but he's too slow.

Bryony's arm arcs like a blade. The corkscrew gripped in her hand like a knife as she brings it down, hard and fast, jabbing it into the side of his neck with a violence that takes my legs out from under me. I scream again, falling back against the wall.

In a second swift movement, she pulls the corkscrew free, then steps back to the counter and picks up her wine glass as though nothing has happened. Dark-red blood blooms at the wound on Alex's neck, then suddenly it's everywhere. Pouring out of him in a steady and sickening flow. Alex's eyes grow wide. His hands grab at his neck. Blood spills through them in seconds. I lurch forward, snatching at a towel on the side. My only thought is stopping the blood and the life from seeping out of him.

'It's OK,' I whisper, pressing the cloth to his neck as he sinks back in the chair, face contorted in pain and regret.

'Jessie,' he says, the words gurgling in his throat in a way I know will haunt my nightmares for the rest of my life.

'Don't speak. You're going to be fine,' I lie as the world

shrinks down to this moment – me still pressing the blood-soaked cloth to Alex's neck, his breathing ragged.

I scream at Bryony, 'Call an ambulance,' even though I know she won't. But if I move my hands away to do it myself, he'll bleed out.

From across the kitchen, Bryony scoffs. 'You're wasting your time.'

She's right. Tears blur my vision and spill onto my cheeks. Alex's fingers fumble around mine, and for an awful moment his eyes lock on me with something like apology.

Then the light goes out in him. He slumps; his hand falls from mine, and his body collapses to the stone floor. I sink into the chair, the cloth in my hands. My entire body starts to tremble, like I'm hooked up to an electrical current. Every breath is a shuddered gasp. Alex was complicit in everything that's happened. In Liam's death. In all these lies. And yet, I didn't want him to die.

'Honestly, Jess,' Bryony says into the silence, 'what is it with both of you? Everything. Every single thing I do, I have to coax and convince, hold your hands all the way through it. For once, could one of you not just have done what I asked?'

I say nothing. Can't speak. Alex is dead. Murdered before my eyes with the same violence and viciousness that Bryony used on Liam.

'So,' she continues, still impossibly calm, 'let's make a plan.' She takes a seat opposite me and sips her wine. 'I'll sort this little mess out, and you'll go back to Skelwick and carry on as normal. I think it will take six months to a year to collect on my life insurance policy and tidy up Alex's estate. His agent will find you the best deals for his art. And contact Jonathon at *The Times* before you sell. He'll do a piece on Alex that will get people talking.'

'Bryony.' I whisper her name, barely listening. 'You can't be serious.'

She rolls her eyes.

'I'm going to tell the police everything,' I tell her.

She freezes. Her eyes narrow to slits. 'You're as caught up in this as I am.'

'I don't care.'

Her lip curls. 'I'll tell them it was all you. That you killed Liam out of revenge and Alex out of jealousy. That you couldn't bear the fact he never loved you.'

'I don't care,' I repeat, even though the words scrape at my throat, even though the fear of not being believed makes my stomach twist inside out. 'You'll tell them your version, and I'll tell them mine. I'm done lying for you. I'm done protecting you.'

My hands shake violently as I reach into my pocket for my phone. It slips through my trembling, blood-soaked fingers and clatters to the floor. In one swift move, Bryony is out of her chair, circling the table, kicking my phone hard, sending it skidding across the room and out of reach. Suddenly, she's towering over me, the corkscrew back in her hand.

I shrink back, and she lets out a brittle, humourless laugh. 'Let's get one thing straight,' she says, tone like steel. 'I don't need you, Jess. I like having you around as my little plaything, but I don't need you. You pretended to be me so easily. Do you honestly think I can't do the same?'

My breath catches.

'I could end you right now,' she goes on. 'Go back to Skelwick as sad little Jess Waters. Keep to myself. Speak only to the solicitor. Be seen around town just enough. I could be poor, pathetic Jess for a few months and collect my inheritance myself.'

'You'd never get away with it.'

She opens her mouth to reply, and that's when I move, scrambling backward, the chair tipping under me. I skid a little in the blood, and nausea rises sharp in my gut. But my focus is getting away from the corkscrew in her hand.

'You can't kill me, Jess,' she says. 'I'm your sister.'

Then she comes at me. Fast. The corkscrew flashes, and I twist – but not quickly enough. A white-hot bolt of agony explodes through my shoulder as the metal punches into me. I scream, the sound torn from somewhere deep and primal, but at least it wasn't my neck.

My hands fly across the counter, searching for anything I can use as my own weapon. My fingers close around the neck of a wine bottle.

Bryony yanks, trying to pull the corkscrew free, but it's stuck. The pain is blinding. Black spots flicker at the edges of my vision, but I grip the neck of the bottle in my hand, teeth clenched through the agony ripping down my arm, and I swing with everything I have left.

The bottle smashes against the side of her skull with a sick, echoing thud. Bryony's eyes widen, mouth dropping open in a surprised O, and then she falls back, head hitting the flagstones with a terrifying crack. I pull the corkscrew from my shoulder, not feeling the pain anymore. It drops to the floor, clattering in the silence, and I stare at her motionless body, at the blood pooling around her blonde hair.

'You're right,' I whisper into the stillness, my voice shaking like I might shatter with it. 'I can't kill someone who's already dead.'

FORTY-EIGHT

Jess

Shock settles over me like a wet, smothering blanket. I sink into the nearest chair without meaning to, my legs folding beneath me, my breath catching in shallow, broken bursts. My hands are still covered in Alex's blood, drying sticky.

I don't know how long I sit there for. Ten minutes. An hour. A lifetime, it feels like. I'm shivering and cold by the time I feel the room swim back into focus. The farmhouse kitchen. The dark wood cupboards. The flagstone floor. The crumpled forms of Alex's and Bryony's bodies. And the blood. So much blood. Huge red puddles. The air is thick with the smell of metal and spilled wine.

Moving slowly, terrified my legs will give way, I push myself up. My feet slide slightly in a smear of blood, and the shock of it jolts me awake enough to stumble to the sink. I turn the tap on and thrust my hands beneath the scalding water.

The heat burns. I don't care. I scrub harder, harder still, until my skin is red and raw, until the last traces of blood swirl down the drain in thin ribbons. When I can't feel my fingertips anymore, I force myself away from the sink. I step over the blood on trembling legs and crouch to retrieve my phone from where Bryony kicked it. The screen is cracked, a jagged line splitting the glass, but it still lights up. I open the keypad and tap 999.

The green call button swims before my eyes. I hover over it, pulse hammering in my ears. If I press it, everything changes. I see it all playing out in my mind like a film I don't want to watch. The police arriving to the scene. Taking in the two bodies. The chaos that will follow. Questions upon questions.

Telling the story over and over. How I helped fake Bryony's death. All the lies I was told and then told myself. Pretending to be Bryony then pretending to be the grieving sister. Then tracking her down.

The first thing any good police officer would ask was if I was angry with my sister. They'd want to know why I came to confront her instead of calling the police first? I don't have a good answer. They'll think I came here out of revenge and killed them both. Not self-defence, despite the injury to my shoulder, but murder. Intent.

I told Bryony I was sick of lying. And I was. I am. But mostly, I was sick of her lying.

I wanted it all to stop. Her games. Her torment. I wanted her to face what she'd done to me and to Liam. But now she's dead, and she can't face anything.

I sink back into the chair, staring at the bodies of two people who the world already believe are dead. And slowly, a new plan starts to take shape. What good can come of calling the police now? The only one left to face any punishment is me. And yes, maybe I deserve punishment for the part I played in all of this. But I didn't mean to kill Bryony. I defended myself. I'd watched her brutally kill Alex. I knew she was going to kill me. It was her or me. And I chose me.

Bryony killed Liam. She destroyed everything Liam and I

built. She poisoned every dream I had, every relationship, every corner of my life. Now I'm done letting her destroy the last pieces of what I have. It's time to look to the future. No one is looking for Bryony or Alex. If I hide their bodies – clean up this mess, erase this nightmare – I can go back to Skelwick. Look after Mum. Start again. Maybe even find a life that feels like it's mine again.

I close my phone, take a long trembling breath and force myself to think. What do I do now? If I bury their bodies, I'll spend the rest of my life waiting for a dog walker or a storm or a farmer ploughing land to dig them back up. I can't live with that fear. They need to be gone and stay gone. Forever. There's only one place that can give me that – the bottom of the ocean.

I don't allow myself to think ahead to what that means I have to do. Instead, I concentrate on one step at a time. I slip out of my shoes – still tacky with blood – and pad through the farmhouse on numb feet, gathering towels, sheets, bedding, anything I can use.

It takes until dawn. Hours and hours of scrubbing until my arms ache and my back screams and the wound on my shoulder throbs in time with the pain in my temple. By the time the first streaks of light slip over the horizon, the kitchen is spotless. Not a speck of blood remains. Not a single sign of what happened here. Alex and Bryony lie wrapped and silent on the floor, swaddled in bedding like grotesque parcels.

I open the boot of Bryony's Mercedes and reverse as close to the door as I can get. The remote farmhouse is a blessing – no neighbours, no early dog walkers, no one to hear me sob as I drag and pull and heave the heavy bundles into the boot. I don't know how long it takes. My muscles scream. My shoulder burns. I fall twice, knees hitting the stony ground. I wipe tears away with shaking fingers.

But eventually, it's done. And then I wait. I spend the entire day inside the empty house, curtains drawn, the silence pressing tight against me. I change into some of Bryony's clothes. Eat just enough to keep from collapsing. Fall in and out of shallow, gasping sleep on the sofa, jerking awake at every bird call. I check the rooms over and over, making sure there's no trace of blood, no trace of me, no trace of them.

Only when the sun begins to sink again do I finally step outside. I'm exhausted and wired at the same time, shaking so badly I have to grip the steering wheel to steady myself. Every second I'm behind the wheel, I expect a police siren, a flashing blue light.

But I must do this. I'll never be free of Bryony's torment unless her body stays gone.

'This is the only way,' I whisper to myself.

Bryony would have killed me eventually. Or she would have kept destroying me piece by piece, the way she always has. It will be a long time before I truly grasp the depth of her jealousy and how it twisted into something worse. Her childhood envy never faded the way Mum and Dad hoped. Instead, it festered. Turning into something grotesque and dark when she was sent away from Skelwick – the home she loved, the place she believed I stole from her by simply existing.

Of course she came back when she did. I was happy. I'd told her about Alex, about our friendship, about how much he meant to me. She saw something bright in my life and – like she always did – she reached out to take it. Everything she's done, even killing Liam, stemmed from her jealousy and hate for me.

It's fully dark by the time I reach the cove, the one tucked miles along the coast from Skelwick. A place Mum used to call the forgotten beach. No soft sand here, no picturesque waves to draw the tourists. It's just coarse shingle, jagged rocks and a narrow hem of calm water.

I park as close as I dare to the curve of the beach. The headlights sweep across the stones, catching the pale shimmer of the tide rolling in. The night air is salty and cool. I draw it in, but it's not enough to dislodge the metallic tang that clings to the back of my throat.

One by one, I drag the bodies from the car, hauling them across the beach, moving only inches at a time. My shoulder throbs, and tears blur my vision, but at last I wrestle them into a deep patch of shadow at the base of the rock face. It's a risk to leave them. If anyone walks this stretch of coastline and comes too close, they'll find them. But it's dark and late, and hardly anyone comes here at the best of times.

I turn back to the car and drive away with both hands gripping the wheel so tightly my knuckles ache. My heart isn't pounding because of fear of being stopped by the police anymore. It's pounding because of what I'm driving towards – the *Odysseus*. But even my fear of being on the water again is nothing compared to the need tearing through me now to finish this. To end her shadow over me once and for all.

When I reach the harbour, the only sound is the masts creaking. My stomach twists. My hands shake. But I force myself up the gangplank. The moment my feet hit the deck, something inside me lurches. I grip the rail so hard it digs into my palms. I don't touch the sails. Instead, I slip on a life jacket and turn on the small engine, the low hum vibrating through the hull. I unhook the mooring lines and steer the boat slowly out of the harbour. The lights of Skelwick shrink behind me, turning into scattered stars against the darkness.

I anchor as close to the cove as I can, the boat rocking in the swell as I lower the dinghy. Back and forth I go, dragging the bodies from the shadows where I left them, hauling them through the shingle. I bring the heavy rocks too. I don't try to get the bodies or rocks onto the *Odysseus*. Instead, I leave them in the dinghy and tie it securely to the boat before I steer it out, further and further, until the lights of the shore disappear completely. The sea swells around me, black and endless – the monster of every nightmare.

Then I climb into the dinghy and use the rocks to weigh the bodies down, tying ropes around the two as best I can with my fingers trembling. Then, one after the other, I push them overboard, just like Bryony did to me. There's a splash and then nothing. I don't jump in after them like she did that day.

Instead, I sit there shaking, unable to move, unable to breathe, until something inside me loosens.

As I guide the *Odysseus* back towards the harbour, the engine humming beneath my feet, I draw in a breath that feels like my first in weeks. Years. A lifetime...

It's done. It's over. I didn't want to kill my sister. I didn't want any of this, but all I can think is how finally I'm free of her.

At last.

EPILOGUE

ONE YEAR LATER

Jess

Morning light pours through the high windows and slides across the reception desk in soft streaks. The little hotel breathes quietly around me, not as grand as the Kilstern but still carrying a Victorian beauty. A ten-roomed building on the seafront with a dining room and a cosy library with leather armchairs and rows of red leather-bound books where I host a book group once a month and wine and whisky tasting events; merging tourism with the community. And best of all, it's mine. Bought with the proceeds from the sale of Alex's art.

Beside me, Helen and Kelly are busy behind the reception desk. Both have taken to hotel work like they were made for it, and I'm grateful every day that they've ignored the rumours and gossip and chose to trust me. Helen manages the bookings and the front desk; Kelly the housekeeping team.

Helen taps on a keyboard before looking up with a satisfied smile. 'I've just taken another booking for next week, so we're now officially fully booked until January.'

I smile, and it almost feels genuine. A part of me is waiting for it all to fall apart, worrying over every little thing. But I take a deep breath of air scented with eucalyptus and sandalwood beneath the aromas of coffee and the pastries we're serving with breakfast. In the dining room, voices talk in murmurs. There are snatches of laughter. Cutlery clinks on plates.

My gaze wanders to the window and the sea beyond the bay. The gulls call their taunt, like they never want me to forget what I did.

As if I could.

Two guests make their way down the staircase. A couple in their sixties with tanned faces and hiking wear.

I step forward and take the woman's suitcase. 'Let me get that for you,' I say, walking with them to the front desk, where Helen checks them out.

They talk animatedly about a cliff walk and their plans to return, and I'm about to step away when the man places the local newspaper on the desk and taps the front page.

My eyes are drawn to the headline. MYSTERY OF SKELWICK COUPLE CONTINUES.

'This is rather an intriguing story, isn't it?' the man says, looking from his wife to Helen to me. 'Did you know them?'

Helen's eyes widen, and she glances at me.

'Everyone knew the Raffetys,' I say with a calm I don't feel. 'It's very tragic.'

'And mysterious,' the man adds. 'Not often the police are stumped.'

They say cheery goodbyes and promise to return before striding away. The newspaper remains on the front desk. I don't need to read the story to know what it says. It's the same one that's been repeated for months.

Because despite my best efforts, the bodies of Bryony and Alex didn't stay gone as I'd planned. In my shock and hurry, I must not have tied the ropes around the rocks well enough. First Bryony's body washed to shore. No one was surprised about that, until the coroner announced the cause of death. Not a drowning as assumed but a head wound.

Even then, speculation began that she'd hit her head before falling off the *Odysseus*. And maybe that would've been the end of it if a second body hadn't washed up a week later. This time with a fatal wound in his neck.

The police came to me of course. Not Sergeant Miller or PC Hughes but two detectives. I lied and told them I had no idea who it could be. But they kept digging. And Addie came forward with the dashcam footage. At which point, the police collected DNA from Liam's parents. It wasn't a match to the body washed to shore. But it was a match to the body in the fire.

They took another DNA sample from the house for Alex, and it didn't take long for them to discover he was the body in the sea. That's when the story exploded and speculation began over how a man who died in a fire at his studio washed up to shore a week after his wife.

The truth of what happened and my part in it sits heavy in my chest. I can rebuild my life, visit Mum, chase new dreams, be whoever I want to be, but nothing will erase the past.

The detectives pushed and prodded, asking me over and over what I thought happened, poking holes in every suggestion I gave them. But I stuck to my story. I told them that I suspected Liam and Bryony were having an affair. I didn't need to explain how jealous Alex would've been. His love for his wife was evident in every speech he gave and in the life-sized canvases on every wall in their house. I hate myself for it, but I told them it was possible that in a struggle, Liam killed Bryony and Alex, threw their bodies into the water and then, racked with guilt, went to Alex's studio to start the fire. It doesn't fit with all the evidence though, and the police know it.

But local gossip took the story, twisting it into talk of love triangles and murder–suicide pacts. The famous artist, his muse and her lover. I hate that Liam has been dragged into the lies.

The detectives still come back every few weeks. I know they suspect my involvement. Like I thought at the farmhouse – I'm the only one left in this awful game Bryony started. But the time in the sea was long enough to destroy any physical evidence tying me to Alex and Bryony. They don't have an exact date for their deaths, and they don't know about the farmhouse Bryony booked online with a fake name. For now, I'm safe.

But the rumours won't die. One about me in particular. How neatly everything worked out for Jess Waters. Living in her sister's house, with her sister's inheritance, wearing her sister's life like a second skin. I see the suspicion when people look at me. The sideways glances. The murmured conversations that stop as I walk past.

At night, when sleep finally claims me, I still have nightmares. But they're no longer about the *Calypso*. The therapist was right about that. Once I remembered everything, those dreams stopped.

Now the nightmares drag me back to that farmhouse kitchen. Bryony swinging the corkscrew. First at Alex. Then at me.

But in the nightmares, she doesn't miss. The metal sinks into my neck. Warm blood pours over my skin. I wake gasping, clammy, fingers scrambling at a wound that isn't there.

In those moments, I see the awful truth. I can rebuild my life however I want to, but even in death, Bryony is still here. Still tormenting me.

I was wrong.

I will never be free of her.

A LETTER FROM LAUREN

Dear Reader,

Thank you so much for reading *I Owe You One* and making it this far. It's always such a thrill to send a new twisty story out into the world, and I'm endlessly grateful to everyone who chooses to spend their time with my books.

If you'd like to be the first to hear about upcoming releases, you can sign up for my newsletter here:

www.bookouture.com/lauren-north

I promise your email will never be shared, and you can unsubscribe at any time.

The idea for *I Owe You One* grew from a simple but unsettling question: *What does it really mean to owe someone your life?* Not in a casual, abstract way but in a way that shapes every choice you make. I was fascinated by the idea of emotional debt, and how it can quietly turn into obligation, guilt and fear, even when it starts from love.

Jess is someone who carries the weight of responsibility everywhere she goes. She worries, she overthinks, she wants to do the right thing. I think many of us can recognise those feelings in our day-to-day lives. Jess truly believes she would do anything for her sister... until she has to confront what 'anything' really means.

And Bryony... oh, she was irresistible to write. Charismatic, complicated and always just a step ahead. Writing her was a balancing act of letting her charm shine while slowly peeling back the layers beneath. She was challenging, unsettling and enormously fun.

At its heart, *I Owe You One* is a story about loyalty, power, and the dangerous line between love and control. I hope it kept you guessing and made you question how far you might go if you believed you owed someone everything.

I love hearing from readers. Your messages, reviews, tags and shares make it all worth it. You can find me on Instagram, Facebook and TikTok, so don't be a stranger!

And if you enjoyed *I Owe You One*, I'd be so grateful if you'd leave a review on Amazon or Goodreads, or simply tell a friend. Word of mouth truly is a powerful thing.

With love and gratitude,

Lauren x

instagram.com/Lauren_C_North
facebook.com/LaurenNorthAuthor
tiktok.com/@lauren_c_north

ACKNOWLEDGEMENTS

Writing a novel isn't the solitary world many believe it to be. Yes, there are plenty of hours spent alone, tapping at my keyboard, lost to my characters. But there are many people on the team that shape and polish and cheer and make sure I never feel alone in this.

I am so grateful for all the support I receive and the many ways it comes. I hope you'll forgive me if I miss anyone.

First and foremost, I'd like to thank my editor, Lucy Frederick. I've lost count of how many books we've worked on together, but I'm eternally grateful that I've had the opportunity to work with you for such a long time. From the first 'what if' of an idea, I know my stories are in the safest of hands. I'm incredibly grateful for your insights and support at every step.

To everyone at Bookouture: thank you for the expertise, energy and belief you bring to every stage of the process. From first draft to final proof, this book has been shaped by a team who genuinely cares, and I'm so proud to publish with you. Please take a moment to read the credits page and see just how many wonderful people have worked on this story.

To Ellis and the Bolinda team, thank you! It's always such a joy to work with you and hear my story come to life in audiobook.

To Amanda Preston, my agent – thank you for your calm reassurance, your fantastic instincts and your unshakable faith in me. And to the brilliant team at LBA who work with you behind the scenes.

And now for the cheerleaders who keep me company, keep me laughing and keep me believing I can do this. Zoe Lea, Nikki Smith and Laura Pearson – not a day goes by where you don't lift me. To Jack Sutherland for her bubbly brightness, keeping me positive and laughing. To B.P. Walter for being my go-to when we want to chat the next crazy rollercoaster we're going to jump on. Kathryn Jones – thank you for the dog walks and the doses of sanity and laughter you bring to my week, reminding me that a world outside of books does exist. Finally to my family – Tommy, Lottie, Andy and Rodney (the dog). Love you guys!

I've dedicated this book to Mel Ewings for his unwavering kindness to me since he became a part of my life when I was an eighteen-year-old psychology student who thought I knew everything. You are a man of few words, Mel, but I suspect that's mostly because Mum and I don't give you much room to speak them. I think the world of you and the solid support you bring to my life.

And last, but by no means least, I'd like to thank you, the reader. You are the reason these stories exist. Grateful doesn't begin to cover it.

PUBLISHING TEAM

Turning a manuscript into a book requires the efforts of many people. The publishing team at Bookouture would like to acknowledge everyone who contributed to this publication.

Commercial
Lauren Morrissette
Hannah Richmond
Imogen Allport

Cover design
The Brewster Project

Data and analysis
Mark Alder
Mohamed Bussuri

Editorial
Lucy Frederick
Kathy Callesen

Copyeditor
Donna Hillyer

Proofreader
Laura Kincaid

Marketing
Alex Crow
Melanie Price
Cíara Rosney
Martyna Młynarska

Operations and distribution
Joe Morris
Kiah Tooke

Production
Hannah Snetsinger
Mandy Kullar
Nadia Michael
Charlotte Hegley

Publicity
Noelle Holten
Jess Readett
Sarah Hardy

Rights and contracts
Peta Nightingale
Richard King
Saidah Graham

RAISING READERS

Books Build Bright Futures

Dear Reader,

We'd love your attention for one more page to tell you about the crisis in children's reading, and what we can all do.

Studies have shown that reading for fun is the **single biggest predictor of a child's future life chances** – more than family circumstance, parents' educational background or income. It improves academic results, mental health, wealth, communication skills, ambition and happiness.

The number of children reading for fun is in rapid decline. Young people have a lot of competition for their time, and a worryingly high number do not have a single book at home.

Hachette works extensively with schools, libraries and literacy charities, but here are some ways we can all raise more readers:

- Reading to children for just 10 minutes a day makes a difference
- Don't give up if children aren't regular readers – there will be books for them!

- Visit bookshops and libraries to get recommendations
- Encourage them to listen to audiobooks
- Support school libraries
- Give books as gifts

There's a lot more information about how to encourage children to read on our websites: **www.RaisingReaders.co.uk** and **www.JoinRaisingReaders.com**.

Thank you for reading.

hachette UK

Printed in Dunstable, United Kingdom

83975421R00173